F

The Wedding Caper

The Wedding Caper

Jo Ann Ferguson

THORNDIKE
CHIVERS

This Large Print edition is published by Thorndike Press®, Waterville, Maine USA and by BBC Audiobooks, Ltd, Bath, England.

Published in 2004 in the U.S. by arrangement with Zebra Books, an imprint of Kensington Publishing Corp.

Published in 2005 in the U.K. by arrangement with Kensington Publishing Corp.

U.S. Hardcover 0-7862-6973-1 (Romance)
U.K. Hardcover 1-4056-3173-2 (Chivers Large Print)

The text of this Large Print edition is unabridged. Other aspects of the book may vary from the original edition.

Set in 16 pt. Plantin by Ramona Watson.

Printed in the United States on permanent paper.

British Library Cataloguing-in-Publication Data available

Library of Congress Cataloging-in-Publication Data

Ferguson, Jo Ann.
    The wedding caper / Jo Ann Ferguson.
      p. cm.
    ISBN 0-7862-6973-1 (lg. print : hc : alk. paper)
    1. London (England) — Fiction.   2. Nobility — Crimes against — Fiction.   3. Large type books.   I. Title.
PS3556.E714W43 2004
    813′.54—dc22   2004055392

For Karen Dennen
who proves big hearts come
in small packages.

Chapter One

"Blood," she whispered. "It is everywhere. Blood and death."

She lifted an upset chair, but froze when a hand paralyzed with death dropped to the floor with a heavy thump. The man lying on the floor had a red spot in the middle of his chest where a knife with a bone haft had been driven into him. An answering echo came from the doorway she had passed through only moments before.

The sound was not another dead man's hand, but the unmistakable rhythm of footfalls.

Pausing only long enough to lower the chair silently to the carpet, she ran into the shadows, drawing the draperies about her to conceal the light color of her dress. She peered around the edge of the draperies, which were the same shade as the blood on the floor.

A tall, black-haired man swaggered into the room. His clothes were finely made, and the buttons on his waistcoat glittered in the bright light from beyond the chair. Putting his hands on his hips, he looked down his long nose arrogantly as he scanned the chamber. A slow smile edged his full lips beneath an unfashionably bushy mustache. The chair was not the only piece of furniture that had been turned over, because a small table was on its side, an empty bottle beside it. Once before he had been in this room. He had argued vehemently with the man who lay dead on the floor.

He went over to the dead man and tapped him with his toe. Turning his back on where the woman hid behind the draperies, he strutted around the room. Triumph oozed from every inch of him.

"Where are the others?" demanded the tall man as he turned to speak to someone unseen.

The answer was just a mumble.

The tall man ordered, "Repeat that."

"They not be 'ere." A shorter man, his clothes ragged and stained, stepped into the light. He crouched, not looking at the tall man. His pose as much as his clothes revealed he normally would not have been received in the elegant room. He pocketed a small statue, concealing it among his tatters.

"Where are they?" Impatience filled the tall man's voice.

"Don't know."

"You don't know?" The tall man crossed the room toward where she stood behind the curtains. "You mean you let them slip away? If one of them goes to seek the constable, even *I* will not be safe." The tall man laughed malevolently. "You shall not drag me down with you. I will see you dead before I pay for your mistakes."

The short man chuckled, and a taint of madness knelled in every word as he said, "Don't worry, m'lord. I will find them 'fore they can sound the alarm."

"How? You do not know them."

His smile was heard in his words. "That be my concern. I will find them."

"And then?"

"Why d'ye ask? Ye know what I will do." The man's chortle deepened with sinister anticipation, slicing through the air as brutally as his knife had cut into the dead man. "I will kill them 'fore they can squawk." He looked past the tall man and called into the darkness on his left, "Was that better, Wiggsley? Surely even you cannot find any fault with this interpretation of the scene."

Lady Priscilla Flanders smiled as the trio

of actors surged toward the front of the stage to listen to comments from the playwright. Sitting in the wings of the small theater for the dress rehearsal of the play debuting tonight was an unexpected pleasure. She was torn between watching the actors and the people scurrying about backstage. One woman was frantically sewing while two men hammered what appeared to be a long bench which they must be readying for an upcoming scene. She had had no idea how much work still needed to be completed when the Prince of Wales Theater opened in less than five hours.

By her feet, her son sat uncommonly still. Isaac must be enthralled by the players and the story unfolding in front of them.

"So how do you think the young miss will escape the villain's evil schemes?" asked a deep, rich voice from behind her.

She looked over her shoulder and held out her hand to the man walking toward her. "Neville, do you honestly believe I would reveal my ideas to you? Think how you will tease me if I am wrong."

Sir Neville Hathaway chuckled. She liked his laugh. It was filled with a *joie de vivre* not even the most dismal situation could dampen. Although the harder years of his life were ingrained into his fiercely sculpted face, his laugh retained a boyish enthusiasm for mischief that often brought her son's to mind. His hair, falling forward on his brow, was the same shiny black as his boots. He carried his dark coat over one arm, for the theater was unseasonably warm. His white waistcoat, brightened with green vines embroidered along the front, seemed too formal to wear with his buckskin breeches. Such vagaries of fashion did not concern him, she was well aware. It was one of the facets of him that fascinated her. He was now a welcome part of the Polite World, but he still retained a part of the man he had been before he had inherited his title.

Kneeling beside her and giving Isaac a wink, he said, "Pris, I had hoped you, as a woman of undeniable courage, had some insight into how the heroine of this play could flee with her life and still unmask the villain to meet his end on the gallows."

"You might ask the playwright for that answer."

"He does not know it." The tall man who had been on stage pushed aside the curtain and stepped over some coiled rope on the floor. He yanked a black wig off his head, tossing it onto a nearby box as he scratched through his fine blond hair. "The fool has changed the ending *again*. He seems unperturbed that the curtain goes up on this production in less than eight hours. Hathaway, do you think you could talk some sense into him?"

"Me?" Neville came to his feet. "Birdwell, you know I never had any luck in persuading Wiggsley that actors need the final script more than five minutes before the play begins." Holding out his hand to Priscilla, he brought her to her feet. "This is my fiancée, Lady Priscilla Flanders, and her son Isaac, Lord Emberson." He smiled at Isaac before saying, "This is, as I am sure you know, Reginald Birdwell, lead actor of the play we shall be attending this evening."

Mr. Birdwell bowed his head toward her because Neville still held her hand. He offered his hand to Isaac, who grinned broadly as the actor said, "Good afternoon, my lord." Being addressed as an adult was a treat for a ten-year-old boy.

Priscilla put her hand on her son's shoulder. Others were impressed by the title he had inherited from her father, but she did not want Isaac to believe such fawning was his due. Her father had gained as much respect for his calm thinking and opinions as for his title. She hoped Isaac would come to be viewed the same way.

"Hathaway," Mr. Birdwell said, peeling off the mustache and dropping it atop the wig, "that is nonsense. You were one of the few among us who ever convinced Wiggsley to listen."

"Listen, yes," Neville replied. "Heed me, no."

"But you are a baronet now. Surely he will be more willing to consider your opinions."

"Wiggsley told me on our last meeting that I was a fool to toss aside a promising career in the theater simply because I was bequeathed a title." He laughed. "Think how scandalized the *ton* would have been if I had continued playing the rogue and the rake on stage."

"All those mamas might have breathed a bit more easily to discover your flirting with their young daughters was confined to scenes behind the lights." Mr. Birdwell's face turned a brilliant crimson that suggested he had spent too much time in the sun. "My lady, I should not have said such an unthinking thing. Forgive me."

Priscilla smiled. "You are forgiven, Mr. Birdwell. I know well what Neville's reputation has been, and I know how much of it is based on fact." She looked into Neville's earth-brown eyes and wondered whom else he allowed to see the truth behind the roguish image. The truth was that he was a man she could trust completely, whether with herself or her son or her two daughters. She knew he would offer up his own life to protect her children. He had been in and out of their lives since they were born, and he had proven again and again how he would allow no harm to come to them.

"Priscilla is, as you can see, a most remarkable woman," Neville said.

She hoped her face was not as scarlet as Mr. Birdwell's had been moments ago. She was saved from having to reply when a very rotund man burst past the curtain. Only Neville's tug on her arm pulled her out of the way before the man could run her down.

"Wiggsley, watch where you are going!" shouted Mr. Birdwell.

The playwright did not slow at the scold, but continued past the seamstress who was cutting a thread. He bumped into her, and her sewing basket fell, scattering threads and pieces of fabric across the dusty floor. A man holding a tray with a single glass jumped out of his way, splashing the boards with drops.

"He appears exasperated beyond expression," Mr. Birdwell muttered. "I hope he composes himself in time to write an ending to the play."

The man with the tray edged closer. He wore a work smock over simple breeches and plain shoes, but his pose revealed his awe of the actor. His brown hair drooped into his face as he bobbed his head toward Mr. Birdwell, who was still watching the playwright storm away. The man held the tray out.

"Hathaway," Mr. Birdwell continued, without acknowledging the man by his elbow, "you have to speak to Wiggsley and persuade him to be sensible. We open in just hours."

Neville glanced at Priscilla. When she smiled at him to let him know she was unhurt, he said, "I told you, Birdwell. He heeds no one but —"

"His muse. I know. I know. He has said that far too many times, but I believe it is an excuse for not knowing what will take place next in the play." He did not look at the man motioning with the tray toward him. "This is becoming ludicrous, and the Prince of Wales Theater cannot afford another flat move. Such a failure will see the doors closed for good."

"Sir . . ." said the man with the tray, his face long with dismay.

The actor ignored him. "You know how hard we worked to make this theater a success, Hathaway. You know how hard *you* worked. Now it is a complete muddle."

"Sir . . ."

"Won't you speak with him, Hathaway?"

"Of course he will," Priscilla said, taking sympathy on the manservant, who was growing more and more distressed. She met Neville's abrupt frown without expression.

Mr. Birdwell smiled broadly and took the glass from the tray. He grimaced when drops fell onto his right shoe. The manservant hastily wiped off the spots and straightened, his expression now like a puppy which was unsure if it was to be praised or beaten.

"Thank you, Reeve," Mr. Birdwell said before tilting back the glass and taking a deep drink. Lowering the glass, he added, "Do bring something for Lady Priscilla and Sir Neville to ease their thirst."

"That is not necessary," Priscilla said. "We were about to leave."

"Leave?" choked the actor. "But,

Hathaway, I thought you were going to speak with Wiggsley. I cannot continue with this uncertainty. I am a professional."

"So is Wiggsley," Neville replied. "But the last two plays he wrote were outright disasters. Not a single good word was said about them in any corner of London. You are right. The Prince of Wales Theater needs a play that will bring more ticket sales."

"For that, we must have a story that holds together from beginning to end."

"From what I have heard," Neville said, "the ending was not the problem with Wiggsley's last play. No one stayed long enough to see it."

Isaac giggled until Priscilla gave him a stern look. She aimed the same expression at Neville, even though she knew it would be futile. When he arched a brow at her and gave an emoted sigh, she had to hide her own smile. She would not have offered for him to speak with the playwright if Neville had not mentioned on the way to the theater that he hoped to have a chance to talk to Mr. Wiggsley.

The actor bowed toward her and strode off as if he still was walking across the boards of the stage with an audience watching him, rapt. His manservant followed behind him, clearly eager to meet his every need.

"Reeve," she heard the actor say, "do see to the props for the next scene."

"Mr. Birdwell, that is not my job," Reeve whined in a tone better suited to someone younger than Isaac.

"Your job is whatever I tell you it is while you are still in my employ. Change the knife in the mannequin on stage. That one was so sticky when I used it, I thought I would not be able to release it."

"But, Mr. Birdwell —"

"Do as you are told," the actor said as he opened a door at the back of the cluttered area. Sarcasm chilled his voice as he added, "It is good practice for when you join the Army and head off to glory on the Peninsula. Not that any woman's head will be turned by such foolish attempts at heroics."

Reeve's eyes sparked with fury.

Mr. Birdwell did not seem to notice. "You know where the others are stored. Go and find one." He slammed the door after him.

Reeve stared at the door for a long minute, then glanced at where Priscilla stood with her son and Neville. Astonishment and vexation combated for prominence on his face. And embarrassment, she guessed, when he whirled and vanished into the shadows, calling for someone to help him get what his employer wanted.

"Hmm . . ." Neville murmured.

"Hmmm what?" Priscilla asked. She recognized his tone, which suggested his thoughts were taking him in unexpected directions.

"Reeve was not so obsequious when I last saw him. The man has more wit than Birdwell. Groveling is the last thing I would have expected of him. He must have done something horrible if he is trying to atone in such an abject manner."

"What could be so horrible?"

He raised his dark eyebrows. "Mayhap he mentioned to one of Birdwell's more ardent admirers that she was not his only ardent admirer."

Priscilla smiled.

"I trust Mr. Birdwell will forgive him."

"Eventually." Neville's dark eyes twinkled with merriment. "And when such forgiveness is to Birdwell's best advantage."

"He will need to hurry if Reeve is joining the Army."

"So you heard that, too? I thought I might have been mistaken. Reeve must have found a sudden dose of patriotism."

"Or a sudden determination to win a reluctant woman's heart."

He grimaced. "There are easier ways."

"I agree. Shall we speak with Mr. Wiggsley?"

"I do believe you owe me an apology for arranging for me to participate in that conversation, Pris."

"And you shall receive one when it is to *my* best advantage." She slipped her arm through his. "Shall we look for Mr. Wiggsley?"

A few quick questions sent them on a tour of the area behind the scenery. The seamstress believed he had gone to the dressing area. One of the actors there suggested looking among the props because the playwright often sought inspiration in that storage room. A lad sitting on what appeared to be a tattered elephant said Mr. Wiggsley had been there, but left to go back to the stage.

Stepping over more coiled rope and around what might have been a prop made to look like a Royal Mail coach, Priscilla caught Isaac by the hand. She noticed how he was eyeing a ladder that reached up toward the top of the curtain. When he grumbled something, she knew she had guessed correctly that he had intended to investigate what could be seen from the ladder's top.

Neville pushed aside the curtain and led the way onto the stage. She stared out into the theater, never having guessed she would see it from this angle. The curved boxes seemed to float in the darkness, and the floor in front of the stage was empty. In a few hours, lamps would send light splashing throughout the theater, and it would be crowded with those eager to see the new play.

A mutter came from just past the edge of the stage. The round shadow must be the playwright. As she stepped closer, she fought not to smile.

Mr. Wiggsley could not hide that he wished he had been born in the time of Shakespeare and Marlowe, when a playwright was revered. He wore commonplace breeches and an unadorned coat, but over them he had donned a short cape. It was appropriate for a courtier in Queen Elizabeth's court, not for a theater during the Prince of Wales's Regency. She wondered if he had had it specially made or if it were truly the child's cloak it resembled.

He turned at the sound of their footsteps. His almost colorless eyes beneath his brown hair widened, then squinted as if he were trying to discern who stood on the stage. "Hathaway . . ." He frowned. "I probably should call you something else now, shouldn't I?"

"Hathaway did before, and it will do for this conversation."

"Did Birdwell send you to dress me down? I never thought I would live to see the day that *you* did errands for *him*."

Neville squatted at the edge of the stage. "By all that's blue, Wiggsley, you are driving the actors quite mad with your indecision."

Mr. Wiggsley raised both of his chins. "They fail to understand the struggle a writer has in finding exactly the right word to convey the meaning of the scene."

"They have no concerns about a few words. They are concerned, however, that you are talking about changing the ending of the play when the opening is only hours away."

"But I have had an inspiration!" He drove his forefinger into the air. "My muse is speaking to me. It must be heeded. If only I had an actor worthy of my work, so I could be certain these words are as inspired as I believe them to be. Then . . ." He laughed with delight, and Priscilla wondered if his muse came from a bottle of something intoxicating, for the man acted foxed.

Neville began, "Birdwell will —"

"Not Birdwell, my friend. You."

"Me?"

"Why not? You always were a far better actor than Birdwell could ever aspire to being. You walked across the stage as if it were a true room or street. You did not strut like a gelding with old dreams of grandeur."

Neville chuckled. "I hope you do not use that comparison in Birdwell's hearing."

"The dolt would not understand the words." Frustration seeped back into the playwright's voice. Abruptly he brightened and motioned to his right toward the chair in the middle of the stage. "If you would stand there, young lady, and have the lad step off the stage, and, Hathaway, you join the boy, and —" He handed the pages to Priscilla. "If you would start at the top of the page . . ."

"Are you asking Priscilla and her son to perform on the stage?" Neville asked as he stood. "Wiggsley, *Lady* Priscilla is not an actress."

"Lady?" Mr. Wiggsley snatched back the pages and held them close to his chest as if he feared she would try to take them. "Forgive me, my lady. I had no idea. Unlike Birdwell, Hathaway is not one who seeks the patronage of —" He flushed. "I should not have said that, either."

Priscilla put her hand on Neville's arm and nodded toward the playwright. Softly she said, "Do ease his embarrassment, Neville. He is flustered, I daresay, and will not be able to write a single worthwhile word."

"Shall we begin anew?" Neville asked. "Wiggsley, this is my fiancée, Lady Priscilla Flanders, and her son, Lord Emberson. Pris, allow me to introduce Wendell Wiggsley, the author of the play you watched being practiced."

Smiling as Mr. Wiggsley bubbled with excitement at the idea she had been viewing his work, Priscilla nodded when he asked if she planned to attend the opening that evening. She started to ask him a question about the scene she had watched, but raised voices from backstage intruded.

"No! I said no, and I shall not have my mind changed." Mr. Birdwell obviously did not care how far his voice carried.

"But, Mr. Birdwell —"

Neville whispered, "That is Reeve."

Priscilla nodded as the actor shouted, "I

24

have had more than enough of your stupid comments. It is time you remembered your position, or I shall find someone else to take it."

Mr. Birdwell charged onto the stage, faltered for only a moment when he saw them looking at him, then continued toward the opposite side. As if on cue, just as he vanished, Reeve burst from behind the curtain. His face became an alarming crimson, but he trotted after the actor, calling his name. Seconds later, Mr. Birdwell reappeared. This time, he walked toward the playwright.

"Wiggsley, where are the final pages of the play? I have to memorize those lines and practice them with my fellow actors to be prepared for this evening." He pressed his hand over his heart and struck a pose. "I must consider my stature in the Prince of Wales Theater, and I shall not have you ruin it with your incompetence."

"Nor shall I have my fine words destroyed by an inept actor." Mr. Wiggsley's face was red again, but this time with anger. He pounded his fist on the edge of the stage, and his chins jutted toward Mr. Birdwell.

When Reeve bumbled into the table set by the overturned chair, Mr. Birdwell fired a scowl at him as fierce as the one the play-wright was aiming at him. Mr. Wiggsley continued to rant at the actor, telling him that he was not submerging his own personality into the part, and Mr. Birdwell ignored him as he vented his own spleen on his servant, who could not hide that he wished he had stayed backstage.

"Neville," Priscilla said quietly, "I doubt there is anything we can add to this conversation."

"I agree." He offered his arm and motioned for Isaac to lead the way off the stage. "Let us hope that they save a bit of that emotion for tonight. If they don't, the play will be rather flat."

"And if they don't, it may be more interesting than we imagined."

"You sound as if you expect them to come to blows." He glanced back at the men, who were still blustering at each other. "And you might not be wrong."

Chapter Two

The watch was calling the hour as Neville entered the Flanderses' house on Bedford Square to escort Priscilla and her older daughter, Daphne, back to the Prince of Wales Theater for the evening's entertainment. A soft light reflected off the yellow walls and flowed down the curving staircase to the black and white tile floor. The cast-iron railing shone from much attention, and not a speck of dust marred the statue, set in a niche, of a young boy and a pair of spaniels.

From the lower level came the scent of roasted meat and spices. Mrs. Dunham, the family's cook, must have been making pies. He hoped there would be a piece waiting when they returned after the evening's outing. No one's cherry pie was as delicious as Mrs. Dunham's.

All thoughts of pie vanished from his head as two shadows came down the stairs like heralds announcing the arrival of a medieval lord. He smiled as Priscilla came into view. Her blue gown swished silken secrets when she turned and said something too low for him to hear. The light danced on her hair, highlighting each golden strand peeking from beneath the turban made of the same fabric as her gown. Her cheeks were rosy with excitement as she hurried down the stairs to where he stood. When she reached him, he cupped her chin and gazed down into her sapphire eyes. He wanted to sweep her to him and kiss her until she was breathless in his arms. He wanted to lose himself in the sweet fires glowing in her eyes. He wanted her. He gently brushed her lips with the kiss he must content himself with for now.

Three weeks from now, they would be wed. Three weeks to restrain the craving that encompassed him each time he beheld her, that consumed him each time he held her. Three accursed weeks until their wedding! Never, not even when he had been a lad watching the pocket of his prey in order to lift a purse, had such a short time seemed so eternally long.

"Can I come down now, Mama?" Daphne called from the top of the stairs.

Priscilla drew slowly out of his arms, and he was pleased to see reluctance in her eyes. He wanted her to want him, too. Her fingers caressed his cheek before he turned his mouth to kiss them.

"Whenever you wish," she replied to her daughter. Her voice was unsteady, and he resisted smiling at the thought that even such a chaste salute could undo her.

Neville turned his attention to the stairs. When Priscilla took his hand, her fingers trembling, he wondered if he was giving his kiss too much credit. She was obviously anxious about her daughter's first evening at the theater as part of the *ton*.

He was tempted to tell her not to worry, but he knew better than to waste his breath. Although Priscilla was a remarkable woman, unlike others he had met, tonight she resembled every mama who was firing-off her daughter. She had taught her daughter well, and now she must trust Daphne to put those lessons to work.

Daphne looked lovely as she came down the stairs. Her hair, the same gold as her mother's, curled around her face and was twisted with pearls to match the ones she wore around her throat. Her white gown was simple, as befit a young miss, and she carried a lacy fan in her gloved fingers. She was every inch a young woman embarking on her first Season, but Neville could not keep from thinking of how she had appeared only a few years ago when she had not been any older than Isaac. That time had flown was a cliché. Yet it was true. Now the little girl who had once popped out from behind furniture to *scare* him was a woman.

Priscilla's hand trembled again. Very little unsettled Priscilla, yet she was in a flutter with her daughter setting off onto her first Season. He squeezed her fingers gently, and she smiled at him as a footman held out a dark blue silk cloak to her.

"Thank you, Juster," she said. When Neville draped it over her, his fingers stroking her shoulders, she added, "And thank you, Neville."

Juster smiled as he opened the door for them. Neville noticed how that smile broadened when the footman looked at Daphne. The young man had suffered a calf-love for Daphne over the past few months, but he wisely knew better than to act on it when Daphne treated him with the same warmth she did her brother.

Turning to Daphne, Neville bowed and said, "Allow me, Miss Flanders." He offered his arm. "I trust you will grant this old man a boon as you go forth to win the heart of each young man you encounter."

She giggled, and, for a moment, the little

girl had returned. "Oh, Uncle Neville, you are so silly!"

"Am I?" He leaned toward her and lowered his voice to a stage whisper. "Didn't you know that your mother had men falling over themselves to get her attention at her very first outing during her first Season? They made quite a pile at her feet." He raised his hand slowly until it was even with Daphne's eyes. "This high, I do believe, as they strove to be the first to gain the pleasure of her company."

"Is that true?" Her eyes were wide as she looked at her mother. "Is that really true, Mama?"

Priscilla laughed as she put her hand on Neville's other arm after he and her daughter had stepped through the door. "After all these years, you should be accustomed to how Neville enjoys exaggerating. At my very first outing, I daresay I did not speak two words and not many more were spoken to me."

"Because you were already in love with Papa?" Daphne giggled again as they paused in front of an elegant closed carriage. "No wonder Aunt Cordelia laments even now that you did not give yourself a chance to find an appropriate husband among the *ton*."

"You should not heed your great-aunt on such subjects," Neville said as he handed Daphne into the carriage. "As you know quite well, Aunt Cordelia is quite prejudiced against the choices your mother has made, both then and now."

With a mock frown because her aunt still was not accepting of him using the name the rest of the family used to address her, Priscilla said, "That is not a matter I prefer to discuss on the walkway, Neville."

He bowed again and held out his hand to her. When she took it, he had to fight his yearning to tug her to him instead of helping her up into the carriage. Never had three short weeks seemed so long.

He kept his groan silent while she stepped in. Motioning to his coachee, Stuttman, he climbed into the carriage. He received only a regretful smile from Priscilla before she turned to her daughter sitting beside her. With no other choice, he sat on the backward facing seat and listened as Daphne pelted her mother with dozens of questions. Priscilla's calm, gentle answers suggested she had responded to her daughter's uncertainty more than once already tonight.

He leaned one elbow on the window frame and watched as the carriage turned away from the garden in the center of the square. Traffic was busy on Charlotte Street, and all of it seemed to be going in the direction of Drury Lane. He wondered how many of these people were bound to see Wiggsley's play tonight.

Blast! Both the playwright and Birdwell should have known enough to hold their animosity in check while in Priscilla's company. He frowned. Birdwell never thought of anyone beyond himself, but Wiggsley usually had the good sense to recall his manners. The playwright must be more concerned than usual about the reception to his work this evening. Was this Wiggsley's last chance to prove he still could create the magic of his earlier work?

"Do you see what a bother you men create?" Priscilla asked, drawing his attention back to her and Daphne.

"And what bother is that?" he asked.

His voice must have revealed his thoughts were not on Daphne's evening, because Priscilla's smile faded as her eyes narrowed. Daphne's expression did not change. Blast! Priscilla was becoming too privy to his thoughts. There were times when he appreciated her guessing what he was thinking before he spoke, but at other times, her insight was inconvenient.

"Oh, Uncle Neville," said Daphne, "Mama was telling me not to fret so much either at the theater or at the gathering afterward. She says she suspects everyone is equally nervous tonight."

He leaned forward to rest his arms on his knees. "I suspect she is right. However, you have no need to worry, other than to make sure you don't step on any of those hearts being tossed at your feet."

Her nose wrinkled. "What a disgusting image!"

Neville laughed when Priscilla arched her brows. He understood what she meant by *that*, because he had seen that expression frequently. She wore it when she did not wish to give voice to her thoughts of how ridiculous things around them were.

By the time they reached Drury Lane, Daphne seemed to be a bit more sure of herself. Neville considered mentioning that she needed only to behave as she customarily did, but decided he should follow Priscilla's lead and wisely refrain. Anything he said might unsettle Daphne further.

"We are here!" Daphne crowed, then clapped her gloved hand over her mouth. "Sorry, Mama."

"It is acceptable to be excited." Priscilla tucked a curl behind Daphne's ear. "You need to curb your reactions around others, but you have no need to impress Neville and me. We know you well already."

"And know that I am a complete block," she whispered past her fingers.

"Nonsense! We know you are excited about your Season, and if you do not show it to us, you will explode."

"Now *that* is a disgusting image," Neville said as the carriage slowed.

Daphne giggled, then tightened her hand over her mouth. She did not lower it until Neville had stepped out of the carriage and offered his hand to assist her out. As soon as he released it, she clasped her fingers so tightly together he was surprised he did not hear her knuckles creak.

The Prince of Wales Theater was bright with lanterns hung from the columns along the front. This was one of the smaller theaters, but he had always enjoyed working here. There was an intimacy between the actors and the audience that he had not experienced in other theaters. People were gathered between the columns, both the Polite World, which was busy sharing the latest *on dits,* and, Neville noted, those who sought any opportunity to relieve the rich of some of their wealth. He fired a scowl at a ragged lad reaching toward Priscilla's bag. The lad scurried back into the crowd, seeking a less observant victim.

"I think going inside would be wise," Priscilla said quietly, and he guessed she had taken note of the boy, too.

"Very wise." He led the way through the heavy doors and into the crowded lobby.

The carpet was well-worn in places, and there was a scent of damp that suggested the roof had leaked. Yet he could smell the lamps burning in preparation for the rising curtain and the tea being brewed so that the audience might have refreshments during the evening. He put his hand on the narrow banister that curved up toward the floors above, where access could be had to the boxes.

"You miss it, don't you?" asked Priscilla quietly as they followed others up the stairs.

"Yes, although it is ludicrous to do so. My life when I was working here was filled with uncertainties, the most dire one being if I would eat that day. I have not had to worry about that since this title was left to me."

She clasped his arm, her fingers stroking his sleeve. "Neville, you do not need to dissemble with me. I know you enjoyed the excitement of such a life, which must have seemed wondrous to you at that time."

"Yes, it was far better than trying to stay one step ahead of the watch."

"You should have Mr. Wiggsley write about your adventures."

"So you could know every detail?" He kept his smile in place, but he was eager to hear her answer. Priscilla never had interrogated him about his past, even though she must be as curious as others were. As a parson's wife, she had seen the darker sides of poverty. She still might be disconcerted by some of the experiences he had had, and he did not want to distress her. Priscilla had a tendency to want to heal everyone's pain. Even though he had come to terms with his past years ago, he was unsure if Priscilla would believe that, for she had mentioned more than once how she would never wish that her son would have to face the challenges Neville had.

"The French say that truth is far more improbable than any tale one could devise," she said.

"Quite true, Pris." He drew back a thick red drapery. "And it is also quite true that we have reached our box."

Priscilla smiled as she looked around the box. The carpet and the wall coverings were as simple and worn as the rest of the theater, but the quartet of chairs appeared comfortable. They would have a view of the whole stage, but were not so far away that they would be unable to see the expressions on the actors' faces.

"Four chairs?" asked Daphne. "Is someone else joining us?"

"Not that I am aware of," she replied to her daughter. She was unsure if Daphne hoped for another person to sit in their box or if she was relieved it would be only the three of them. "It is always a good idea to have an extra chair in case someone pauses for a bit of conversation."

"And," Neville said with a wink, "you can use it to fight off admirers, Daphne."

Her face screwed up as she gave him the disgusted look she had since she was young. While he teased Daphne about her face freezing that way, Priscilla went to the front of the box.

She rested her hands on the edge, where paint was chipping off. Below, the theater was filling rapidly. Most of the boxes on the far side remained empty, and she knew the members of the *ton* were using every minute before the beginning of the night's entertainment to share the latest gossip.

"This is so exciting," said Daphne as she

came forward to stand beside her. "I cannot believe I am here tonight. I have waited so long for my first Season. Do you think it will be my only Season, Mama? I know you are concerned that I will fall in love too quickly and too easily and that I am young and that I have much to learn and —"

Priscilla interjected, when her daughter paused *finally* to take a breath, "You always have been fond of the theater."

"But this is different! Tonight is different. Everything is different. I am not standing on the outside of the Polite World wondering when I will have a chance to be part of it. I *am* part of it tonight, and that makes everything and everyone different."

Priscilla put her arm around her daughter's shoulders and gave them a squeeze. "Do not let being part of the Season make you think *you* are different. If you stay true to Daphne Flanders, you will find yourself enjoying the whirl of events much more." She chuckled. "That is advice I was given by my mother when I began my Season."

"Did you heed it?"

"As best I could. Neville can tell you how important it is to —" She looked behind her. "Bother! Where did he go?"

"He said he would be right back."

Daphne's eyes glittered like twin jewels in the lamplight.

Swallowing her vexation, which would do neither her nor Daphne any good, for Neville would not change to meet the expectations of the Polite World, Priscilla wondered if he had slipped away to visit the actors before the play began. She had not been able to ignore this afternoon how much he was enjoying himself among the thespians. It was a life he had aspired to and one he would have gladly remained a part of if he had not inherited the obligations of his title.

"Is anyone within?" came a female voice from outside the box. The drapery was pushed aside before Priscilla could answer.

"Harmony, how kind of you to stop by our box," Priscilla said, hiding her surprise as she sat and motioned for her guest, Lady Lummis, to do the same.

The viscountess, a pleasingly round woman with graying hair and an indulgent smile for Daphne, sat beside Priscilla. "My dear Priscilla, it is grand to have you return to London for the Season."

"We were here last year, if you recall."

"For only a short time, and you were involved with that most unpleasant business about bodysnatchers." She gave a genteel shudder as she pressed her hand over the ornate gold and sapphire brooch she wore on the bodice of her dark blue gown. "This year, you are here for a far more engaging reason." She smiled again at Daphne. "You may have heard that my stepson is looking for a bride."

"Is that so?" Priscilla kept her smile in place, but glanced at Daphne. She was relieved that her daughter had turned to look back out at the theater. She was unsure if Daphne could hide her reaction to such a statement.

"Yes, and, as he is his father's heir, the lucky woman who becomes his bride need never worry a moment about her comfort."

"That is true."

"He will be attending the gathering at Lord Mulberry's house this evening after the conclusion of the entertainments here at the Prince of Wales Theater. I trust you will be coming."

Priscilla continued to smile only because of the years of practice she had at keeping a smile in place when she had been a parson's wife. Harmony Lummis reminded her of one lady, Mrs. Stone, at her late husband's church. Mrs. Stone believed everything would be perfectly right in the world — mayhap even peace with the French —

41

if everyone would do exactly as she suggested. Priscilla had known Harmony for many years, so she indulged her friend's belief of knowing what was best for everyone around her. Both Harmony and Mrs. Stone were well intentioned, but Priscilla knew where paths cobbled with good intentions led.

"It will depend on Neville's plans," she said, glad to be honest, although not completely. She knew Neville intended to go to Lord Mulberry's house. The two men were friends, and Neville was looking forward to the chance to introduce Priscilla to the baron.

"I do hope we will see you there." Harmony leaned toward her and whispered in a voice that would easily reach the next box, "Your daughter would be wise to consider a match with my son."

"My daughter is only beginning her first Season. I suspect she will wish some time for harmless flirtations before she allows some young man to win her heart."

"Her heart?" Harmony fanned herself as if the very idea of marrying for love made her swoon. "My dear Priscilla, I trust you will not allow her to involve herself in a youthful indiscretion, which is all too often the result of letting a young woman believe she knows better about these matters than her elders."

"My daughter has a good head upon her shoulders."

"Even a good head can be turned by the nothing-sayings of a rogue." She set herself on her feet and put her hand over the gold brooch on her bodice. "I hope you will heed the advice of someone who is more familiar with the *beau monde* than you may be."

"Thank you for your concerns." Priscilla would not get into a brangle with the viscountess. It would be futile, because Harmony was quite assured of her beliefs and would not allow anyone or anything — not even rational discussion — to alter them. "We will see you at Lord Mulberry's, I am sure."

Harmony immediately brightened. "Yes, and I shall introduce my beloved son Elwen to you and your daughter. Oh, it shall be a most pleasant evening."

"Yes, it will be." She hoped the viscountess would not hear the doubt in her voice. There was no need to worry, she discovered, when Harmony took her leave, smiling more broadly than when she had come into the box.

Bother! Being the mother of a young

woman taking part in the Season was going to be more complicated than she had imagined. She should have known better, because she had been part of one Season herself and witness to at least a dozen more. Somehow, amidst Daphne's prattle about how wondrous the Season would be, she had allowed herself to overlook how her daughter would be of interest to men who were unworthy of the title gentleman. It would be simple to dismiss them, except when one of her friends was involved in the matchmaking. Hurting Harmony's feelings must be avoided, but at the same time, Priscilla needed to safeguard her daughter from rakes who would damage her reputation and possibly break her heart as well.

Her disquieting thoughts were interrupted when Daphne dropped into the chair the viscountess had vacated. "Oh, Mama, this is so exciting! I cannot wait until we reach Lord Mulberry's house. Do you think there will be dancing? Do you think Lady Lummis's son will ask me to stand up with him?"

"Let us take one matter at a time," Priscilla said, her smile growing genuine. "Right now, we are going to enjoy the performances." She was going to add more, but the drapery drew back again.

She expected Neville, but was astonished to see a young woman she recognized from a hop Daphne had attended in Bath. The redhead's maid, who wore an anxious frown, followed close behind her, and Priscilla wondered if the young woman had slipped away unseen from her companions.

Daphne jumped to her feet and embraced her friend. They both began talking, so excited they chattered at the same time like a pair of birds in a tree. The maid slid along the wall and waited in the shadows for her young charge to return to where she belonged.

"I see we have a fourth," Neville said as he came into the box. He glanced at the frantic maid. "And a fifth."

"We have had many callers while you have been busy upon whatever errand that called you away," Priscilla replied.

He grinned. "Is that your way of chiding me for pausing to speak with an old friend before I joined you here in the box?"

"I would not chide you," she said, letting her voice become prim.

"But you are distressed with me because you think I went off without telling you where I was bound."

"It would have been polite to tell me."

"I did."

"You did?" Priscilla did not doubt him. Neville was honest . . . usually. If he were to tell her an out-and-outer, it would be for a good reason, not just to ease her dismay as what appeared to be an uncharacteristic discourtesy.

He smiled. "No doubt your ears were filled with Daphne's excitement."

"As they have been all week."

When the redhead squealed with un-bridled delight, Neville shook his head. "We shall have everyone in the theater wondering if that young woman is in need of rescue."

"Rather I would say it is Daphne who is in need of rescue."

"The girl is loud, but Daphne seems to be enjoying her company, so I doubt we need to hurry to save her from being prattled to death."

Priscilla shook her head. "I do not speak of Daphne's friend, but of a previous caller. Harmony Lummis."

"Lady Lummis?" His nose wrinkled. "Is she here with her vexing husband or her loathsome son?"

"She was by herself, although she was eager to let me know that her son is ready to find himself a bride. She hopes to introduce him to Daphne this evening at Lord Mulberry's house."

"Pris, you should know that —"

She put her fingers to his lips and glanced at where Daphne and her friend were giggling. "There is no need to denigrate the young man here. I have been friends with Harmony for more years than either of us would wish to own to, and I am aware his reputation is even more discolored than yours, Neville."

"You do not know the half of it."

"Yours or his?"

"Both."

Her smile returned. "What you know that I do not about Harmony's son is most likely something I do not wish to be enlightened about."

"True, although usually you can handle even the most sordid tidbits of information." He became serious as he glanced at Daphne. "However, you need to heed *on dits* in this case, Pris. Lummis may wish to marry, but I doubt he wishes to put an end to his bachelor's fare or his liaison with his convenient."

"You are fretting like an apprehensive father, Neville. I do not intend to allow Daphne to as much as dance with a man of questionable character."

He gave her a rakish smile. "How can you say that when you have let her dance with me?"

"Neville, you have exulted in your roguish reputation, but I fear it has been cleaned up quite thoroughly since you most honorably asked me to marry you."

A rumble of voices from beyond the box followed by an abrupt quiet warned that the entertainment was about to begin. Daphne's friend, with her maid following close behind, hurried out of the box. Neville shifted the chairs so all three of them had an excellent view of the stage.

Priscilla sat between him and her daughter. Putting a hand on Daphne's arm, she wondered if her daughter was trembling or if the quiver came from her own fingers. She appreciated Neville's teasing more than she could say. Did he guess that she had become distressed that he had vanished because she needed his banter to keep her from thinking of all that awaited Daphne in the hours and days ahead as the Season unfolded? On one thing, she agreed wholeheartedly with Harmony. A young woman must never be allowed to do anything indiscreet. The Polite World was often unforgiving, and it never forgot a faux pas.

A pair of singers began the evening. They were well received, and Daphne applauded loudly even as she asked Neville's opinion of them. A short ballet seemed to have no connection with the music being played. The audience began to talk among themselves, revealing their ennui with such amateur entertainment.

It became quiet again when the new play was introduced. A buzz of anticipation filled the theater.

"Will this play be as good as Wiggsley's best or another disaster?" Neville murmured. "You can almost hear them asking each other that."

"And your opinion?" Priscilla asked.

"I will wisely wait and see for myself." He chuckled. "After all, the ending is certain to be a surprise."

"Even to the actors?"

"One would hope not, but with Wiggsley one can never be completely certain."

Priscilla wondered if that uncertainty was why the actors seemed so stiff while they spoke their lines. Even the scene where the young woman hid behind the draperies and the audience was shown the identity of the killer — Mr. Birdwell, once more in his black wig and magnificent mustache — was without any tension. At the end of the scene, the applause was tepid. She clapped more enthusiastically, but she had to agree with the majority of the audience. The play was convoluted and much of what was happening on stage was meaningless. Even so, the evening's entertainment might have been redeemed if Mr. Birdwell did not make each entrance as if he expected a standing ovation simply for appearing on the stage.

"Do you think Mr. Birdwell is intentionally trying to ruin the play?" asked Daphne, revealing her thoughts matched Priscilla's.

"You should not say such things!" Priscilla returned.

"But, Mama, it is the truth. Tell me, do you think differently?"

She would not be dishonest with her daughter. "No, for the same thought has been plaguing me for the past fifteen minutes. But one should not speak so of people who are trying so hard to do their best."

"And why not?" asked Neville, folding his arms on the front of the box so he might look at the audience below. "It is a valid question, especially when anyone with only half a brain — and I know you are not in that category, Pris — can see that tonight Birdwell would be better suited to the role of the bumbling fool."

"Oh, bother, Neville! How shall I ever instill in Daphne the need to guard her tongue in public when you have never done so?" She laughed, unable to maintain her scolding pose.

Daphne giggled.

"Do you think anyone else in the theater," he asked, "is speaking of anything else? Look at how many people are not waiting for the conclusion of the play." He pointed to the slow line edging through the audience toward the back door. "Dash it! I had hoped Wiggsley and Birdwell would set aside their dislike of each other and remember their love for performing in the Prince of Wales Theater. By all that is blue, they are going to leave me no choice."

"No choice?" Priscilla shifted on her chair to face him.

"I told Robertson earlier that I would do what I could to keep the Prince of Wales Theater from closing."

"Mr. Robertson? He's the theater's manager, isn't he?"

Neville nodded. "Now he is going to be eager to get me to put my money where my promise is."

"Are you saying that you will be buying the Prince of Wales Theater and trying to keep it open?" Her smile broadened. "Neville, that is a wonderful idea. It will allow you to keep a toe in the theatrical world while you still remain in the Polite World."

"Wonderful idea? I was a beef-head to suggest it, but I thought when Wiggsley and Birdwell saw how dire the situation was, they would rise to the occasion with brilliant performances. I was wrong. Now —"

A woman screamed.

Priscilla glanced toward the stage, but it was empty.

Neville's chair crashed to the floor as he jumped to his feet.

"What is happening?" cried Daphne, grasping Priscilla's arm.

As if in answer to her question, another scream erupted through the theater, followed by the shout, "She is dead!"

Chapter Three

Neville tore aside the drapery and took a single step out of the box. He was struck by several people, sending him back into the box. Shouts from the hallway rose in panic.

He pushed the drapery out of his way again to survey the people crowding the narrow corridor. It appeared that half the people wanted to go toward the stairs while the other half were determined to reach the far end of the passage. No, he corrected himself. They were gathering near the entrance to a box closer to the stage.

"What do you see?" asked Priscilla from behind him.

"A frightened herd of sheep unable to figure which way to go."

A woman screamed. The same woman who had called out moments ago. He heard a thump. The woman must have swooned. The corridor was so crowded. Why hadn't someone kept her from striking the floor? Were all of them frozen in place?

Priscilla shoved him aside and went out into the corridor. She would not wait in safety when someone needed assistance. Dash it! Would she ever think before she acted? There must be a reason for the screams.

"Stay here," he said to Daphne, who nodded as she sank slowly to a chair.

He did not linger to hear if Daphne asked him a question. Pushing his way out into the crowd, growing ever thicker in the constricted passage, he saw to his left lamplight glittering on gold. That must be Priscilla. Her hair refused to remain decorously beneath her turban.

Elbowing aside two men who seemed sewn to the carpet and apologizing to a woman who glowered at him as he pushed past her, he did not pause as he tossed his apologies back over his shoulder. He edged around a dowager. There was no one in front of her, he realized. Then he looked down and saw Priscilla on her knees by a woman who had swooned.

"Does anyone have *sal volatile?*" she asked. When nobody responded, she pointed to the dowager. "Lady Topplington, will you sacrifice the feathers in your hair to bring Miss Sawyer back to her senses?"

Neville did not hear the woman's answer, because his arm was seized. He started to yank it away, but halted when he heard a frantic whisper.

"Hathaway, praise heaven it is you! I have been trying to keep everyone away." Rimley, a dark-haired baron, who had recently inherited his title from his spendthrift father, was babbling like a young miss.

"What is it?"

The man, who was as thin as a jackstraw, motioned to the drapery behind him. "In there, Hathaway."

"What is in there?"

"It is . . . it is horrible." His mouth worked as if he were trying to keep his stomach from humiliating him. "You know more about how to handle these things than I do."

Neville translated *these things* into some sort of crime. Rimley might be a presumptuous pup at times, but he was clearly alarmed by what awaited in the box behind him. The words, "She is dead!" rang in his ears.

"Stay here," he said, as he had to Daphne.

Rimley nodded, gratitude blossoming in his eyes.

"I will go with you," Priscilla said as

Neville reached for the drapery.

"What of Miss Sawyer?"

"She is coming around."

Her glance led his eyes to where the prone woman was being helped to sit by two men under the dowager's close watch.

Knowing it was futile to try to keep Priscilla from investigating what had distressed Rimley and caused a man — Rimley, he collected — to shout, he did not bother to suggest she might wish to remain outside the box to comfort the women who were not made of the same stern stuff she was. He did put his arm around her waist as the drapery was drawn back to allow them entrance into the box.

He heard her breath's sharp intake over the curse he muttered. On the floor by an upset chair, Harmony Lummis was sprawled in a most inappropriate manner. Blood from the slash in her chest was turning the carpet a deeper red. Someone had driven a knife deeply into her.

"Oh, Harmony," Priscilla moaned.

He drew her to him and held her. As she shivered with shock and sorrow, he could say only, "I am sorry, Pris."

"Harmony . . ." She shuddered so hard he was surprised the floor beneath their feet did not quake. Pushing herself away from him, she walked to where her friend was lying. "Who could she possibly have vexed enough to cause this?"

He was not surprised her thoughts mirrored his own. Only someone with a deep grudge would plunge a knife fiercely into the woman's breast. Or, he had to own, someone who had been startled by her resistance to whatever the murderer had planned.

The former suggested the person who had killed her knew her well. The latter could mean she had been slain by a stranger. That the lady's death might have resulted from either scenario did not help to pinpoint any possible suspects.

"I don't know," he said, having nothing else to say.

"I have known Harmony for so long. I cannot imagine any enemies she had who would do this. Can you?" Priscilla asked, again too quietly for anyone beyond the drapery to hear. As nobody had followed them into the box, she did not need to worry about her words being repeated.

"No." He squatted beside the dead woman and twisted his neck to examine the haft of the knife. He did not touch it or Lady Lummis. There was no reason to check to see if her heart beat when the tip of the blade must have pierced it. Her skin was already growing gray with death. "If you asked me that about her son, I could give you a long list, but the lady herself seemed to be in good pax with everyone. Her only crimes were a blind eye to her son's behavior and a tongue that seldom was kept behind her teeth."

"Mayhap we should consider that her son's enemies might have wished her ill in order to inflict a wound on him."

"Possible, but it would be simpler at this point to assume this has nothing to do with anyone save the lady herself and the person who wished her harm." He shook his head as he stood. "You and Daphne may have been the last to see her alive. Did she act oddly?"

"No more so than usual." Priscilla arched her brows. "It is unseemly to speak so of a woman who has been murdered, but Harmony was often a figure of fun among the Polite World. She seemed not to care that others believed her to have a bee in her bonnet. Do you see anything unusual about the knife? Does it offer any clue to the murderer?" Her voice caught on the word, and she quickly added, "Tell me there is something that will point to the one who did this."

"I wish I could, but it is a simple blade. There must be hundreds, mayhap thousands, of similar knives in London." He looked toward the stage. "Even the corpse on stage was stabbed by a knife with a handle that resembles this one."

"On stage?" She put her fingers to her mouth as she stared out at the theater. "Do you think someone saw the body there and decided to . . . oh, sweet heavens, it is too appalling even to speak of."

He put his arm around her and drew her to him again. She leaned her cheek against his shoulder. Longing to tell her everything would be all right, he did not. She would not want to be fed lies, and he would be a fool to try.

"Daphne?" she whispered.

"I told her to remain in our box. With the tempest in the corridor, I thought her safest there."

"Thank you for watching over her." She tilted her head back, giving him a view of her lustrous eyes.

Their dark blue depths dared only the bravest man to discover what thoughts were hidden there. He wondered how many lifetimes it would take for him to tire of gazing into them. He stroked her cheek and curled his fingers around her nape.

"Neville, we must do something about Harmony," Priscilla said, shattering his thoughts.

Reluctantly, he released her. He was amazed he could forget, even for a moment, the dead woman on the floor. But he should not have been astounded, because Priscilla could weave a spell around him that he did not want to break. "Yes. We —"

He was shoved aside rather roughly. Stepping forward so the man rushing into the box did not run over Priscilla, he grasped the man's arm.

"Stay back," Neville ordered.

"I wish to see what has happened. It is — Hathaway!"

Neville was unsure whether to curse or to be relieved Birdwell was here. That the play had obviously come to an end meant the rest of the audience did not need to continue to be tormented by scenes that made no sense. Birdwell was not, however, the best man to have present in a crisis. He often spouted off comments more nonsensical than what he had been saying on the stage tonight.

The actor's face lengthened as he yanked off his mustache. His skin might have grown pale, but it was impossible to tell beneath his theatrical cosmetics. He made a pitiful sound, then whispered, "Is she all right?"

"Does she look all right to you?" Neville asked.

Priscilla put her hand on his arm, and he knew his voice had been too sharp. It was not easy to suffer fools when a woman was dead with a knife in her chest.

The actor dropped to his knees and pressed his hands over his mouth. "I never imagined anything like this could happen here. I thought the Prince of Wales Theater was safe. How could something like this happen to her?" His shoulders stiffened, and he scrambled to his feet as if he had just recalled they were watching.

"Mr. Birdwell," Priscilla asked, "do you know Lady Lummis?"

"We have met," he said, staring at the corpse. "She often attends — attended — performances here. I cannot believe someone would kill her." He glanced at her quickly before looking back at the dead woman. "Who could have killed her?"

"That is something we must find out. Mr. Birdwell, would you please send for the beadle and the watch?"

"There is no beadle in the parish."

"Still? There was nobody in that job when we were in Town last year."

Birdwell shuffled his feet. "There was a new one, but he died a few months ago."

"Then send for the watch!"

"What good will they do? A patron was robbed last week during the closing night of our last play, and they did nothing to recover the man's money. And that was not the first robbery. There have been several near the theater recently."

Priscilla drew in a quick breath as she looked back at the corpse.

"Send for the watch!" Neville wondered how any person could be such a block. "And tell Robertson I want to see him."

"He may not even know anything is amiss," Birdwell choked out. "He stays in his office once the tickets are all turned in."

"He is the manager of this theater! He needs to know. Now!"

As Birdwell turned to leave, Neville seized his arm. The actor froze.

"Where have you been since the intermission began?" Neville asked.

"With Wiggsley. Trying to get him to relent on the stupid ending he wrote to that accursed play."

"Did anyone see you with him?"

Birdwell shuddered, but yanked his arm out of Neville's grip. "You know well how all the actors stand around dissecting the first act while waiting for the curtain to rise for the second. Besides, I am not the only one appalled at the reaction from the audience. So many have never walked out on a Reginald Birdwell performance before."

Neville could have argued that point, but this was not the time.

"Get Robertson," he ordered.

Birdwell rushed out, shouting for his valet.

Neville let a grim smile loosen his taut lips. For once, Birdwell was showing good sense. His valet could go to alert the watch while the actor brought Robertson to the box. Whether either the Charleys or the theater manager would be of much use was debatable, but he could not stand here and do nothing. Not for the first time did he wish that the stalwart constables who upheld the law in the country also oversaw the law in Town.

His frown returned. Robertson usually being in his office once a performance began offered an excellent alibi for the theater manager. But what reason would Robertson have for killing Lady Lummis? Murder at the theater would keep patrons away, and Robertson needed to bring more in if he hoped to keep the theater open.

"Pris," he began as he turned back toward her. The rest of what he intended to say fled from his mind when he saw how pale she was. Her cheeks had as little color as Lady Lummis's corpse. "What is it?"

"Mr. Birdwell spoke of a robbery last week." Her voice had become steady. Steadier than his own, he must own.

"Yes."

"Harmony was robbed."

He frowned. "How do you know that?"

She pointed at the dead woman. "Her brooch is gone, Neville. It was a large brooch of gold with sapphire stones. It was quite out of style, which suggests it was a family heirloom."

He knelt and looked beneath the chairs. He saw something glitter. Even though it was too small for a brooch, he picked it up. Slowly he stood and held out his hand.

"A clasp," Priscilla said as she picked it up from his palm.

"It must have broken off her brooch."

"When it was ripped from her." She sat on a chair and stared at her hand. "She must have tried to fight off her murderer, and her brooch was broken then."

He shook his head. "No, Pris, don't assume that. It was just as likely he ripped it off her when she was dead. If he was in a hurry to escape before someone chanced upon this box, the clasp would have slid under the chair without him noticing."

"So you believe she was not killed while someone was trying to rob her?"

"I would like to believe that, and it is possible, but there are no signs of a struggle here."

"Harmony could have been surprised by her attacker before she surprised him by fighting back. It could have been very quick."

"That is true." He appreciated Priscilla's clear thinking. "We should not dismiss any possibilities out of hand."

Priscilla pointed to a bag beside another chair. "But why didn't the murderer take that as well? It does not look as if it has been touched."

He picked up the bag and opened it onto the chair. A lacy handkerchief fell out. He turned the bag inside out, and a single coin bounced across the chair. He caught it before it hit the floor.

"A shilling," he said.

"She would have had more than a shilling in her bag."

"I agree. The coin must have caught in the lining, so it did not come out when any others she was carrying did."

"Mayhap you should send for someone from Bow Street," Priscilla said as she came to her feet. She set the chair against the wall of the box and glanced out at the theater. "One of their men might have some insight into the circumstances."

"An inspired idea, Pris." He pushed aside the drapery again and signaled to Rimley. The baron had shown at the card table that he had a calm head upon his shoulders. "Rimley, did you see anyone other than Lady Lummis in this box?"

"No." He swallowed so hard that Neville knew he was still trying to keep the contents of his stomach down. "I thought this was where Miss Sawyer was sitting. I looked in and saw — I saw —" He gulped and turned a vivid shade of green. "I came back out. When Miss Sawyer emerged from her box next to this one, I realized she was not the victim. I looked in to be certain I had seen that unspeakable sight, and she must have peered around me. We both saw Lady Lummis lying there bleeding. Miss Sawyer fainted, and I — I —"

"Wisely called for help."

The baron nodded, again appearing pleased that Neville was giving him a chance to escape humiliation. With Neville's words, he could pretend with the rest of the *ton* that his shout had been to bring assistance rather than giving in to panic.

"And I need you to be wise again," Neville said. "Send someone to Bow Street."

Rimley nodded and pushed his way through the still thickening crowd. Had anyone remained in the seats below? Clearly even those who had been scurrying away at the first screams had decided to return, anxious not to miss a moment of the dreadful excitement.

Neville looked in both directions. Where was the blasted theater manager? Counting the evening's receipts from tickets was far less important than persuading this crowd to disperse. He frowned when he looked toward the stairs leading to the manager's office and saw a tall man. Light glistened on his blond hair, so Birdwell had divested himself of his black wig. His valet was shadowing him. The actor must not have sent Reeve to get the watch.

He signaled to another man he recognized and asked him to go to inform the watch. Birdwell was right. The watch was useless, but at least the Charleys might get this gawking crowd to disperse. Glad that the second man did not ask any questions, he went back into the box.

Priscilla was coming to her feet after draping Lady Lummis's cloak over the lady's corpse. Tears glistened in Priscilla's eyes, and he was tempted to enfold her to him again and hold her until her grief went away. Not grief, he realized when she turned to face him, but fury. She was furious someone had killed her friend and escaped without leaving a clue to his identity or why he had done such a horrible crime.

"I sent Rimley to get someone from Bow Street," he said, knowing his words sounded lame. Or mayhap it was that he wanted to be able to offer her an answer to the puzzle presented by a dead woman who had been robbed of her brooch but nothing else.

"That is good." She rubbed her hands together, and he could think only of Lady Macbeth trying to erase the spots of the king's blood from her palms.

But Priscilla was not the guilty one, and he should not be thinking of the stage. The play was most definitely not the thing. As the Bard would say, however, the game was afoot. It could take awhile for this investigation to unwind and the answers to become clear.

Quietly, he said, "Pris, why don't you take the carriage back to your house? I will stop by after I have spoken with Robertson."

"That might be a good idea. Daphne needs to get away from here." She sighed. "I had not guessed her first excursion into the Polite World would end like this."

"Think of the stories she shall tell her grandchildren." He curved his hand along her face. "Be careful, Pris."

"I realize the murderer may still be within the theater."

He flinched. He had not given that idea any thought, for he had assumed the murderer would have made good an escape while everyone milled about in distress. If the killer were among the *ton*, the whole of the situation would be far more complicated. He did not fool himself into believing no member of the Polite World would stoop to murder. Both he and Priscilla had learned that lesson very quickly, both here in Town and in the countryside.

Drawing aside the drapery, Neville was pleased to see the hallway was nearly empty. Either the audience members had come to their senses, or — more likely, he had to own — they had perceived that there would be no more excitement to gawk at. His smile broadened when he saw a familiar face.

"Reeve!" he called to Birdwell's valet.

The brown-haired man flinched and whirled, terror in his eyes. His knee-length work smock flowed around him like a lady's gown. It was stained with food, and a dark patch along one side was damp. Neville was about to question him, then saw Reeve carried a half-filled teacup. Tea made small waves on the saucer as the man's hand shook. Even as Neville watched, more splashed onto his smock.

"Over here," Neville said. "Come here."

"Mr. Birdwell —"

"— Is letting Robertson know what has transpired. Did you send for the watch?"

Reeve shuffled his feet. "I was on my way."

"Good. Wait a moment."

"Wait?"

Neville turned back to Priscilla. Holding out his hand, he said as she took it, "Come with me."

"But . . ." She looked back at the draped figure on the floor.

"There is nothing you can do for her now."

70

"Her family should be informed."

His mouth tightened again. "I shall do that."

"No." She put her other hand on his arm. "I will do that. Harmony was my friend, and I am unfortunately accustomed to the task."

"But Lummis was not one of Lazarus's parishioners. He may not accept the news well."

The sad smile that settled on her face each time her late husband's name was mentioned did not ease the steely resolve in her eyes. "All the more reason I should be the one to tell him. He would be less likely to take out his sorrow and rage on me."

"Blast it, Pris. You are vexing when you are right."

"Then I must be vexing much of the time."

He started to laugh, but the sound froze in his throat. Putting his arm around her waist, he herded her out into the hallway where Reeve wore the expression of a man who could not decide whether to remain where he had been asked to wait or to make good his escape while he had the chance. Neville understood why when the valet looked past him, his face losing all emotion.

"Mr. Birdwell is coming toward us," Priscilla whispered needlessly, for Neville had guessed that already from looking at the valet. "If you will excuse me, I shall go and get Daphne."

Again he was tempted to jest with her about trying to avoid the obnoxious actor. Doing so would only add to her disquiet, and he wished to avoid that. As she slipped past him, he turned toward Birdwell.

"Where is Robertson?" Neville asked.

"He will be along as soon as he can."

"As soon as he can? What is more pressing than *that?*" He flung a hand toward the drapery.

"You will have to ask him." As he had when Wiggsley was dressing him down, Birdwell turned to his valet. "What are you doing here still, Reeve? I told you to go and find the watch."

Neville did not allow the valet a chance to reply. Instead, he walked to where Priscilla stood with her arm around a very ashen Daphne. "Reeve, will you escort Lady Priscilla and Miss Flanders to their carriage?"

The valet nodded, making sure that the wet spots left by the splashed tea touched no one. "I would be glad to." He frowned at Birdwell.

He could not blame the valet for being furious at Birdwell. The actor needed to realize the murder was not part of some play where he was the lead, ready to uncover the truth and be draped in the laurels of a hero.

"Pris, if you want to wait until I can go to Lummis's house with you . . ." Neville said.

"Do what you can here to find the murderer." She gave her daughter a bolstering smile when Daphne whimpered at the word *murderer*. "Come to our house as soon as you can."

"I will." He touched her cheek, hoping he could strengthen her — and she could strengthen him — with the simple touch.

She offered him the same smile she had her daughter, then brushed her fingers against his. Neville said nothing as the valet, after handing him the cup and saucer, cleared a path through what was left of the crowd for Priscilla and Daphne to slip through. With her arm around Daphne, Priscilla followed.

Neville fought his feet, which wanted to send him after them. The throng at the top of the stairs would make any killer think twice before striking again. Lady Lummis had been in her box, out of view of most people.

He frowned. Had she been alone? They had seen no sign of anyone else within the box, but the garrulous woman would have been averse to watching the play alone. Mayhap she had been expecting someone to join her. If that was so, the person whose arrival she had been anticipating could be the very one who had driven the dagger into her.

Dash it! There were too many questions and not a single answer.

He kneaded his forehead as Birdwell continued to squawk about what had happened. Not waiting for the actor to pause to take a breath, he asked, "Where are the other actors?"

"Huddling backstage."

"And Wiggsley?"

"He is with them."

He should have known. Wiggsley always lingered backstage during an opening, hoping that his whining and pleading would urge the actors to give better performances. Tonight Wiggsley was fortunate. He had plenty of witnesses surrounding him to prove that he had had no hand in any disaster but the one on the stage. "Go and get them and bring them here." He gave the actor a cold smile. "Unless, of course, you are avoiding Wiggsley."

"Why would I do that?"

"You did nothing tonight to help make the play a success."

"I could do only so much with the material I was given."

On that, Neville had to agree. It was not the time to discuss tonight's performances. "Go to Wiggsley and the others, and tell them to come here."

Birdwell scowled. "Now see here, Hathaway. You do not give orders at the Prince of Wales Theater. Who do you think you are? The owner?"

"It appears I shall be."

"What?"

"It is a matter between Robertson and me. Where is he?"

"I told you. He was busy in his office, and —" At the sound of footsteps, Birdwell looked over his shoulder. "Here he comes now."

Gordon Robertson was a small man, barely taller than Priscilla's young son. What little hair was left on his head was the same black as the thick mustache that drooped over both his lips. Ink stained his fingers, and he wore a pair of spectacles balanced at what appeared to be an impossible angle on his forehead. His clothes were rumpled and well-worn. His shoes, however, were brightly polished. Had he just cleaned them to wipe away the lady's blood?

Without a word to either Neville or Birdwell, he pushed his way past them and shouldered aside the box's drapery. He took one step inside before halting to snarl a curse.

"Where have you been, Robertson?" asked Neville, following him.

The theater manager did not answer. He stared at the blanket covering Lady Lummis. Groping, he clutched the drapery, his face growing as pale as the paint on the walls.

"I thought Birdwell was exaggerating," he whispered. "Nothing like this has ever happened here."

"I hope not."

"The Prince of Wales Theater will be ruined."

"I think that is not as important as the fact you have a dead woman in this box." Neville rested a hand on the molding around the doorway. "I have sent for help in finding the identity of the person who carried out this crime."

Robertson looked at him for the first time. "Hathaway! I did not realize you were here."

76

"Compose yourself, man!" He wanted to shake some sense into the manager's head, but suspected such an action would undo the man's equilibrium further. "We have to figure out who killed Lady Lummis and why."

Looking at him, Robertson said with a wobbly smile, "*You* need to figure it out, Hathaway. With the disaster tonight — and the requests already coming in for refunds on tickets sold tonight and for tomorrow as well — it is clear that the Prince of Wales Theater is going to be your responsibility." He glanced at the dead woman. "All of this is going to be your responsibility."

"When I spoke of helping the Prince of Wales Theater —"

"I took you at your word. So what do you want to do now, boss?"

Chapter Four

Priscilla had long been of the opinion that a person's home either reflected their true thoughts or was a mirror image, showing the exact opposite to allow the owner to hide behind a façade. When she stood in the foyer of Lord Lummis's house near Soho Square, she was unsure whether the elegant marble floor and exquisite staircase flowing upward like an inverted waterfall were camouflage or an accurate image of the family residing here. Even though she had long known Harmony, she had met Harmony's husband only a handful of times, and, since he had become a man, her son fewer times.

Chiding herself for her fanciful thoughts, she looked at the footman who had opened the door. His heavy eyes and tousled hair suggested he had been asleep, although he should have remained awake and at his post until Harmony returned home. He was dressed in livery of a light blue that matched the walls.

"Lord Lummis is not at home at this

hour," the footman said with the indifference of a man who had repeated those exact words more times than he wished to count.

"I suspected that, but these are extraordinary circumstances. Will you let him know Lady Priscilla Flanders wishes to see him and his son, if the young man is at home, without delay? It is a matter of utmost importance."

"Lord Lummis is not at home at this hour. If you wish to leave your card, my lady, I —"

"I understand he is not accustomed to receiving callers at this hour, but he does need to see me without delay."

"My lady —"

She assumed the tone she used whenever she had tired of an argument given to her by a lady in her late husband's church. It always brought the end to any brangle and persuaded the woman to do as she should. Priscilla hoped that tone would have the same result here.

"Young man . . . what is your name?"

"Shelton, my lady."

"Shelton, I must see Lord Lummis and his son immediately. Please inform them of that."

"But —"

"Immediately. You should know, so you can convey this to the gentlemen, that I do not intend to leave until they receive me."

The footman's eyes grew wide, and he mumbled something as he backed toward the stairs. He bumped into the lowest riser and almost fell. Spinning, he rushed up the stairs so quickly he was nearly going on his hands and feet.

Priscilla would have smiled if the reason for her call was not so dreary. She must collect her thoughts before she spoke with Lord Lummis and his son. Bother! What were their given names? As Harmony's friend, she should know, for she had heard the names repeated often, albeit in a disgusted voice. Tonight it did not matter that the son was a prime rake and the father a complete block.

She hoped the call would be brief. Daphne had wanted to come with her, but Priscilla had insisted her daughter remain on Bedford Square. Only the reminder that tomorrow evening Daphne would be attending her first assembly silenced her daughter's protests. Priscilla had told Gilbert, her butler, to allow nobody to enter the house until Priscilla returned.

"Not even Sir Neville?" the butler had asked, his face, as always, serene.

"Yes, of course, you should let Neville in."

"And Lady Cordelia?"

Priscilla grimaced now, as she had when the butler posed the question. Although it was unlikely her aunt would call at such an hour, Aunt Cordelia seemed to have a way of discerning when her arrival would most complicate Priscilla's life. Her aunt no longer schemed to put an end to Priscilla's betrothal to Neville, even though she still disapproved. It would have been simpler if Aunt Cordelia had remained at her house near Bath, but she would want to reassure herself that Priscilla was doing all she should for firing-off Daphne into the Season.

Neville had teased Priscilla often about letting her aunt aggravate her. Aunt Cordelia deemed herself an expert on raising Priscilla's children, even though she had, in three marriages, no children of her own. Priscilla's genuine affection for her father's sister stilled her tongue when her aunt made one of her outrageous comments.

Hearing the footman coming back down the stairs, Priscilla was astonished. He was returning far more quickly than she had expected.

His expression was grim. "My lady, neither Lord Lummis nor his son are at home now."

"Are they within the house?" She must set aside the canons of propriety, and she was doubly glad Aunt Cordelia was not here to witness this. And Neville, as well, because he would find her disregarding good manners amusing after the many times she had reminded him that etiquette was of utmost importance.

Shelton stared at her, shocked that she would ask such a question. "Y-y-yes," he stuttered, before recalling himself enough to add, "But they are not at home."

"Thank you."

As she had expected, the footman walked past her and reached to open the door.

She went in the opposite direction and began to climb the stairs. His shout from behind her echoed through the foyer. She heard his footsteps following her, and she hoped that *he* would remember the strictures of good manners. As she continued up the steps, he pleaded with her to heed him. She wished she could turn and say that she wanted to, but she must appear unstoppable in her resolve to speak with Harmony's husband and son.

The odor of smoke from a cheroot led

her to the right at the top of the stairs. The corridor was so dimly lit she could not tell if anything hung on the walls. A pair of tables appeared as lumpy shadows. Beneath her feet, a thick carpet might have had a pattern, but it was lost in the shadows.

Priscilla paused in front of double doors. One door was open wide enough to give her a view of two men facing each other across a hearth. They sat in matching chairs upholstered in a garish green. Even if she had not seen both men previously in Town, she would have recognized them as father and son. Lord Lummis's black hair was threaded with silver, but it remained as thick and curly as his son's. Both men were stocky, looking as if they could wrestle any beast to the ground. The younger man had not inherited his father's nose that resembled a parrot's beak, but Lord Lummis had bequeathed him his long jaw.

"My lady," Shelton said in a whisper, "please come with me. Lord Lummis is not —"

Sorry to upset the footman, but not willing to be stopped, Priscilla walked into the room. Shelton followed her, pleading with her to heed him. He halted in midword when the two men looked, astonished, at them.

"Lord Lummis," Priscilla said quietly, "I beg your indulgence with my intrusion into your evening."

The viscount came to his feet, squinting at her through the cloud from his cigar. "Priscilla Flanders, isn't it?"

"Yes, my lord."

"Why are you calling? Harmony is not here."

Priscilla almost blurted out that she was well aware that Harmony was not at home. She must choose her words with care. "I need to speak with you and your son."

Lord Lummis looked down at his dressing gown, pocked with spots where ashes from past cigars must have scorched the material. "I am in no condition to be receiving. I thought I told you that, Shelton. Why didn't you — ?"

"Do not fault him," she interjected as the footman started to make his apologies. "He tried to stop me."

"Then why are you here?" asked Elwen Lummis as he came to his feet, wearing the same puzzled frown as his father.

"I think you should sit down," she said, abruptly wishing she had not come here alone. Who else could she have brought?

Leaving Daphne on Bedford Square had been a wise decision, and Neville needed to remain at the theater to investigate Harmony's murder. She bit back the sob the thought elicited. Shattering into tears now would not make this any easier.

"What is wrong?" asked the viscount, clearly impatient for her to take her leave.

"Please sit."

"Has Mother wagered more with you than she could afford to pay?" Elwen swaggered toward her. "You show no patience, my lady, in coming to collect that debt at such an hour. I know you are friends of long standing, but her other creditors have had the decency to wait for daylight."

"Please sit," she repeated.

Lord Lummis's eyes narrowed as he motioned to his son. "Do as she asks, Elwen. It is clear she will not go until she has said what she has come here to say."

For a moment, Priscilla thought Elwen would balk; then, with a glower, he drew out a wooden chair for her. She thanked him quietly and sat, her hands folded in her lap, as she waited for the men to retake their seats.

"All right, my lady," the viscount said with another puff on his cigar. "We are sitting as you requested. Will you please spit

85

out what you feel is so necessary for us to hear that you have come in with five eggs and four of them rotten?"

"Excuse me?" she asked, wondering if he were in his cups.

"Do you have anything worthwhile to say or not?"

Assuming that was what his other words meant, she said, "I am sorry to come here with bad news."

"Bad news?"

She faltered, wishing she could find a good way to tell these men what had taken place at the Prince of Wales Theater. In the more than sixteen years she had been a parson's wife, she never had learned how to make such sad news acceptable.

"Yes," she said, her voice cracking on the single word. Tightening her hands, she went on, "I am sorry to tell you that Harmony is dead."

Both men stared at her. She heard the footman make a choking sound. She did not look at Shelton as she waited for some reaction — any reaction — from Harmony's family. The men kept staring as if they had forgotten to speak.

Into the silence, Priscilla said, "I am very sorry."

The lady's son came to his feet.

Slamming his fist on the back of his chair, Elwen snarled, "Was she foxed? Did she step out in front of a carriage again, expecting it would stop in time?"

"No!" Priscilla stood, ignoring that Lord Lummis remained seated. He had excused her lack of courtesy, and she would his amidst these extraordinary circumstances. "You don't understand, Mr. Lummis. Your mother died at the Prince of Wales Theater. In her box." She dampened her lips as he glowered at her. Delaying would not make the tidings any easier for the men to accept. "She was murdered."

"Impossible!" roared Lord Lummis as his son was shocked into silence. "No one would have any reason to murder Harmony."

"She was robbed as well." She took a step toward the dismayed viscount. "Lord Lummis, if you wish, I can arrange for someone from St. Julian's Church to retrieve the body from the theater."

"No, this is impossible!" Lord Lummis erupted to his feet, and Priscilla backed away hastily. "I have no idea why you would come here with such a tale, my lady. You are Harmony's friend, and I had guessed a parson's widow would not be a party to such a story." He scowled. "But you are planning to marry Hathaway, aren't you? Did he put you up to these lies?"

She ran her tongue along her lips again, before swallowing her reaction to his insult to Neville. "Lord Lummis, I would never be a party to such a horrible prank. I would be glad to go with you and your son to the theater. My carriage is waiting below."

"To the theater? Do you mean what you are saying is true?" The viscount groaned and pressed his hand over his heart.

She rushed to his side when he dropped back into his chair. Calling for his son to bring him some wine or brandy, she knelt by the chair. She took Lord Lummis's hand and chafed it.

"I am sorry," she murmured. "She was a lovely lady."

He ripped his hand from hers and, shouting to his son to come with him, he stood again. Without another word to Priscilla, he rushed out of the room, calling for his valet and his carriage at the same time. His son followed.

Shelton, the footman, wavered between following his lord's orders and staying to escort her back to the door. When she gestured for him to go after Lord Lummis and his son, he nodded with a grateful smile.

Priscilla came to her feet slowly. She had made a complete bumble-bath of revealing the news to the lady's husband and son. But every way of explaining what had taken place at the theater likely would have elicited the same response.

She glanced at the bottle of wine. Pouring herself a glass to strengthen herself for what was sure to lie ahead was impossible. She had overstepped propriety's bounds too far already this evening. The best idea would be to go home and have a bottle of wine waiting when Neville returned from the Prince of Wales Theater. She sighed. That might not be before the morning, because there would be many details to deal with. Gratitude flushed through her. Neville had spared her much of the hullabaloo taking place in the theater box.

Turning to the door, she was astonished to see a woman there. The woman's face was as white as the paint on the doors. Her plain gown labeled her a servant, but the bits of lace at the light blue collar announced she ranked high among those seeing to the needs of the Lummis family.

"Are you Lady Priscilla?" the woman asked, her voice strained and unsteady.

"Yes."

"I am Blake, Lady Lummis's abigail." She wrung her hands. "I heard . . . I mean . . ."

Priscilla took her arm and drew her to sit on the closest chair. The abigail started to resist sitting while Priscilla remained on her feet, but Priscilla insisted in the tone that always persuaded her children to heed her.

"Blake," she said, "I regret having to tell you that Lady Lummis is dead. I am sorry."

"Dead? She was in perfect health when she left for the theater."

Wishing again there were other words she could use, Priscilla said softly, "She was murdered."

"Murdered? I warned her!" The abigail put her hands over her face. "I warned she was inviting trouble by letting him seduce her, but she would not heed me. Now she is dead, and I wonder if he even cares."

"He? Lord Lummis?"

"No! That actor." She shuddered as her voice broke into sobs.

Priscilla gasped. She had not guessed Harmony would fall prey to a thespian's fascinating arts. Not a hint of such a relationship had been whispered among the *ton*. Was it possible only the lady's abigail was privy? That seemed impossible. *On dits* were filled with details of any recklessness, especially when a husband was cuckolded.

"Which actor?" she asked, carefully keeping her voice tranquil. "Do you know his name?"

"Of course I do!" Blake lowered her hands and raised her head. Fury burned in her eyes as tears washed down her cheeks. "Reginald Birdwell!"

Priscilla stared at her, as speechless as Lord Lummis had been when she told him of his wife's death. "Harmony Lummis and Mr. Birdwell have been lovers?" she struggled to choke out. Even more horrific than the lady's abigail speaking of such a liaison was Blake's suggestion that the actor might be connected with Harmony's murder.

"You must not speak that name here." Blake glanced around the room as if expecting dozens of ears to heed every word they uttered. "Nor must you repeat here what I have told you."

"I will not."

"Nor must you speak of it to anyone else, my lady." Blake grasped Priscilla's hands. "Promise me, my lady, that you will let my lady's secret die with her."

"I cannot promise that. Lady Lummis's

killer must be found and brought to justice. The truth about your lady's *affaire de coeur* with Mr. Birdwell may need to be revealed in order to do that."

"No, my lady! You must not. If Lord Lummis were to find out —"

Priscilla put her hands on the abigail's shoulders. "Blake, he cannot do anything to harm her now."

Blake's shoulders sagged beneath her fingers. "That is true, but even after her death, I do not want my lady's name blemished by scandal."

"I suspect people will be much more interested in the circumstances of her murder than her recent indiscretion." She hesitated, then asked, "How long have she and Mr. Birdwell been lovers?"

"My lady, you cannot believe I would speak of such matters!"

"Don't you wish for her murderer to be caught and brought to justice on the gallows? You must trust me, Blake, to be discreet with what you have to tell me, but I need any information you can share in order to find her killer."

The abigail stared at her shoes, then nodded. Without looking up, she whispered, "Lady Lummis spoke more than once about you, my lady. She said you were warmhearted, and she was glad you had set your mourning for your late husband aside with the passage of time."

"That was kind of her to say," Priscilla replied, not wanting to correct Blake. Even in the midst of her joy while planning her wedding to Neville, she could not forget her sorrow at losing Lazarus. That grief was a part of her for the rest of her days, just as her love for Lazarus was. Fortunately Neville understood, because her late husband had been his best friend.

Still not meeting Priscilla's eyes, the abigail said, "My lady was first seduced by that blackguard more than six months ago."

"And Lord Lummis has no idea she was having these assignations?"

"No, for thoughts of her never cross his mind unless he decides she is spending too much money. For the past five years, the two of them have been living separately, although in the same house, if you perceive what I mean."

Priscilla nodded. Blake's words made the situation in the house quite clear, and it was not unusual. Arranged marriages far too frequently dissolved into acrimony after an heir was produced.

Thanking the abigail and expressing her

sympathy, Priscilla took her leave of the preternaturally still house. She did not look back as her carriage turned toward Bedford Square. She was relieved to be done with the duty of bringing the disturbing news to Lord Lummis and his son. But now she had another problem.

How was she going to tell Neville that his friend, albeit a friend who vexed him to no end, might be a heartless killer?

Chapter Five

Neville yawned as the door opened and he stepped into the familiar foyer on Bedford Square. He had called here several times while Lazarus was assigned to St. Julian's Church, not far from the square. During Priscilla's previous trip to London, he had been at the house more than he had expected. Watching over her and her children had started as a pleasant pastime. He had not expected to become heart-smitten with her; in fact, he would have laughed at any man who dared to suggest that was destined to be his fate. Now he could not wait for the moment when there would be no need to knock on her door and wait for it to be answered.

"Good morning, Sir Neville," came Gilbert's always calm voice. Almost always, Neville amended, for there had been a few times when the butler lost his serenity.

"Good morning," he replied. "I assume you have Juster and Layden busy with chores if you are answering the door yourself."

The butler closed the door. "Lady Cornelia is calling later today."

Neville chuckled. Priscilla's aunt never failed to create a commotion anywhere she went. It was not that she was a termagant with everyone, as she could be with Priscilla, Lady Cornelia simply assumed everyone would do as she wished and meet her high expectations. That was one of the reasons she despaired at Priscilla's accepting his offer of marriage.

"Is Lady Priscilla in?" he asked.

"She is in the front parlor. If you wish to come with me, I —"

"I know the way, Gilbert, and I suspect you have many other matters to consider with Lady Cornelia's impending call."

Gilbert nodded, and, for only a second, Neville thought he saw the butler's mouth twitch with a smile before Gilbert walked toward the stairs leading down into the kitchen.

With another laugh, Neville climbed the curving stairwell. He did not hear the children's voices wafting from an upper floor. No doubt they intended to make themselves scarce during their aunt's visit. They had affection for the old tough, but they dreaded her exacting standards and queries about their day. Queries that often seemed more like interrogations.

He came around the top of the stairs and walked toward the door near the front of the house. Pausing in the doorway, he saw Priscilla standing by one of the pair of windows offering a view of the garden at the center of Bedford Square. He had been surprised when Gilbert said she was in this room rather than the more comfortable chamber behind it where the family customarily gathered, but he was even more astounded when she did not turn to acknowledge his presence. She must be deep in thought.

The cloths that covered the furniture while the family was away from Bedford Square had been removed, revealing a light green settee near the hearth and a writing desk next to where she stood. He walked past two wooden chairs opposite the settee and waited for Priscilla to face him. She continued to look out the window, and he said nothing as he admired how her simple ivory dress accented her alluring curves and gave a richer glow to her golden hair. When he saw her dab a lace handkerchief against her eyes, he rushed to her side and put his hands on her shoulders.

"Why are you crying, Pris?" he whispered as he breathed in the scent of her sweet, light perfume. "I am sorry for the silly question. I know Lady Lummis was your friend."

"Yes, she was, but I cannot rid my mind of the sight of Lord Lummis's face when he realized I was not lathering him with out-and-outers last night."

"He thought you were lying?" He bit back the expletive he longed to snarl.

Slowly she turned to look at him. Stains from her tears emphasized the dark arcs beneath her eyes, and he wondered if she had slept at all. He had not.

"That is unimportant, Neville," she whispered. "He was in shock." She dampened her lower lip, then added, even more softly, "I know how difficult it is to lose a spouse."

He put his crooked finger beneath her chin. "You are assuming Lummis had the same affection for his wife you had for Lazarus."

"Whether he did or not, she was part of his life."

"True."

"What happened after I left the theater?"

"Nothing." He sighed. "Pris, the watch was useless. The two of them stood around and wrung their hands and muttered about how sad it was."

She smiled weakly. "You knew you should expect nothing more from them. What of Bow Street?"

"Thurmond, whom I have worked with before, did come to the theater, but he found nothing more than we had." He shook his head, trying to let the frustration weighing heavily on his shoulders slip off.

"Can we meet with him to determine if he has any suggestions about what we should do next?"

"We?" He regarded her with astonishment. "Pris, I turned the matter over to the professionals at Bow Street. I thought we would be busy with wedding plans, and there would be little we could offer to help."

"You know the incompetence of the watch."

"Yes, but I also know the competence of the thief-takers at Bow Street."

"We are not seeking just a thief."

"We? Are you suggesting *we* should be helping the authorities find this murderer?"

"Yes."

His amazement doubled. In the past, they had been thrown into the search for a murderer, but each time it had been because they were personally involved in some manner with the victim or the circumstances.

"But why?" he asked. "I know Harmony Lummis was your friend, but what information would we have to offer to find her murderer?"

She looked away and walked to the settee. Sitting, she said, "I did learn something interesting while at Lord Lummis's house, something that might be of great value in the investigation." She patted the other cushion. "I would rather not speak of it at such a level that everyone in the house can hear."

Neville did not need that invitation to sit beside her, but first he went to the door and drew it open farther. That would prevent Gilbert from eavesdropping, a practice he shared with Mrs. Moore, the housekeeper. His own servants on Berkeley Square had learned such actions would not be tolerated, but he suspected they still had ways of discovering every word he spoke and every action he took.

That reminded him of a matter he needed to discuss with Priscilla. Having two houses in London was unnecessary. Would she be willing to move into his house, or was she assuming he would join her and the children here?

That thought vanished from his head when Priscilla said, "This may be difficult for you to hear, Neville."

"Why?"

"Because it is about your friend, Mr. Birdwell. He was Harmony Lummis's lover."

He digested the fact without comment. When he had worked on stage, there were many unhappy women who sought happiness with an actor glad to provide it in exchange for expensive gifts.

"Bother!" Priscilla said when he did not answer.

"Bother what?"

"Why can't I ever surprise you with a fact you were unaware of?"

He took her hand. "Pris, you surprise me in many ways. Far more delightful ways than the discussion of a faithless woman and her insipid paramour."

"Fine words when you do not want to own you were unaware of that most remarkable fact."

"True."

Priscilla smiled as she put her other hand over his. "Much better."

"I have vowed to be honest with you, Pris, and it is not my way to break my word."

"When you would be caught in your lie."

"I have been caught in many lies, but I would never tell one when I thought it might bring you or the children harm." He drew his hand from between hers when she opened her mouth to protest. "We have had this discussion before, Pris, and there is no reason to have it again. You know as well as I do that, until we know the identity of the person who killed Lady Lummis, no one is safe."

"I realize that." She folded her hands in her lap. "And I realize as well that Mr. Birdwell was with the other actors at the time of the murder."

"True, which means he could not have killed her himself."

"Although he could have had arranged for someone to kill her."

"What reason would he have for killing a rich patroness?"

Coming to her feet because she could not sit still while speaking of such matters, Priscilla said, "Her abigail mentioned that Lord Lummis had flown up to the boughs when he discovered how much money his wife was spending. Could it be she was no longer able to provide for Mr. Birdwell as she had in the past?"

"Birdwell has had many rich women

panting after him," Neville replied, standing. She drank in the sight of him, strong and determined. The shade of the coat he wore over a green waistcoat was a poor copy of his ebony hair. "If Lady Lummis could not give him the luxuries he wanted, he could easily have found another who could."

"You speak with obvious knowledge of such arrangements."

When he smiled, the skin around his eyes crinkled. She loved that expression, which was one of the reasons she teased him whenever she could, even at the most uncomfortable times, such as now.

"I daresay, Pris, that you are trying to poke your charming nose" — he tapped it — "into my past."

"If a guilty conscience causes you to assume my words mean something other than they did, I cannot help that."

"Guilt?" His smile broadened. "Pris, you know I have never been inflicted with that emotion before this very moment."

Startled, she asked, "Why at this very moment?" She wanted to take back the question as soon as she asked it. To hear him speak of other women while they stood so close would be almost more than she could bear when her emotions were raw.

"Because I am guilty of failing to kiss you as soon as I walked in."

When he tugged her to him, she gave herself to the demand on his lips. She sighed as his mouth left hers and sprinkled a trail of heated sparks along her face before finding pleasure on the sensitive skin of her neck. Her hands rose to encircle his shoulders.

He murmured something wordlessly into her ear before his tongue teased its crescent shape. His breath sent swells of delight through her. When his lips touched hers again, she tasted their delicious warmth and yearned to lose herself in the rapture he offered.

"You should feel guilty for not doing that sooner," she whispered when he raised his mouth from hers. Locking her fingers behind his nape, she smiled.

"I shall try to rectify that mistake on my next call."

"And the one after that?"

"It sounds as if you wish me to make this a habit, Pris, whenever I come in the front door."

"Or the back." She brushed his lips with hers. When he smiled, she leaned her cheek against his chest. Being in his arms helped her keep the horrors beyond the house from haunting her. In spite of herself, she shivered.

His thumbs slanted her head back. "Sweetheart, I want you to feel warm when I hold you, not quiver as if with a chill."

"I cannot keep from thinking about . . ." She stepped away, the moment shattered.

"Nor can I." He took her hand and led her back to the settee. "You asked me how things progressed at the theater, but I did not ask you how your call on Lord Lummis unfolded."

"You must have seen him at the theater." Sitting, she clasped her hands in her lap. If she reached out to him again, she doubted she could restrain the tears burning in the back of her throat.

"I did, and he was all in a flutter, as I would have expected."

"So you believe his shock was sincere?"

Neville frowned. "Are you suggesting the viscount was putting on a performance which was far more successful than his wife's paramour's?"

"I am asking you because you know the man better than I do."

"He is a lout, poorly spoken and with habits that would appall a pig." He grimaced. "Like father, like son, I should add, because Gerald *and* Elwen Lummis are everything you have heard them rumored to be."

"If her husband learned of her *affaire* with Mr. Birdwell, he might have gone into a rage."

"It is true he has a frightful temper."

"I saw no sign of it last night. He appeared truly horrified by the death of his wife. That brings us back to Reginald Birdwell."

Neville shook his head slowly. "I know better than to discount anyone out of hand, but Birdwell is no more a killer than you are, Pris."

"Thank you . . . I think."

"The only thing Birdwell considers important is performing before ever larger audiences."

"You must own that hangings draw a huge crowd of spectators."

"True, but I doubt he is ready to give his final performance in such a venue. He —"

Voices from the ground floor drifted into the room, each word growing louder. When Neville rolled his eyes and came to his feet, Priscilla knew he had recognized the assertive voice, as she had.

Cordelia Emberley Smith Gray Dexter swept into the room with an entrance any actor would envy. Her black hair was without a hint of gray, and her face belied her age as well. She was dressed in a pale purple gown that, like everything she wore, was of the latest style.

"My dear Priscilla, I have been very eager to discuss the latest *on dits* with you," she gushed as she kissed Priscilla on the cheek. Her voice became a bit harder when she drew off her gloves and added, "I should have guessed you would be here, Sir Neville."

"Aunt Cordelia," Priscilla said, "I thought you were going to address him as Neville now that he and I are being wed."

"I suppose that would be more seemly." Every word was begrudging, and she frowned when Neville's grin broadened. Her own smile returned as she asked, "Where are my dear nephew and nieces?"

"They were planning to go for a walk in the garden in the middle of the square after they finished their midday meal," Priscilla said. "I am surprised you did not see them." She went to a window and smiled when she saw Leah skipping on the walkway alongside Isaac, who was bouncing a ball. Daphne watched both of them, walking with one of the footmen. "Here they come now."

"You give the children too much

freedom," chided Aunt Cordelia. "This is not Stonehall-on-Sea, you know. They should be guarded more closely in Town."

"They never go out without a footman." She paused when the children halted on the walkway at the very spot where they would have caught sight of her aunt's carriage. A hasty, fervent debate was under way. No doubt Daphne was reminding her younger brother and sister of the need to greet their aunt. No doubt, as well, both Leah and Isaac were giving her numerous reasons why they should delay.

When Daphne pointed toward the house, she glanced at the window where Priscilla stood. She said something to her sister and brother, and they turned to look up also. At Priscilla's quick motion for the children to come inside, the crestfallen younger two nodded, while Daphne wore a superior smile. Priscilla hoped her daughter would rid herself of it before she came into the parlor. It was certain to cause her aunt to question why Daphne, so newly launched on the Season, was wearing it.

"They should be here soon," Priscilla said as she turned from the window. Hearing the door open below, she smiled. "That must be them now."

"Before they arrive, Priscilla, I wish to speak to you." Aunt Cordelia took Priscilla's arm and drew her as far across the room from Neville as possible.

Priscilla gave him an apologetic look, and he winked. Her consternation that Aunt Cordelia had seen it oozed away when her aunt began asking questions about Daphne's first evening among the *ton*. As Priscilla answered the questions, she grew puzzled.

"Aunt Cordelia," she said, "we did not attend Lord Mulberry's soirée."

"I should think not, for it was not held." Her nose wrinkled. "That dreadful situation at the Prince of Wales Theater. I am glad not to hear the names of anyone in this family connected with that." She scowled again at Neville. "I trust you will discontinue such low pursuits as stalking killers when you have wed my niece."

"I am quite ready to let others handle it," Neville replied, bringing Aunt Cordelia a glass of wine. Offering Priscilla the other he carried, he raised a single brow.

Bother! She could not fault him for trying to avoid her aunt's wrath. Setting the glass untasted on the table beside her, she said, "Neville was quite willing to let others handle it until I asked him to help me find the truth."

"You?" gasped Aunt Cordelia. "Have you taken a knock in the cradle, Priscilla? You have a daughter beginning her first Season, and you are . . . getting married." She choked on the last two words. "You have to concern yourself with your clothing for the ceremony and the seating arrangements for the breakfast and which guests you will invite back to your home after the ceremony and so many other details. This is absolutely the worst time for you to become engaged in finding a murderer."

"I doubt there is a good time."

"Do not be flippant with me, Priscilla!" She started to wag her finger, but looked past Priscilla. Her glower became a smile. "Ah, here are three good children who heed the wisdom of their elders. Come and let me see you."

Isaac was wide-eyed as he glanced from his great-aunt to her. Priscilla motioned exactly as she had at the window, and he gave his aunt the required kiss on her cheek. The two girls did the same.

Putting her arm around her son's shoulders, which seemed to be higher each day as he sprouted up so quickly she wondered how long it would be before he was taller than Neville, Priscilla said, "Let's go into the back parlor and have a nice coze. I believe Mrs. Dunham has some cakes left from last night if the three of you did not finish them for lunch."

"There are enough left if we share," Isaac said, wearing the same guilty expression as his sisters.

Neville tousled her son's hair and smiled. "What do you say to allowing these pretty ladies to have the first choice of cakes?"

"That is not fair." He glanced at his great-aunt and hurried to say, "But it is what gentlemen do, isn't it?"

"So I hear," Neville replied with a grin sure to irritate Aunt Cordelia.

Now it was Priscilla's turn to roll her eyes, but she refrained. That would give her aunt another reason to lament what a poor example Neville — and Priscilla while in his company — provided for the children. She wished she could persuade Aunt Cordelia to see how Neville had brought the whole family out of their dismals in the wake of Lazarus's death.

"Daphne," she said before Aunt Cordelia could release the words behind her pursed lips, "please lead the way into the back parlor. I am sure Aunt Cordelia would like to see how you escort guests into a room."

Daphne beamed at showing off her recently refined skill to her great-aunt. As she went with her sister and brother following to the door connecting the front parlor with the back, Priscilla did not move. She simply watched them go.

"Spit it out, Pris," Neville said as he picked up her glass.

"Are you taking that because you are afraid I might throw its contents at you?"

"Because I told your aunt the truth? Dash it, Pris. Aren't you the one always demanding I be honest?"

She laughed softly. "You have a very vexing way of using my own words against me."

"I would rather have *you* against me." He gave her a heated kiss before handing her the wine that could not cool the fire left in his wake. "Shall we go and keep your aunt company?"

"If you would prefer to take your leave . . ."

"I would be labeled cow-hearted to flee her company."

"Or wise."

He drew her hand within his arm. "Pris,

your aunt needs to accustom herself to me as a part of this family."

Priscilla's answer was forestalled when a lanky footman appeared in the doorway. "What is it, Layden?"

"A man named Reeve is here to see you, my lady."

"Reeve? Mr. Birdwell's valet?"

Layden shrugged his shoulders. "I cannot say, for he gave me no more message than that."

"What do you say, Pris?" asked Neville. "Will you receive him?"

"Of course." Looking at the footman, she said, "Have him brought to the front parlor."

"Yes, my lady."

As he started to leave, she added, "Oh, and tell Lady Cordelia that we will be joining them in the back parlor as soon as we can."

"Yes, my lady." He walked toward the door.

Feeling foolish, she called after him, "And, Layden?"

He turned to face her again. "Yes, my lady?"

"Please alert Mrs. Dunham to have cakes and tea brought to the back parlor." As soon as Layden had gone out, she added, "What do you think Reeve wants, Neville?"

"I have no idea, but I hope whatever it is may lead us to answer at least one of the questions we have."

Chapter Six

Reeve slipped into the room as if afraid he would be caught somewhere where he should not be. For once, he was not wearing his work smock. His coat was dusty, and his shoes had given up any hope of a shine. Pushing his brown hair back from his face, he halted just inside the doorway.

Priscilla watched as Neville motioned for his friend's valet to sit on one of the wooden chairs. Reeve complied, and she said, "I am sure you will understand when I state this is most unexpected."

"Forgive me, my lady, for being so forward as to come to your home uninvited." Reeve looked at Neville who was regarding him without expression. "I went to your house first, Sir Neville. They told me I could find you here."

"They did, did they?" He added something under his breath that sounded like, "I shall have to speak to them about that."

When Reeve began to shrink into himself like a dog that had been beat too many times, Priscilla sat on the settee and said, "If you have chased Sir Neville from Berkeley Square to Bedford Square, I trust your errand is of great importance."

"Oh, yes, my lady!" Relief eased the lines in his face, and she wondered how long it had been since he last slept. The gray arcs beneath his eyes seemed too dark for losing a single night's sleep.

"And what is it?" asked Neville with impatience.

Reeve gulped. "It is said you and Lady Priscilla have been successful solving other crimes."

"We have found ourselves in the company of a murderer before and needed to prove that person did the appalling deed," Priscilla said. "It is, however, not a task we take upon ourselves gladly."

"Mayhap we should" — Neville chuckled — "start a service to seek out those who break the law. What do you say to that, Pris?"

"I say we should allow Reeve to tell us what he came here to say." She gave him a frown which she hoped he would understand meant that teasing her was hardly appropriate when the valet was listening.

"Yes, Reeve," Neville said. "Do tell us what you came here to say."

"I had hoped you would speak with Mr. Birdwell. He is refusing to return to the Prince of Wales Theater."

Neville leaned forward. "Did he say why?"

"Mr. Birdwell was distraught that Lady Lummis mentioned putting an end to their love affair."

"Birdwell said nothing of that last night. He owned to knowing the lady, but nothing else."

"He is not a complete widgeon, Sir Neville."

"True." Nodding, he asked, "Where is Birdwell?"

"At his house." The valet looked at the carpet. "He has locked himself in his room and refuses to come out. He may heed you, Sir Neville, for you are longstanding friends."

Neville laughed without humor. "I would not describe us in those exact terms, but I have known him for many years."

"He idolizes you, Sir Neville. When he has seen how you have remade your life, he imagines himself doing the same."

"I had help with my family's title."

Reeve shook his head so hard, his hair fell back into his eyes again. "No, it is more than that. He speaks of how you

117

came to perform on some of the finest stages in London. He wants that for himself." His mouth tightened. "Although I do not know why. He seems to have everything he could possibly need and more. What adulation he has not received on stage, his convenients have showered on him." He straightened his shoulders as his face reddened. "I should not have spoken so about him."

"The more you tell us," Priscilla said, "the more we will be able to help him."

"Mr. Birdwell and Lady Lummis exchanged some very strong words when last they spoke."

"When was that?" Neville asked.

"Two nights ago. No, three nights ago."

"What sort of strong words?"

"The lady wished to be done with their relationship, and she spoke to him of moving from the home she had provided for him."

Neville's mouth twisted. "With her husband's money. A very good arrangement for the two of them, because they had no need to find a place to sneak to for their trysts."

"So you will give him a look-in this afternoon?" The valet could barely contain his excitement, and she wondered why *he* was not the actor. He seemed to possess a far greater range of emotion than his employer.

"Yes," Neville replied. "Reeve, did I hear rightly? Are you about to join the Army in hopes of being sent to the Peninsula?"

The valet's chest swelled as he shoved his shoulders back. "I have seen too many make-believe battles on the stage. It is time I did my duty for king and country and went to fight some real ones."

"All real battles do not end on the side of good."

"I know that."

"Running off to battle to create an *amour* in a woman's heart is a lousy method of finding love."

"How did you — ? I have many reasons for wanting to get away from the Prince of Wales Theater."

"Including Birdwell?" asked Neville.

"Yes." Reeve's shoulders sagged. "Pardon me, but may I ask what hour you plan to call on Mr. Birdwell? It might be for the best that I am not present. He has resisted all my attempts to persuade him to come out of his rooms."

Neville smiled as he looked toward the door connecting the two parlors. "I would say straightaway is the very best time.

What do you say, Priscilla?"

"I would say you are asking for more trouble." She did not need to add that Aunt Cordelia would be furious at being kept cooling her heels in the back parlor.

He became abruptly serious. "More trouble is the very last thing we need, Pris."

Neville was unsure what excuse Priscilla used to persuade her aunt that the call upon Birdwell was so important it could not be delayed. Whatever it was, Aunt Cordelia must have accepted it because, within the hour, Priscilla was sitting beside him in his phaeton as they drove toward the address Reeve had given them.

An address near Grosvenor Square. That had been a surprise. Few actors could afford to live in a grand neighborhood. Then he had realized Birdwell could not have bought the house himself. Drawing the carriage to a stop, he looked in the other direction and saw the fine façades of the houses edging Grosvenor Square.

"You might wish to suggest," Priscilla said as he handed her out of the carriage, "that Mr. Birdwell become the patron of the Prince of Wales Theater instead of you."

He straightened the brim of her bonnet, which was decorated with small pink roses. "His money may not be his own."

"All the more reason for him to risk it on his next play."

"Pris, sometimes you put your finger right on the crux of the problem."

She slipped her hand on his arm and smiled. "Surely these are thoughts you have considered yourself."

"Do you think I would own to it if I had not?" He savored her lyrical laugh while he chided himself. Instead of letting his mind dwell on how Birdwell was living in such luxury, he should have been focusing on what they might learn about Lady Lummis's death.

The door was opened by a footman who had the appearance of a man wishing he was anywhere but where he was. He bowed his head, not meeting their eyes as he murmured, "Mr. Birdwell is not at home."

"Not again," muttered Priscilla.

Neville patted her hand on his arm as he recalled what she had told him during the drive about her call at Lord Lummis's house. "Reeve requested we call at this hour. I believe we are expected."

"*You* are Sir Neville and Lady Priscilla?" The footman's head snapped up, revealing freckles splattered across a pug nose.

"Did you expect someone else?"

"No," the footman said, even though his expression belied his words.

Had the man feared he would find Lord Lummis standing on the steps? Or some other capricornified husband ready to demand satisfaction on the dueling green? Birdwell needed to be more circumspect with his affairs.

"Come in! Come in please." The footman stepped back and yanked the door open so wide that the hinges protested with a squeal.

Neville drew Priscilla into the house with him, not letting her lift her hand off his arm. As long as there was the slightest possibility Birdwell had arranged for Lady Lummis's murder, Neville intended to keep Priscilla in sight at all times. He almost laughed at the thought. He did not need a reason to want to keep her close, but he would take advantage of any excuse.

When the footman excused himself to announce them, Neville looked at the gold leaf decorating the plaster of the ceiling medallions. He could not keep from grinning. "Birdwell's mistress kept him well cared for. Or, should I say, his mistresses?"

She did not answer, and he saw her

staring at where black velvet portieres fringed with six inch long tassels smoothed the sharp corners of the doorways. Crystal and silver glistened in the multitude of candles burning on every available surface with the scent of sweet herbs.

"I knew Birdwell liked an extravagant life, but I had no idea he had illusions of living at Versailles," Neville continued.

"This is finer than Lord Lummis's house," she said, walking toward a niche that held a golden statue of a barely draped woman. "Do you know what dowry the lady brought with her into the marriage?"

"No, but it could not have been overly generous. Her family is not as rich as a nabob's. I would describe them as comfortable. Nothing more."

"Her abigail did say Lord Lummis was distressed with the amount of money his wife was spending. He —"

When Priscilla clamped her lips closed, Neville heard footsteps on the marble risers of the staircase. The footman returned, wearing a dismayed expression. Listening to the man babble about how Mr. Birdwell would not receive anyone now, Neville allowed him to go on until he took a breath.

Then Neville said, "Thank you for announcing us. You need not escort us to where Birdwell is hiding. You need only to direct us there."

He thought he would get a refusal, but the footman nodded and gave directions to where Birdwell was. As soon as he was done, the footman rushed toward a door beneath the stairs, opened it, and vanished through it. The door slammed behind him.

Neville laughed. The footman could not have made his message more clear. He did not want to be nearby when Neville and Priscilla routed Birdwell from his hiding place.

"Ready, Pris?" he asked.

She nodded, and he frowned. It was unlike Priscilla to be tight-lipped. He was accustomed to her having a perceptive comment on everything and everyone around them. Her face was blank, and her gaze turned inward. She must be deep in thought.

Putting his foot on the first riser, Neville slid his fingers on the smooth banister which flowed up from the ground floor. The white marble risers were immaculately clean. He looked back when he did not hear Priscilla following. She was standing on the bottom step, but had not put her foot on the next one.

"What is wrong, Pris?"

"I don't know. Something is not right, but I am not sure what. I have this unmistakable feeling of dread."

"Mayhap your own good sense is telling you to flee from Birdwell's company."

"It is not amusing, Neville. We are overlooking something. Something vitally important."

"Standing here will not help you remember it. Speaking with Birdwell might."

"Possibly."

He walked back to her. Putting his hand under her elbow, he urged her up the stairs. She went without comment, astounding him again.

A maidservant waited at the top, but said nothing as she scurried past them down the steps, averting her face. Was she trying to hide her thoughts or simply attempting to be as far from Birdwell's room as possible when Neville insisted the actor receive them?

The upper hall was bright with sunshine and the glint of more gold. He whistled tunelessly. "One would guess King Midas resided within these walls. How much gilt does one man need?"

"Gilt!" gasped Priscilla as her fingers dug into his sleeve and his arm. "That is what we have not considered. Harmony was robbed of a gold brooch. I believe after the other thefts reported, it is safe to assume her murderer took it."

"Yes." He tapped his chin. The thievery had fallen out of his thoughts, because it seemed such a minor crime in comparison with murder.

"Why would Birdwell wish to steal from a woman who gave him all of this?" She spread her hands out to encompass the hallway and the gilded tables along the wall between the doors.

"We can only conjecture which items are from the late lady. Birdwell has many very good lady friends who feel they need to give him gifts in return for his performances."

"That is one way of describing such an arrangement." A smile tugged on the corners of her lips.

He wondered if he had ever seen a more welcome sight, but said, "Birdwell is one more floor above." He held out his hand as he began up the stairs.

She did not take it. Instead she walked toward a door that was half ajar. When she drew in a sharp breath — the same sound she had made when she saw Lady Lummis's corpse — he jumped down from the stairs and ran to her. He steeled himself to look over her head, preparing himself for the horrible sight of Birdwell lying in his own lifeblood.

All he saw were wooden crates.

"He is packing," Priscilla said. "He may be getting ready to leave London."

"Or planning to sell a few items to hire himself good legal counsel."

"If he believes he is the primary suspect —"

"Which is because of his relationship with Lady Lummis."

"Then he wisely is bolting from Town."

He pushed the door open wider, but, before it went far, it struck what he assumed was a box. "Making himself scarce is sure to aim the finger of accusation at him."

"Better to be accused than to be hanged."

Such logic Neville could not argue with, and he did not try. Birdwell had been in a panic last night when Lady Lummis's corpse was discovered. Had it been the honest emotions of a man who had affection for a generous woman, or had he been acting with a skill he had failed to show on the stage?

Going into the room, which was painted dark blue, Neville stepped around two wooden crates, then paused by a third that was open. Inside were china cups and a pair of gold candlesticks. On the walls, outlines revealed where paintings had been hung. He guessed they were now in the narrow boxes leaning against a black walnut table of the perfect height to be set by one side of a settee. If there was other furniture in the room, he could not see it past the boxes. The floor was bare, and he thought he saw the fringe of a carpet peeking around crates almost covered by blue brocade draperies.

"Either Birdwell is fleeing," he said, "or he is clearing the house of everything valuable before his mistress's husband comes to throw him out."

"He must know to do that would be enough proof in some people's minds to label him as the murderer."

"But not in mine, and, I daresay, not in yours."

"No." She winced as she jerked her hand back against a crate. "Bother!"

"A sliver?"

"Yes." She squinted as she raised her finger closer to her face.

"Allow me, Pris." He took her hand, settling it on his much broader palm. Easily, he plucked out the sliver. He raised her finger to his lips and kissed it. "Better?"

"Much better." Her voice had softened to the timbre that resonated with luscious longing throughout him.

His other hand curved along her cheek, and he wondered why he was wasting time trying to track down the killer of a woman he had met only a few times. He could be gazing into Priscilla's eyes and reveling in the eloquent emotions afire within them. He groaned silently. Three more blasted weeks until he could sample what he wanted to share with her. Yet not all was denied him. He tilted her mouth beneath his. When her lips eased into a smile, he explored their sweetness and smiled.

Her fingertip traced his lips when he raised them from hers. "Are you trying to distract me, Neville?"

"Distract, befuddle, captivate, whatever word you would like to use." He splayed his fingers across her cheek. "For you do all of that and more to me."

"Such charming words, Neville."

"I *can* be charming when I choose."

She gave a hushed laugh. "So I have seen. If you would exert some of that charm on Aunt Cordelia —"

"Egad! It is not the charming prince's job to charm the dragon, but to slay it." He regretted the words as soon as he spoke them. The beguiling glow in her eyes vanished as she looked away from him and at the crates stacked in the room. Dash it! He had wanted the moment to last longer, but his own words had reminded her of the reason why they had come to Birdwell's house.

Without saying more, Neville led the way out into the hallway. As they climbed the stairs, Priscilla slipped her hand into his, and he gave her the best smile he could.

"Do not berate yourself," she said. "Everything reminds me of why we are here."

"Everything?" He touched her lower lip while he brought her to stand beside him at the top of the staircase.

"Almost everything."

His answer was overmastered by a string of curses, many of them the low cant of the streets. Past Priscilla, he saw a shadow. The oaths came from that direction.

"Birdwell sounds in a vile mood," he said.

"You would be, too, if you were accused of murdering your paramour."

Her voice was so matter-of-fact, he was tempted to laugh. He did not when he saw

Birdwell by a door at the far end of the hallway.

"What are you doing here?" Birdwell lurched toward him, a nearly empty bottle in his left hand and a full one in his right.

The odor of cheap gin struck Neville like a blow. Birdwell had set aside his taste for blue ruin when he rose through the ranks of actors to enjoy the company of the *ton*. Mayhap he had given every bottle of wine in the house a black eye, and now he had no choice but to drink gin. Neville stared at the actor's dishevelment. He had seldom seen Birdwell when the actor was not in prime twig. Even backstage at the theater, when others were wearing old clothes to paint scenery or to practice a scene, Birdwell always appeared ready to enter Almack's.

"We thought we would give you a look-in to see how you fared," Neville said.

"A look-in?" His lip curled. "Do not lie to me, Hathaway. Reeve sent you to persuade me to change my mind."

"Yes."

"You are wasting your time. How can I change my mind? All the music has left my life. There is no rhyme nor harmony remaining in the world." Birdwell dropped to sit on a chair near the staircase railing.

Neville was puzzled, then realized the actor was speaking of Lady Lummis.

"How many times," Birdwell continued, "have you told me, Hathaway, that I need to understand the depths of emotion if I am to achieve the highest acclaim as an actor? I have found the depths of this hell without my beloved Harmony. Will I be cheered when I reveal this pain on the stage? No, for it will chase away patrons who cannot bear to see anyone suffer as I am suffering. People come to the theater to be entertained, not to be made despondent."

"Shakespeare did not think so."

Birdwell raised his hands in the air and shrugged. "That was hundreds of years ago. Mayhap the audiences loved tragedies then, but would they have loved a real life tragedy like the one I am enduring?"

"We are sorry for your loss," Priscilla said with a sincerity Neville doubted he could emulate.

"Thank you." Birdwell focused his eyes on her. They widened in astonishment. "Lady Priscilla, I did not realize you were here, too. If I said anything that should not be heard by a lady —"

"Mr. Birdwell, this is a trying time for all of us."

"I appreciate your kind heart, my lady. Few others see my pain." He fired a scowl at nobody.

Neville wondered if Birdwell, in his drunken state, saw people who were not present. "They will," he said quietly, "once you start moving everything out of the house."

"Move?"

"We saw crates in the room downstairs. We assumed you were arranging to leave the house Lady Lummis provided for you."

Birdwell wove on his feet, but steadied himself against a chair. "Yes, I'm planning to leave. However, most of those crates have been there for weeks. Harmony and I had noticed her favorite gold statue of Pan was not in its usual place on the mantel in the bedroom, so I had the cases opened to see if we could find it."

"Did you find it?" Priscilla asked, her voice revealing as little emotion as her face.

"Not yet, and I am not taking the time to look now. Mayhap later. For now, I must find somewhere else to live."

She glanced at Neville with an arched brow. He was sure her thoughts, once again, matched his. Birdwell intended to take as many of those crates with him as he could before Lummis arrived to have him evicted.

"Have you noticed any other things missing, Mr. Birdwell?" she asked.

"Yes. No." He shrugged and had to grip the chair harder to stay on his feet. "Mayhap. What does it matter?"

"There were some robberies at the theater."

"I know, but what does that have to do with Harmony's missing statue?"

Before Priscilla could answer, Neville asked, "How many people from the theater call here?"

"I don't keep an accounting."

"Just an estimation would do."

Birdwell scratched his chin that was covered with a low mat of whiskers. "In the past month or two, Harmony has asked for me to invite the whole cast of whichever play I am the lead actor in."

"Just the actors?"

He swore before asking, "Why do you care? Harmony shall not be the hostess of another gathering here."

"Were Wiggsley or Robertson or any of the other backstage workers in attendance, too?"

"Probably." He lowered his head. "Harmony loved everything to do with the theater. Lord Lummis does not feel the same, I have learned from his terse note to me this morning." He tilted back one bottle and took a deep drink. Setting it on the chair, he reached for Priscilla's hand. His fingers closed almost an inch from hers, but he bowed as if he held her hand. Releasing the hand only he could see, he took a drink from the other bottle. "If you will excuse me, I must prepare for this evening's performance."

"Will you be going on tonight?" she asked, her eyes wide.

"The show must not be allowed to fold."

"Birdwell, Robertson has already closed the show," Neville said.

"Nonsense. Wiggsley wrote a new ending." He released the chair and raised his hand. "We will be cheered. The audience will love us. We will . . ." He took one step and collapsed.

Neville caught him before he could strike the floor. Gin splattered everywhere. With a grimace, he lowered the unconscious man onto the flowered carpet.

"That answers one question," he said as he lifted the bottle which had sprayed them. Setting it on the chair beside the almost empty bottle, he wiped his hands against his spotted coat. "He is not planning to flee from London, but he is getting what he can out of here before Lummis arrives to evict him."

"So we have learned nothing to help us find Harmony's killer."

"No, we are at a dead end."

"I wish you would choose other words."

"I cannot think of any better ones."

With a sigh, she whispered, "Neither can I."

Chapter Seven

"Mama, it is perfect!" Daphne was lying on Priscilla's bed with her chin propped on her hands.

Aunt Cordelia walked around Priscilla and pinched the pleats in the pale yellow sleeves and readjusted the fall of the skirt. "I do wish you had chosen some other color, Priscilla. Yellow does not seem right for a wedding."

"Why not?" Priscilla asked, turning with care to look at her appearance in the cheval glass. The dress still had many pins, because the modiste had not finished it. Neither the creamy yellow in the sleeves and underdress nor the richer yellow lace draped over the skirt were garish. The square neckline was modest as befit a bride. "I love this sunny color."

"And you cannot be thinking to wear *that* chain." Aunt Cordelia shuddered.

Looking down at the gold chain Neville had given her, Priscilla said, "It goes well with the dress."

"But wearing the ring you received the day you and Lazarus wed is absurd."

"I would like to think Lazarus is part of this wedding, too." She went to the bed and smiled at Daphne. "In so many ways."

"That is absurd," Aunt Cordelia insisted. "If he were there, then you would not be wedding *that man.*"

Priscilla decided her aunt was the one being absurd, but to say that would hurt her aunt's feelings. So instead, she changed the topic to what Aunt Cordelia would be wearing to the ceremony.

When Daphne jumped off the bed and went to get the gown she had chosen for a soirée that evening, Priscilla undressed. The gown still had work to be done, but the seamstress had assured her it would be completed before the wedding.

Aunt Cordelia waited until Priscilla's abigail had left the room before saying, "Priscilla, there is far too much talk about how you have become enmeshed in another investigation of murder."

"You know Harmony Lummis was my friend. If Daphne were not being fired-off, I would have gone to the country to attend her funeral." She brushed her messed hair, giving her an excuse not to face her aunt.

"The very least I can do is help find her murderer."

"That is a task for Bow Street."

"Which they are not doing well."

"Do you think *you* can do better, Priscilla?" Aunt Cordelia moved to where Priscilla could not avoid her stern face. "If you will not consider your reputation, think of your daughter's."

Priscilla put her brush on the dressing table. "I am thinking of my children. I have tried to raise them to do what is right."

"Even Neville believes you should not be chasing a killer now. You should listen to him. He is going to be your husband, and it is a wife's place to heed her husband's counsel."

She was unsure which outrageous statement to respond to first. Aunt Cordelia had always been headstrong, and, if she had ever obeyed the counsel of any of her husbands, Priscilla had seen no sign of it. Even more amazing was her aunt supporting a decision Neville had made.

Saying something that her aunt must have taken as assent, Priscilla quickly changed the subject again. She could not wait to tell Neville about her aunt's comments. How he would laugh!

Or would he? He had been sincere when

he said he did not want to be part of another investigation. Was it possible that he and her aunt were right this single time that they were in agreement? Yes, it was possible, but that altered nothing, because one thing remained the same and it would not change. Priscilla owed her friend the duty of finding out the truth.

The high-ceilinged room was hot and too crowded and shrill with voices trying to be heard over the orchestra. The scents of perfume battled with sweat and cigar smoke drifting from a nearby room where the gentlemen could withdraw to raise a cloud and enjoy gambling.

Priscilla waved her fan in front of her face. Even that gave her little more than a hint of fresh air. She would have moved toward one of the trio of open doors, but none would allow her as clear a view of the dance floor as she had here.

She smiled when Daphne glanced in her direction from where she was dancing beneath a great brass and crystal chandelier and waved to Priscilla. Her daughter was thrilled to be attending her first assembly and even more agog that she had been approached by a young gentleman before the beginning of each dance.

Priscilla was not surprised. Daphne was a comely sight in her pristine white gown. Even the lace on her sleeves and the ruffle at the dress's hem were white. Small flowers of the same hue were twisted through her blond hair, where a single curl glided down to her shoulder to accent her flawless skin. She was smiling as she took the hand of a handsome young man whose tawny curls edged his face. There was nothing effeminate about the man, for his jaw was straight and his shoulders wide enough to make Daphne appear fragile beside him.

An illusion, Priscilla knew, for her daughter had shown in recent months that she had inherited her mother's strong will and her father's quiet determination. Any young man who failed to perceive that would be in for a jolt the first time Daphne spoke her mind.

With a smile, Priscilla recalled her own first assembly. Aunt Cordelia and her father had been there to watch over her, but she had paid them little mind once she was introduced to Lazarus Flanders. He had recently completed his divinity studies and was looking forward to being assigned to his first church. His easy wit and sense of humor had shown her that he might be serious about his calling, but he had a cockeyed view of life she found very appealing. Within minutes, she would have sworn she had known him for years. Within weeks, she had known she wanted to spend the rest of their lives together.

"I wish you could be here tonight, Lazarus," she whispered. "Would you be a protective papa as Daphne seeks what we were so lucky to find?"

Tears filled her eyes, blurring the image of Daphne swirling about with the young man whose hair was only a shade darker than hers. Not sad tears, for she would not have wished for Lazarus to linger in pain, but happy tears that they had been blessed with those years together.

"How could such a lovely lady be ignored by all the young bucks?" asked a deep, dear voice from behind her.

"There are many lovelier and *younger* women to draw the attention of those dashing young men, Neville."

He stepped forward to stand beside her. No matter how many times she had seen him dressed in his finest, the sight threatened to steal her breath as her heart pounded against her chest. The same style of black coat and white breeches were worn by many of the gentlemen in the room, but they seemed designed specifically with Neville in mind.

"I will agree with the latter, because one cannot argue with the passing of the days." He chuckled as he lifted her gloved hand to his lips. "But I shall never accede to the former. There is no woman lovelier than you in this room or any other."

"They do say that love is blind."

"Rather blinded by your beauty."

She laughed. She could not halt herself.

"Pris, other women would be flattered by such flummery." His smile was boyish. "Why do I have to be inflicted with one who can see it *is* flummery aimed at getting her to give me the smile that makes her more beautiful?"

"I ask you to be honest with me, Neville. I cannot treat you with less than the same honesty."

"An occasional slip in that direction would not hurt my feelings."

She raised her fan to her face and fluttered her eyelashes as she looked over it. "My dear Neville," she said in a simpering voice, "I daresay I shall swoon if you continue."

"Egad, spare me, Pris."

"I have until you asked otherwise."

"And you will always do what I ask?"

He gave her a rakish leer.

"Yes, whenever it proves to you that you are wrong."

He roared with laughter, and heads turned. As women bent to whisper behind fans, Priscilla put her hand on Neville's arm. He was like no one else in the room, and she did not want him to change, even if his ways often shocked the *ton* . . . and her.

Lowering her own voice, she asked, "Have you seen anything out of the ordinary?"

"No, but if robbery was the reason for the lady's death," he answered, taking care not to speak Lady Lummis's name, which would draw more attention to their conversation, "this evening's gathering is a paradise to a finger-smith."

"Why would a thief bother to pick pockets when there are so many baubles glittering on the guests?"

"As long as no thief takes this." He lifted her left hand where she wore the sapphire and pearl ring he had given her two months before.

"I doubt that either of us will allow that to happen."

He smiled, but then asked, "Who is that dancing with Daphne?"

"Burke Witherspoon."

"The marquess?"

"Yes." She laughed. "You sound like a suspicious father, Neville."

"Suspicious?"

She patted his arm again. "That some other man might be paying attention to Daphne."

"It is our obligation to act as chaperons, is it not?"

"Yes," she said in the same jesting tone she had used before. "Do you know Lord Witherspoon, Neville?"

"I have seen him occasionally at the homes of mutual friends. He inherited his title almost at the same time as your son did, and he appears to take his duties seriously. All in all, I would say he is a good chap with a fine sense of humor."

"He will need one if he decides to call on Daphne."

His eyes grew wide. "Aren't you making plans quite early on, Pris?"

"This is the second time they have danced tonight." She smiled. "I believe he has spoken to some of his friends and asked them to step aside and let him dance with Daphne."

"How do you know others planned to dance with her? Not that I am surprised

Daphne is the center of attention. She resembles you, after all."

"I received calls from several mothers and sisters in the past week. Each was interested in arranging for their sons or brothers to have a dance with Daphne tonight. It would appear, in spite of Aunt Cordelia's concern, the family's reputation remains sparkling."

He slipped his arm around her waist. "Those admirers may be waiting their turns."

"No, for they have allowed Lord Witherspoon to dance with Daphne twice now."

"Can I assume you have spies throughout the room?"

She laughed as she touched his cheek lightly. "Dear Neville, how can you be so much a part of the *ton* and yet be unaware of how it works? Daphne has dozens of watch-dogs tonight, each one reporting to me anything they deem out of the ordinary."

"And Witherspoon's arranging to dance with her more than once is something quite out of the ordinary?"

"Very much so." Her smile fell away. "I am glad it is the only peculiar thing tonight."

"It is not."

"What?"

He lowered his voice. "Have you noticed that nobody speaks one lady's name?"

"No, I had not."

"That is because you are too intent on your daughter." Slanting toward her, he drew her hand with her fan up as if he wanted to examine it. "Don't you find it odd, Pris, that there is no bibble-babble about the late lady?"

Priscilla scanned the room. The smiling dancers turned through the pattern dictated by the music. Clumps of guests gathered along the walls, talking while they watched the dancers. No cloud of worry seemed to linger over any brow.

"Her husband and son were not well received," she said.

"But the lady was a member of the Polite World, and she suffered an appalling fate. When servants died under curious conditions on Bedford Square last year, the *ton* talked endlessly of it. Why would they be silent about one of their own?"

"They might believe if they ignore the matter, it will be as if it never happened."

He grimaced. "I shall never understand the *ton*, Pris. Hiding like a fox in a hedgerow does not keep the hounds from the chase."

"I would like to believe her death was a singular incident."

"So would I." His voice was as grim as his face. Then his smile returned, suggesting his only care was finding a glass of something cool to drink.

Priscilla looked over her shoulder to discover a man she did not know walking toward them. His hair was a brownish-red, and his face suggested he had spent too much time in the sun. Not only was it almost the same shade as his hair, but it was peeling across his cheekbones. Although she thought his riding boots out of place, the rest of his clothing, from his dark blue coat to his silver breeches, were appropriate for the gathering.

"What happened to you, Dentford?" asked Neville.

"Too much sun, as you can see." The man rubbed at his face, and she guessed the flaking skin was itchy.

Neville put his hand on Priscilla's arm. "Dentford, have you been introduced to Lady Priscilla Flanders?"

"Your betrothed?" The red-faced man grinned as he bowed over her hand. "It is a pleasure, my lady, to meet the woman who finally snared such a wily man. He has long avoided finding himself standing in front of a parson."

"Pay him no mind," Neville ordered with

a chuckle. "Pris, this is Theodore Dentford, fourth viscount."

"It is a pleasure," she said.

The viscount smiled in her direction, but became serious when he turned back to Neville. "Have I heard rightly? Are you involved in that messy business involving Harmony Lummis?"

"If you speak of her death, then, yes, we are involved in trying to figure out who did such a horrible thing." He put his arm around Priscilla's shoulders.

"We?" squeaked Lord Dentford. He recovered himself enough to add, "I mean no insult, my lady. Such pursuits are usually not of interest to women."

"Nor to most gentlemen," Priscilla replied. "It is fortunate that Neville has an aptitude for seeing what others overlook."

Lord Dentford cleared his throat. "I heard Lord Lummis and his son have left Town."

"Not surprising." Neville sighed. "No doubt they wish to bury the lady in the family's private plot."

"True, true. So you think Lummis had nothing to do with the crime?"

"It is too early to say."

"Oh, my."

Priscilla asked, "What is wrong, Lord Dentford?"

"Nothing to worry yourself about, my lady." He squared his shoulders. "My wife has been unsettled by the attack on Lady Lummis. She had intended to attend the theater that night and spend some time in conversation with the late lady, and now she is distressed by the multitude of rumors flying in every direction."

"Rumors?" she asked.

"Rumors of infidelity and jealousy and retribution."

Neville's laugh sounded forced. "There is always such talk in the wake of such a tragedy."

"True, true."

"Who has spoken these rumors to Lady Dentford?"

"Her friends, I suppose."

"And they are?"

Lord Dentford frowned, his face growing a deeper crimson. "Why are you interrogating me, Hathaway?"

Priscilla answered, hoping she could calm the viscount before his rising voice was noticed by others. "Neville and I were speaking of how nobody here tonight seemed to be discussing Lady Lummis's unfortunate death. That fact makes us curious who is speaking of it."

"Forgive me, my lady," the viscount said,

bowing his head toward her. "The whole of this matter is so upsetting that I find myself on edge. My wife earlier today received Lady Cordelia Dexter. I believe they spoke of the rumors."

"Thank you, Lord Dentford." She managed to smile but she was disappointed. She was unsure why, because having Aunt Cordelia discussing the murder with Lady Dentford was more commonplace than the guests ignoring it.

"You are welcome." He scratched his cheek, then jerked his fingers away as if abruptly realizing what he was doing. "Good evening, my lady, Hathaway."

As he walked away, Neville cursed under his breath.

"Have pity on him," Priscilla said almost as softly. "He is seeking comfort for his wife."

"Foolish woman. Whether she was present or not might have made no difference about what took place. She has no reason to wallow in guilt."

"But I understand how she feels."

He turned her to face him. "Pris, I thought you wiser than that."

"I *know* with the logical part of my brain that there was nothing I could have done to halt the murder. Even if I had spent

151

every minute with her, the murderer might have stalked her at another time to steal her brooch and slay her. I know that! But still, there is a small voice within me that says there must have been something I could have done differently to insure the lady remained alive."

"I understand."

She clasped his hands and lifted them between their chests. "You do, don't you?"

"How many times have I thought if I had peeked past the draperies at the back of our box sooner that I would have seen the murderer emerging from her box?"

"But would you have known he was the murderer? Such criminals do not wear brands upon their foreheads to show their intentions."

"If the man had been out of place there —"

"Do you think that likely? I would suspect, because nobody noticed anything out of place, the killer is either a member of the theater troupe or a member of the *ton*."

"A most unsettling thought." He shook his head. "It is simple to consider what might have happened, but we must focus on what *has* happened, so we can halt it from occurring again."

"Do you think it will?"

"I have to keep that consideration at the forefront of my mind. If I do not . . ." He looked to his left and smiled.

Priscilla released his hands as her daughter came toward them. Lord Witherspoon was escorting her, and they were laughing together. A pinch of something she could not quite describe rushed through Priscilla as a far younger image of her daughter lay like a translucent portrait over Daphne. It seemed like such a short time ago when she had cuddled Daphne on her lap and sung a lullaby. How could the years have passed so quickly since she sat beside her daughter and guided her hands to make her first embroidery stitches? The woman in an unblemished white gown should still be wearing a guilty expression while Priscilla scolded her for ripping yet another dress while climbing trees and running along the strand in Stonehall-on-Sea.

Neville's arm settled around her shoulders again, and she raised her eyes toward his. In a hushed tone that would not reach Daphne's ears, he said, "She will never grow up so much that she will grow away from you, Pris."

Her eyes filled with tears, but she had no time to tell him how much she appreciated his astute words. Blinking the tears away, because she did not want to embarrass her daughter, she smiled as Daphne introduced her to Lord Witherspoon.

"How do you do, my lady?" The marquess bowed over her hand with a grace that spoke of much Town polish. When he straightened, she noted he was of Neville's height. "I wanted to thank you for allowing Miss Flanders to attend this assembly. She has been telling me about your many adventures and how handily you have solved each mystery, bringing a killer to justice."

"I am sure Daphne made the situations sound more exciting than they actually were." She glanced at her daughter, who did not seem to notice, for Daphne was beaming with happiness. "I believe you know Sir Neville Hathaway?"

"Of course." Lord Witherspoon's pleasing tenor voice lightened with amusement. "Sir Neville has been teaching me the foolishness of betting against the odds, especially when luck favors him."

"Uncle Neville!" gasped Daphne. She put her hand over her mouth, instantly contrite at her outburst.

Neville smiled. "You need not worry on this young man's behalf, Daphne. He is a quick student, and I would say luck favors him often."

When Lord Witherspoon smiled, Daphne did, too.

Priscilla watched her daughter closely. Daphne's eyes were alight with happiness and excitement. When her daughter nodded in agreement with everything Lord Witherspoon said, Priscilla glanced at Neville, who gave her only a raised eyebrow in return. Daphne's smile dimmed when the marquess took his leave after bowing over Priscilla's hand, then Daphne's. It did not return as brightly even when a baron whom Priscilla recognized as a friend of Aunt Cordelia's asked Daphne to stand up with him for the next dance.

Neville lifted a pair of glasses from a tray held by a passing servant and handed her one. Tapping the rim of his against hers, he said, "I believe your worries about your daughter are about to increase tenfold."

"Daphne is overawed by everything around her."

"Especially one young marquess — who seems to have taken a liking to her as well."

Priscilla followed Neville's gaze toward where the dancing had begun again. Although Daphne was being twirled about by the baron, she was looking at Lord Witherspoon who was watching her.

"Bother!" Priscilla muttered.

"Yes," Neville said with the hint of a smile, "I think he is quite bothered by Daphne, and I suspect he will be bothering you in short order."

"This is not funny, Neville."

"I did not mean to suggest that it is."

"And," she said with her own smile as she tapped him on the arm, "the problem soon will be yours as Daphne's stepfather."

"By all that's blue, I had not thought of that."

At his dreary expression, Priscilla could not keep from laughing. "You should have considered that you would take on that role when you married me."

"I did, but I did not give thought to the idea that I would be put into the position of granting young men leave to call upon your daughters."

"A worthy recompense, I am sure many would say, for making other fathers worry about their daughters." She wagged her finger at him. "Don't tell me again that your reputation was undeserved."

"I never said that." He grinned. "Not exactly."

"Whether your reputation was undeserved

or well earned, it mattered little to those fathers who worried about your intentions toward their daughters."

"And now the worry is mine."

"Yes."

He took her hands between his and led her to where chairs by the wall would offer a view of her daughter. Seating her, he took the chair beside her and entwined his fingers with hers. She gazed into his dark eyes, as fathomless and mysterious as the night. The warmth of his gaze surrounded her and seeped into her, tempting her to forget everyone in the room but him. Drawing her hand out of his, she raised it to caress his cheek. He turned his head and pressed his lips against her palm.

She jerked back her hand at a shriek from the far side of the room, then realized, when she heard it again, the sound was only a shrill laugh.

"I am sorry," she whispered. "I fear I am fretting my gizzard."

"Such language, Pris!" He smiled gently.

"Something I heard Isaac say. I should know better than to repeat what my son says."

"What you should do, Pris, is calm yourself before you suffer a *crise de nerfs*."

"You know I would never give in to

worrying to the point I swooned. If I did such a thing, I would feel ashamed to be seen in public again."

"I have to own that I would not be distressed to have you remain behind closed doors now."

She stared at him, amazed. "Neville, it is not like you to fret so much either. There is no reason to believe the murderer considers me a target."

"True, and that is not the reason I would like to keep you behind closed doors far from the rest of the world." He pressed his heated mouth to her palm again.

"You are a rogue."

He raised his head and regarded her with the craving she understood all too well. "If a rogue is a man deeply in love, then I accept the reference."

She touched his cheek again, knowing any other signs of affection must wait. She wanted to thank him for drawing her out of her doldrums with kisses, but, like him, she needed to pretend his attentions had been aimed only at delighting her instead of keeping her — and himself — from thinking about the killer who might be near and plotting the disposition of his next victim.

Chapter Eight

"You look as if you have ridden a hag-hound through perdition," Priscilla said as Neville walked into the back parlor.

"Thank you for the compliment."

She came to her feet from where she had been writing out instructions for Mrs. Moore. Although the housekeeper could run the house efficiently, Mrs. Moore was eager for a list of specific directions as the date for the wedding breakfast approached. Priscilla had not guessed so many preparations would be required. Her previous wedding breakfast had been a quiet gathering of family and a few friends. The upcoming one was certain to be a social occasion involving the *ton*. The guest list was growing every day.

Putting the page on a table, Priscilla went to where Neville stood. He looked . . . haggard. There was no other word for it. His mouth was turned down in a weary frown, and the arcs beneath his eyes were as dark as the whiskers on his unshaven chin. She would have said his clothes looked as if he had slept in them, but she doubted he had slept.

"Has something happened?" she asked, not sure she wanted to hear his reply.

He grabbed her by the shoulders and kissed her hard. Before she had a chance to put her arms around him, he released her.

"What is it?" she asked. "What is wrong?"

Walking slowly past her, he went to a chair. He looked back at her, and she realized, even exhausted, he would not sit until she did. She wanted to tease him about being a gentleman, but his empty, haunted eyes silenced her.

She sat on the settee and held up her hands. He stared as if unable to guess what she intended with the gesture. Reaching out, she took his hands. She drew him down to sit beside her.

"Tell me," she said in little more than a whisper.

"There is not much to tell. I spoke to Thurmond, and he has come to a dead end with the investigation. He has been given another assignment." He laughed sharply. "That is that, as they say. 'All's well that ends well,' as the bard wrote."

She could taste his bitterness as if it

stung her own tongue. "You know you do not mean that."

"No, I don't." When he sighed, his shoulders rose slowly. She guessed they were heavy with invisible burdens. "It galls me, Pris, to know a woman is dead, and there is nothing being done to find her killer. We have let our indifference bring us to this point."

"You are not indifferent to this murder. Neither am I."

"That is not what I meant. I am talking about the whole of the Polite World, which acts as if the rest of London's population does not exist, unless a member of the *ton* seeks them out for a specific task or to be entertained. On those rare occasions when the *ton* and the lower classes come into contact, the Polite World pretends nothing has happened. Now even Bow Street is doing that."

She frowned. "Do you think Bow Street was pressured by someone to halt their investigation?"

"No." He sighed as he propped his fist on the curved arm of the settee. "I asked Thurmond that myself and drove him into a pelter. The problem is, Pris, that this is beyond Bow Street's scope. They are thief-takers, not investigators. What we need is a skilled group of men policing the city. If they existed, there might be hope of capturing this murderer. Now . . ." He winced.

"What is it?"

"Nothing."

"You look ill, Neville."

"It is nothing." He gave her a crooked smile. "Nothing more than an aching head. I would not mind it half as much if I had enjoyed a few bottles to earn it."

"Here." She put her hands on either side of his face. "What you need is to rest."

"I don't have time for that. If Bow Street is unwilling to continue the search for —"

"Neville, a few minutes will make no difference to the murderer, and they will make a great difference for you."

He did not resist when she drew his head down onto her lap. When she began to massage his temples, he murmured, "Thank you, Pris. That helps more than you can know."

"I doubt you have been sleeping well as you try to puzzle out the identity of the murderer."

"That is true." He opened one eye and looked up at her. "What of you, Pris? You know your aunt will have my head and other equally precious parts of my anatomy if you are so overwhelmed that you fall asleep when the banns are next read on Sunday."

"I am sleeping as well as one might expect." *Especially when I cannot stop thinking of you,* she added silently. She almost said the words aloud, but speaking them would be a guarantee that Neville would not rest. Her lips still tingled from his fiery kiss, and she wanted more.

As his eyes closed and his breathing slowed from its tense pace, she knew postponing his next kiss was a sacrifice she must make. She had never seen him as exhausted, not even when he had first inherited his title and had come to Stonehall-on-Sea to escape the endless forms he needed to review with his solicitor and estate manager.

Priscilla relaxed back against the settee and closed her eyes. She savored the brief respite as she imagined how they could share more times like this after their marriage. Sunny mornings in the garden behind Mermaid Cottage in Stonehall-on-Sea as they looked out at the sea beyond the chalk cliffs. Long afternoon walks on the rough shore beneath his ancestral estate in Cornwall while they marveled at the bizarre sculptures wind and water had made from the rocks. Quiet evenings when they sat in this very room and enjoyed the company of the children. Enchanting nights when they were alone in their bed, whether it was in a seaside cottage, distant Cornwall, or in London.

But that was for the future. Today, she doubted Neville would remain still for long. Not only would he soon grow uncomfortable with his legs hanging over the settee's arm, but it was unlike him to rest when there was a task to be done.

As if he had heard her thoughts, he said quietly, "I cannot believe there is nothing more we can do."

"We never said there was nothing else. Bow Street did."

He turned his head to smile up at her. "Sweetheart, I knew you would have some insight that I would find comforting." He curved his arm up around her shoulders. "Not as comforting as your touch, I must own."

"You *must*, must you?"

He laughed, the sound more like his everyday laugh. "Give this poor, exhausted man a chance to regain his wits before you engage him in battle."

She kneaded his forehead where the lines were deep. When he closed his eyes again, she said, "You never are without some portion of your wits, Neville."

"A good half of them are missing just now." He smiled. "By Jove, Pris, that feels good."

"I am glad." She faltered, not wanting the delightful moment to pass, but knowing he would want her to share her thoughts. "Neville?"

"Hmmm?"

At his contented tone, she almost pulled back her unspoken words. She could not, for she owed every opportunity to bring Harmony's killer to the gallows.

"Neville, did anyone discover what happened to Harmony's brooch?"

"It was sure to have been sold by now."

"To whom?"

His eyes popped open, and he sat up. "A jeweler or a two-to-one shop —"

"A what?"

"A pawnbroker. The murderer may have even contacted a fence." He arched a brow. "I collect you know what a fence does."

"Yes, I know what fences and pawnbrokers do. I would guess those two would be the likely destination for a murderer trying to sell a piece of jewelry." She rose and went to the sideboard. Pouring him a glass of wine, she said, "Harmony's brooch was unique. It would be easily recognized if any member of the *ton* donned it."

"If the gems were removed and sold separately from the gold, it would never be found."

"How long would that take?"

"It would require a skilled craftsman, so the gems were not ruined. Whoever received it would have to obtain the gemsmith's services, and that often takes a few days."

"Then we have no time to waste, do we?" She smiled. "Does your friend Morton work at the Prince of Wales Theater?"

"Yes." He grinned as he took the glass. "Pris, I know what you are thinking."

She hated how her hands trembled as she filled a glass for herself. Setting the bottle down, she forced a smile as she picked up the glass. "If you are thinking that in order to find out where a murderer had disposed of his stolen goods in exchange for money, we must appear to be thieves ourselves, then you are right."

"Morton does work at the theater. However, it would be awkward for us to sneak costumes out without raising suspicions. The theater is closed until another play can be prepared." He grinned wryly. "Wiggsley was fortunate the rest of the play was never seen. It would have been his ruin."

"And, mayhap, a reason to divert attention?"

"With murder?" His brow furrowed. "Unlikely, because Wiggsley is more apt to slice into someone with his pen than with a knife." He laughed. "Also, knowing Wiggsley as I do, I suspect he believes the audience would have been won over if they had seen the whole play."

Priscilla smiled. What little she had seen of the playwright told her that Neville — as usual — had well taken the measure of someone else. Sobering, she asked, "Neville, how well do you know Morton?"

"I have known him for years." He shook his head. "If you are asking if he could be the murderer we seek, the answer is no. In spite of his rough ways, he has a kind heart."

"As long as you are sure —"

"Pris, I *am* sure about Morton. I wish I could be as sure of the others at the theater."

Wanting to apologize for doubting him, even though she had been right to pose the questions, she asked, "And Mr. Robertson?"

Neville did not answer for a long minute. Taking a deep breath, he released it slowly. "Robertson has no alibi save for his own word. He was seen going into his office and coming out, but everybody I spoke with at the theater owned that he could have skulked out without anyone noticing during the performances."

"Do you accept his word?"

"I always have. I always believed his vow had great value."

She nodded, again faltering when she longed to find the words to ease his doubt about a man he had considered a friend. "I am sorry to have to ask that question, Neville."

"You have to ask it. I am asking it myself, even though Thurmond is convinced Robertson is telling the truth."

"I am glad to hear Mr. Thurmond's opinion. His insight has been invaluable before," she said.

Neville nodded. "I agree, but I am keeping my eyes open when Robertson is nearby, just the same."

"Would it be awkward for the owner of the theater to sneak into the theater?"

He shook his head. "Let's not speak of the ownership of the Prince of Wales. I hope to find a way to persuade someone else to take over the theater." He took a drink. "Your faith in me is always amazing, Pris. I believe, if we are cautious, we will be able to sneak past Robertson and persuade Morton to part with a few items as he has in the past when I asked for a favor. He will keep his lips closed, so Robertson is no wiser. I have no need for the theater manager to nag me about putting up the funds for the theater. Let's go and see Morton."

"Now?"

"Why not?" He came to his feet.

She put her glass on the sideboard. "You are exhausted."

"Touching you has exhilarated me." His arm around her waist tugged her to him. This time, when he kissed her, he did not hurry. And when she caressed his shoulders, it was not to ease his stressed muscles.

He was right, she decided, as his lips drifted along her neck, setting every inch of her on fire. When he touched her, she felt so exultant she could have danced around the room without touching the floor. Each kiss added to the luscious enchantment he spun around her. The magic of his mouth matched the bewitchment of his fingers coursing down her back and then slowly toward her nape, bringing her even closer. She could imagine his wondrous lips touching her in places which pulsed at the very thought.

Their wedding seemed like a lifetime away. She hoped each moment beyond his arms would fly by as swiftly as each moment within them. Even so, their wedding night could not come soon enough.

Priscilla wondered how long she could hold her breath. The lane behind the theater was dotted with puddles of what was not water. One rat skittered away while another watched her and Neville boldly, unwilling to give up its treasure of moldy bread.

When Neville opened an unmarked door, she hurried through, releasing the stale breath. She took another, then wished she could have waited. All the odors from the alley had followed her into the theater.

She was astonished to hear voices beyond the piles of boards and a trio of battered trunks. Although no play was scheduled, the back of the theater was filled with people practicing and working and talking. Each of them looked expectantly toward Neville.

He paid them no mind as he steered her to the left. "This way. Watch out for the coiled rope."

Priscilla was glad for the warning because she was trying to scan every inch of the area behind the curtain. Was there a clue here to identify the murderer? If so, she had no idea where to begin to look. Everything was ajumble. Mayhap the stacks of wood and cloth made sense to the actors. To her, it appeared to be a higgedly-piggedly bumble-bath.

"Is that Mr. Birdwell's dressing room?" she asked, pointing to a door that gleamed with fresh paint in contrast to the rest of the dusty, unpainted backstage area.

"Birdwell fancies himself the most important player in this company, and he wants everyone to know that. He keeps his dressing table and dressing box locked away."

"What is a dressing box?"

"It contains everything he needs for the stage. His cosmetics and wigs. He has Reeve guard it as if it were the crown jewels. I suspect only his valet has a key to that room."

"Should we try to talk to Mr. Birdwell again?"

"What else do we have to ask him?" Neville grimaced. "We have not discovered anything new."

A savage oath came from behind her, and Priscilla whirled. Something flew past a door, shattering into white and blue pieces on the floor. It might have been a vase or a dish. She could not tell because a piece of bright red wool landed on the shards.

"Morton?" Neville called, keeping her from stepping forward.

She wanted to tell him that he need not worry. She had no interest in being within range of some other flying prop.

A wizened man with white hairs sprouting from his skull and cheeks stuck his head out of the room. His dark brown waistcoat was open, and a dressmaker's measuring string dropped down the front like an outlandish necklace. Gnarled hands and wrinkles gouged into his face announced his advanced age. He moved toward them like a cricket, leaping forward on each bouncy step.

"I am busy. Can't ye see that? Go away. I don't 'ave time fer —" His rheumy eyes widened. " 'Athaway, m'boy! The sight of ye is just the thin' for these sore eyes. Are ye 'ere to reopen the Prince of Wales?"

"Can we talk in the props room?" Neville asked.

"Ah, don't want all of *them* to be listenin', d'ye?" He fired a glower at the workers.

Priscilla was astonished when the others

drifted away to the far side of the back-stage area. Neville had never given her any clue that his friend was a tyrant.

"'Oo is she?" Morton asked.

Neville introduced the props master to her. Morton simply hurrumphed and motioned for them to come into the room.

Priscilla stepped over the broken ceramic and around the scarlet wool. When she reached the door, she paused to stare in disbelief at the mess within the room. Every shelf was swept clean, and trunks had been emptied. The floor was covered with torn fabric and broken props.

"What happened?" asked Neville. "I have never seen this room in shambles."

"The actors are 'elpin' themselves to whatever they want."

"I understand."

"I don't," Priscilla said.

Neville smiled. "When a show closes abruptly, actors still have to eat."

"And they be eatin' their way right through m'props like a swarm of moths," muttered Morton. "Not just the clothes, but everythin'."

"Anything of value missing?"

He shrugged. "'Tis too soon to tell much. I 'ave t'get everythin' put away in the proper place. Then may'ap I can see."

He swore again and pointed toward an empty shelf. "All the props fer Wiggsley's latest masterpiece were there. Now they all be gone."

"They did not wait long to pick the place clean, did they?"

"They would've taken more if I 'adn't 'alted them. Don't know why anyone would want broken plates and tableware. They won't get much fer wot they stole. Dirty whelps, the lot of them."

"Speaking of dirty whelps, Morton . . ."

"Wot d'ye need?" the old man asked. "The same as when you 'ave needed costumes before, 'athaway?"

"Yes, for me and Lady Priscilla."

Morton eyed her up and down before nodding. "I think I 'ave the very thin' for ye."

With a quick efficiency that Mrs. Moore had tried to instill in the household staff, the props master dug out clothing for them.

Priscilla's nose wrinkled as she took the dress that smelled as bad as the alley behind the theater. "Do you have shoes?"

Morton hooked a thumb toward a dark green trunk. "Ye can look in there t'see if anythin' be left."

Setting the clothing on the floor,

Priscilla went to the trunk and peered in. Shoes of different styles and sizes were haphazardly thrown into the trunk. She knelt and began lifting them out. Red satin slippers were fine enough for a cyprian's ball. She set them next to a single flannel shoe that had holes worn into the sole.

"Anything for me in there, Pris?" asked Neville from behind her.

"How about these?" She held up a pair of men's shoes with wooden heels that would serve someone playing a dandy or a member of the old French court.

He took them and laughed. "I would fall off these and break my neck in about three steps." Tossing them atop the other shoes she had pulled out, he said, "I can wear my boots if there is nothing in the trunk. All I need to do is scuff them up a bit and —"

She yelped in pain and pulled her hand back. Blood slipped down her thumb.

With a curse, Neville grabbed a strip of cloth off a shelf and, dropping to his knees beside her, pressed it against the incision along her thumb. She winced, but bit back her gasp of pain.

"Wot is 'appenin'?" called Morton.

"She cut herself," Neville said through clenched teeth.

"On wot? Just shoes in there."

"I think something else is in there." More gently, he asked, "Can you hold this, Pris?"

"Yes," she replied. "It looks worse than it is."

As he reached into the trunk, she urged him to take care. He lifted away the shoes that had fallen when she jerked her hand back. Slowly he lifted out a knife. Its blade was stained with her blood.

"It looks like the one that killed Harmony," she breathed.

"And the one in the murder victim on stage." He wiped the blood on the other end of the fabric.

Morton stepped forward and squinted at the knife. "I was wonderin' where that got to." He picked up a wooden box with more knives and held it out to Neville. "Ye can put it in 'ere. One less I 'ave to look fer."

"You are missing other knives?" Priscilla asked.

"The box was tipped over when all this —" He gestured to the messy room. "When all of this was wrecked. I found most of them, but a few are missin'."

"How many?"

" 'Oo knows? I 'aven't counted the lot yet."

"Are the knives you use for props this sharp?" she asked.

The old man scowled as Neville drew another piece of fabric across the blade and watched its edge slice through the material. "They are supposed to be dull," Morton said, "but someone 'as sharpened this one." His eyes widened again. "Do ye think one from m'room killed the lady in the box?"

Neville turned the knife over and over in his hands. "It is possible, but it is just as possible the murderer brought the knife with him. This is a common sort of blade." He tossed it into the box Morton held. "That is no help."

"We 'ope someone finds that blackguard," the props master said. "One lady be dead, but we will starve if we don't get back to work."

Trying to tear a smaller strip off the fabric, Priscilla said, "We hope to find a solution to both."

The old man chuckled. "I wager ye do." He took the material from her, ripped off a piece, and with care bound her thumb. "There ye be, m'lady."

"Thank you, Morton." She picked up the clothes she had dropped on the floor. Breathing shallowly, she asked, "Where can we change?"

"I don't think 'is 'igh-and-mightiness is in right now."

"Has Birdwell been here?" Neville asked.

" 'E comes and 'e goes."

"Where does he go when he is not here?"

Morton shrugged. " 'Oo knows? Probably drinkin' 'imself 'alf-blind in 'is fancy 'ouse. Doesn't matter. 'E isn't 'ere. Ye can use 'is room." He pointed toward Mr. Birdwell's dressing room.

As Priscilla was about to step out of the props room, Neville put a hand on her arm. She was about to ask him what was wrong, then saw the actor's valet come out and look around the open area.

"But his man is standing guard," Neville murmured. "Reeve will not let anyone in there."

"Why?" she asked. "Could he be trying to protect Mr. Birdwell? But that makes no sense if Mr. Birdwell is not at the theater."

" 'E must be 'ere." Morton shook his head. "Probably foxed, so Reeve is protectin' that door as if a king's ransom be behind it. Guess 'e's tryin' to practice for 'is soldierin'."

"When is he planning to leave for the Army?"

"Don't know. 'E just talks 'bout it. Talks 'bout it all the time and 'ow she won't be able to resist 'im once 'e's a soldier."

"She who?"

"No idea. One of the gals 'ere at the theater, I suspect, as 'e is 'ere most of the time. I don't think 'e's gone to sign up. I thought 'e'd be gone by now. 'E is right eager to get away from Birdwell. As soon as 'e gets the money 'e needs, 'e'll go."

"Money?" asked Neville. "What does he need money for? He cannot be considering buying a commission, can he?"

"May'ap 'e be tired of bein' ordered 'round by 'is 'igh-and-mightiness. May'ap 'e wants to order folks 'round."

"And," Priscilla said softly, "being an officer might be what he needs to do to impress his lady fair."

He pointed in the opposite direction. "There be some small chambers over there. Ye can use them."

"I know where they are," Neville said.

The old man chuckled, the sound like a rusty rasp. "I forget. Ye know yer way 'round this theater." He turned back to gathering up the scattered costumes, clearly dismissing them. "Jes bring back them things in the same condition I gave'm to ye."

Priscilla smiled. Such an order was sure to make Mrs. Moore happy. The housekeeper would not want such malodorous garments in her laundry room.

Neville led her out of the room and toward the shadows at the right.

"He is watching us," Priscilla said.

"Reeve?"

"Yes," she whispered. She stole a glance back at where the valet was staring after them, his eyes narrowed into slits. "Why is he distressed to see us?"

"Anyone with half a brain would be distressed by what has been happening at the theater. He is no fool. He knows we are trying to find who killed Lady Lummis, and he knows Birdwell is a suspect. It must be galling him that he cannot protect Birdwell from the suspicions."

"It is more than that."

"Then what is it?"

"I am not sure I can put it into words."

He opened a door she had not seen. "You can change in here. I shall be next door and will meet you back out here." He lowered his voice to a husky whisper. "Unless you would like some help."

"Are you offering?"

"Who else?"

"I thought, as I am in the theater, I might have a dresser of my own."

"Like Reeve?" He gave an emoted shudder. "Heaven forbid."

"Heaven or you?"

He gave her a quick kiss, then, as she turned to go into the room, drew her back to him. Edging her cheekbones with his thumbs, he smiled. "Most definitely me, Pris. I don't want to share you with any other man."

"*I* would forbid that." She laughed.

"Go and change."

"If you will let me go . . ."

"In a moment." He caressed her mouth with a gentle hunger that swept through her, taunting her to surrender to their longing. Not satisfied with her mouth, he tasted her cheeks, her eyelids, the sensitive line of her neck. Whispering her name against her lips, he captured them again. She clung to him, having all she wanted, but aching for more.

She was trembling as she stepped away before she could not fight her desires any longer. He gazed down at her as if trying to memorize every facet of her face. He started to say something, then opened the door just beyond where she stood. He went inside, closing the door after him.

Priscilla shut her eyes and drew in a deep breath. Releasing it slowly, she reminded herself why they had come here. They must think about finding Harmony's murderer.

As she opened the door and started in, she looked again at Reeve to realize he was still staring toward her. What was bothering the man? Was it more than his employer still had not completely cleared his name? His hands were tightened into fists at his sides, and, even from across the backstage area, she could see his chest heaving with his rapid breathing. He seemed ready to explode. Why? Did he fear Neville had come to shut the theater down for good? That made no sense. He must have heard Morton's laugh, and the old man would not have been in a jolly mood if Neville was putting him out of a job.

The valet's gaze caught hers. She tried to pull hers away, but he held it for the length of three heartbeats. He stood too far away for her to read the emotions in his eyes before he rushed back into Mr. Birdwell's dressing room, closing the door without a sound.

Something was not right with the valet. With him, or with his employer? Reeve had been a mirror for Mr. Birdwell's emotions each time she had seen them together. He was overly solicitous of Mr. Birdwell's concerns, a toad-eater in everything he did for the actor. Did Reeve suspect his employer of being the murderer and wanted to make sure no one else had the proof that would send Mr. Birdwell to the gallows? Her fingers gripped the door. Did Reeve *know* that Mr. Birdwell was involved in the murder of his mistress?

More questions she had no answers to. Mayhap finding the person who had bought the stolen brooch would give them the clue to unravel the web of lies and half-truths around this crime.

She hoped so.

Chapter Nine

Priscilla hated how she smelled and how Neville smelled and how the street reeked worse than both of them. She wondered how Morton had ingrained the odors into these rags. It would have been as simple as dragging them through the puddles behind the theater, but she hoped he had found another way.

The same type of puddles were scattered along the street where they walked as if accustomed to such a setting. Hearing a screech from her left, she stared at a building leaning toward the street. Half the glass in the windows was broken, and the steps were covered with the contents of a recently emptied chamberpot. This section of London had burned in the Great Fire less than two hundred years before. Setting a torch to it again to drive out the rats and the bugs and the odors might not be a bad idea.

"Don't gawk, Pris." Neville's voice was a low hiss. His face was covered with dirt he had gathered up from the theater floor and spread across his cheeks. With a floppy hat pulled low over his brow, she would not have recognized him. She hoped no one else would. "You will attract eyes we need to avoid."

"Every time I come to one of these sections of London, I cannot help staring." She pulled the brim of her tattered bonnet down to shadow her features. "I feel sorry for these people."

"Some of them would not feel sorry for you if they knew who you really are." He put his arm around her shoulders and held her closer.

As he guided her around broken cobbles, he did not need to remind her to watch what she said and how she said it. This was not the first time she had dressed in such clothes and come with him into the bowels of the city. The last time, her abigail had insisted on washing Priscilla's hair over and over until the odors had been battered away by the soap.

"Watch where yer goin', twit," snarled Neville with a low accent that seemed natural. He pushed aside a drunken man who had almost walked into them.

The man lumbered into the broken railing on a set of steps. When his feet went out beneath him and he landed hard on a riser, he grinned and held out his hand in fingerless gloves. "A tonic, old chap?"

Neville shook his head. "If I 'ad a 'alfpenny, I'd be spendin' it on m'self and m'lady."

"Lady?" The drunkard laughed, blowing fumes of cheap gin in their direction. "Yer doxy be a fair one, but a lady she is not." He crooked a finger. "Come 'ere, m'pretty one, and lift yer skirts fer me. I can pay ye far better than that clutch-fisted chap."

"Ye don't 'ave as much as a tonic," she retorted, tilting her chin with feigned pride as she hoped her fake accent would not make anyone question that she belonged on these streets. She linked her arm with Neville's. "Come along, dearie. I 'aven't got all day, ye know."

"Come back later when yer done with 'im," called the foxed man. "Mayhap I will be 'fore the wind then, and I will show ye wot a real man be like."

Priscilla swallowed a chuckle when she heard Neville's curse as they hurried along the street. "Really, Neville," she said as soon as they were out of earshot of the man who had begun singing a bawdy tune loudly. "You cannot be distressed by such a comment about you."

"I am not upset about anything he said about me." He put his arm around her waist and leaned her toward him again. "I do not like hearing my future wife being mistaken for a cyprian."

"Better to be mistaken for that than to be seen for what I truly am. Isn't that the advice you just gave me before we encountered yon gentleman?"

"Blast it, Pris. Do you always have to be so reasonable? Can't you allow me the chance to play your dashing hero once in a while?"

She rested her ragged bonnet against his shoulder and heard the stiff straw crack. "You are always my dashing hero. I thought you knew that."

A church bell ringing silenced his reply. His face closed up, and she wondered what he was thinking. Was it the passing of the hour or something else that was making him withdraw behind that mask?

"Let's go," he said, his voice grim once again.

Priscilla had dozens of questions, but did not ask a single one when she saw a band of men and young boys gathered near an alley. She noted Neville glancing at them and away several times as he hurried her around the corner of the next street.

"Resurrectionists," he murmured, not slowing.

"But we are not in a churchyard, so we need not fear bodysnatchers."

"Those louts do not haunt just churchyards in search of their prey." He looked back over his shoulder. "We look too healthy for them to cudgel in the daylight, most likely, but they may be bold enough to attack anyone whose path crosses theirs."

"The drunk man!" she gasped.

"He knows enough, even as soused as he is, to look out for Jamie and his boys."

"You know them?"

"I recognize some of them from when we went to talk to Ben Crouch last year."

She was astonished. When she had gone with Neville to visit the leader of the bodysnatchers, she had paid no mind to the other men crowding the low tavern. She had wanted only to complete their errand and leave.

"Are we near that tavern?" she asked, rushing with him around another corner. She had no idea how he was finding his way through the maze of streets. All the houses and piles of garbage looked alike to her.

"No, we are going toward the river, where the theater-folk often take their treasures to sell or to pawn."

"And stolen goods?"

"Some of the people in the theater deserve the wicked reputation given to all. They would take stolen items to a pawnbroker or to a fence they knew."

"I should not be surprised you know where to find such men."

He laughed and eased the pace to a comfortable stroll along the crowded street. The houses crowded together around courtyards, so he had to weave a path in and out of the fetid yards. No sign of whitewash or paint remained on the rotting boards along the front of the buildings. Some were made of stone, as had been required after the Great Fire, but even those were filthy.

"Before I was allowed to walk on the stage," he said, "I had a variety of jobs."

"I have heard of a few." She wondered where all the people they passed were bound. Some carried ragged packs on their backs; others were followed by children of various ages, many scantily clad. More people sat on the steps and leaned on open windows to watch the parade passing.

"So you have, but my first job in the

theater was to make sure out-of-work actors had a steady income."

"From selling articles stolen from theater patrons?" She sighed with relief when they emerged from the throng to where the street was a bit more open. Hearing a door slam, she saw several of the nearby steps were abandoned.

"Now you understand," Neville said, drawing her attention back to him.

"I understand you are a man of many skills."

He gave her a rakish smile. "You have no idea how many skills I have to share with you."

"Dearie," she said, adopting the low-class accent again, "ye'll 'ave to show me some of them soon. Might show ye a few of mine, too."

With a laugh, he tapped her on the nose. "Just the idea I had hoped you would have." Suddenly he cursed. Taking her arm, he said, "Hurry!"

"What is it?"

"The street is empty."

She was astonished to see he was right. The bustle had vanished. As he pulled her along at a near run, she asked again what was wrong. He did not answer as he led her through the decrepit streets. Her breath was sharp under her ribs, and she paid no attention to the horrible odors filling each one. She was too busy trying to keep pace with him.

Neville went through a low arch and to a wall taller than the top of his head. It was constructed of planks with very little space between them for finger- or toeholds.

"Is this where we find the pawnbrokers and the — whatever the other one is called?" she asked.

He chuckled, even though his face remained rigid. "A *fence*, Pris. You need to remember the low cant I taught you."

"I fear I do not recall it with the same ease Isaac does."

"Can you climb as well as he does?"

"He does not climb well, if you recall. He often goes up on his own, but needs help coming down." Her eyes widened. "You want us to go over *that* wall?"

"Going over this may save our lives."

She grasped his arm. "What is it, Neville?"

"Jamie and his boys are following us." He swore again and did not apologize. "He must have recognized us, too. He may believe we are rival resurrectionists."

"If we tell him —"

"He is not a man who likes to talk. Action is more his way of life." He grabbed one of the boards and shook it. "Can you climb over?"

"I think so."

He cupped his hands and said, "Let me give you a leg up."

She raised her skirt high enough so she could put one foot on the lowest plank. It creaked beneath her.

"Be careful," he urged.

"I will be," Priscilla said, watching where she put her other foot. As fast as she could, she climbed to the top. She swung her leg over it. "Climb up, Neville!"

"I doubt the wall will hold both of us! Go! Hurry!"

She groped with her toes for a lower board. Shouts came from beyond the courtyard. Male voices slurred with drink. She could discern only a single word, but it was surgeon-anatomist. She knew that term for the doctors who bought from the bodysnatchers and did dissections in their hidden laboratories.

She jumped the last few feet to the ground. Her ankle twinged, but she tried to shake out the pain as she called lowly, "Neville, I am down. Come over the wall!"

A board bowed as he put his foot on it. She saw his fingers through the cracks. He climbed only a single board before she heard more shouts. Then Neville yelled as his fingers vanished from between the boards.

When she heard someone land a fist against bare flesh, she cried, "Neville!" She reached for the boards to climb back over. She yanked her fingers back. He doubted the wall would hold both of them, so she must give him a chance to scale it.

She tried to peer through the cracks between the boards. She jumped back as the wall was hit. A man grunted with pain, and the wall shivered again as something — or someone — struck it. Wood cracked, but not on the wall. Splinters rained down on her as a crate struck the house near the top of the wall. She cowered, holding her arms over her head.

At a thud on her side of the wall, she looked up. "Neville!"

He grabbed her hand. "Let's go."

She did not need him to say it twice. She ran as fast as she could past more houses ready to tumble down. She did not dare to look back to see if the body snatchers were following.

When they entered a courtyard, she groaned at the sight of another wall. This one was only as high as Neville's waist.

He gauged it, then started to turn. Pounding footsteps echoed toward them. He cursed, then said, "Follow me." He scaled the wooden planks in one easy movement, then held out his hands over the wall. "Now you."

"You make it sound easy."

"Just put your foot on the lowest board and hold out your arms."

She did as he ordered. He grabbed her at the waist and swung her up and over the wall. She gasped when he set her down only long enough to tighten his hold on her. Then he swung her past a muddy puddle close to the wall.

He jumped over the puddle, falling to his knees on the stones beyond it. She rushed to him. He waved her aside as he stood, the knees of his breeches ripped. Seizing her hand, he drew her behind a stack of barrels that smelled of ale. She squatted down beside him.

"Not 'ere!" she heard someone call from the other side of the wall.

"They could 'ave gone over the wall."

Footsteps came toward them. "Nay, fer there be no sign of them over there. They must've gone toward the alley."

Priscilla breathed out a sigh of relief when the footfalls vanished into the distance. She gasped when Neville's hand slid down her leg; then she realized he was brushing her skirt back over her ankles. She looked up to thank him. When she saw the glow of appreciation in his eyes as they slowly moved along her, she did not lower her gaze. He held out his hand, and the gentle pressure of his fingers closing over hers sent renewed heat trilling through her in a luscious melody that beckoned her closer. Her fingers rose to brush his bewhiskered cheek.

Tilting his chin so she could see his cheek better, she said, "He hit you hard."

"Just a glancing blow, because I ducked. Unfortunately, I did not duck quickly enough." He drew her to her feet. "Thank heavens, you are always up to any challenge, Pris."

"Not any one. That first wall was more than enough, but I must own my feet were spurred by the thought of resurrectionists having designs upon us while our hearts still beat." She walked with him across another cluttered courtyard. "Can we get to where the pawnshops are without meeting up with them again?"

"I hope so." Neville motioned for Priscilla to follow him along the narrow passage between two buildings. They seemed to grow closer on every step, and he was relieved when the walls did not touch before they reached the street.

He was glad to see this street was as crowded as the other had been before the bodysnatchers appeared in search of prey. He ignored the people who watched them pass, but he was aware of each, gauging whether any of them presented a danger to Priscilla. He would have rather left her in the comfort of Bedford Square. Making such a suggestion would have been futile, because she would have insisted on coming with him. She was not squeamish, although she was unsettled by the sights around them.

He sneezed as some hideous odor tickled his nose. Even in his darkest days, he had not lived in a wretched neighborhood like this. In addition, he had grown accustomed to the finer areas of Mayfair.

The first three pawnshops they went into had nothing for sale similar to Lady Lummis's brooch. Two other shops were filled with broken furniture and torn linens. Neither of them pawned jewelry.

"Pawnshops are a waste of time," Neville announced after leaving the fifth shop. "I think it is time to pay a call on a fence who is well-known among those who work in

Covent Garden and Drury Lane."

"Who is that?" Priscilla asked.

"He goes by the name of Carter. I am not sure if that is his given name or his surname or not related to his real name at all."

She dampened her lips, and he found himself watching the tip of her tongue, wishing his was brushing her lips. He shook the thought from his head. Keeping his wits about him was necessary, because Carter was not easily fooled. The man did know how to keep secrets, which was why people used him to dispose of valuables that had come into their possession illegally.

"What is he like?" she asked.

He paused as he waited for a wagon to pass. Whatever it was carrying was even more putrid than the street. With a smile, he said, "A very ordinary man. If you saw him amid a crowd, you would take no notice of him. Then you visit his shop, and it is an experience like walking down a familiar street and discovering something you have never seen before, even though it has been there all along."

"Are you suggesting I might have walked many times near the man we are about to call upon?"

"I am saying it is possible."

Neville kept the teasing banter going as they continued toward the river. He doubted he betwattled Priscilla, because he saw her scan the streets as he did. There was no sign of pursuit, but the resurrectionists were not the only ones they needed to worry about.

The sight of Carter's tiny shop, tucked between two pawnshops, lifted a weight from his shoulders. Once they were done here, he would hire a vehicle and have them driven back to Bedford Square. It might be a vegetable wagon or some other sort of dray, but he did not want to chance meeting Jamie and his boys again.

"Is this the street?" she asked.

"Yes. Why don't you give me a kiss for good luck?" he whispered. Giving her no time to answer, he brought her mouth to his to taste her warm lips. She sent his desires soaring. Curling his fingers around her nape, where golden tendrils brushed his skin, he longed to discover every inch of her.

Pain erupted through his head as he bent to trail kisses along her neck. Releasing her quickly, he kept his arm around her waist as she wobbled. He touched his aching cheek.

"Does it hurt badly?" asked Priscilla.

"Not bad," he lied. "It is my fault for not ducking more quickly. My reflexes are getting too rusty. The soft life of the Polite World is ruining me." Without a pause, he asked, "Are you ready?"

"I think so . . . if you think that was enough good luck."

"I will need more later, no doubt."

Her smile sent lightning through him. "No doubt."

Pulling his hat even lower, Neville opened the heavy wooden door that looked as if someone had tried to break it down with a battering ram. He ushered Priscilla in, keeping his hand on her back.

A dark-haired man was sitting behind the counter in front of a black curtain flanked on both sides by rows of drawers. His clothes were remarkably clean and well-made for the riverside neighborhood. His fingers sparkled with rings he was not afraid to wear because he was certain to have weapons beneath the counter.

The man, whom Neville knew was Carter, looked up, revealing a well-formed face except for a nose that appeared to have been pummeled as hard as his door. A pair of spectacles were balanced on his nose, and his light blue eyes were lost in the reflection from a lamp set next to him.

He had a pocket watch in front of him.

Carter frowned and bent back over his work. "You are in the wrong place."

Neville winked at Priscilla before walking to the counter, keeping his head down. "We need 'elp."

"You are in the wrong place." He continued to tinker with the pocket watch.

"We be interested in doin' some business with ye, sir."

"You are in the wrong place," he repeated again, but his hands paused. He did not look up, but he was obviously listening.

"Ye may sell only to quality, but ye buy from anyone. So we 'ave 'eard at the Prince of Wales Theater."

Carter lifted his head and scanned the shop. Neville doubted he had ever seen anyone — even young Isaac when deep into some mischief — look so guilty. "The Prince of Wales Theater?" he asked.

"Man there said ye'd buy without askin' questions."

"What do you have to sell?" He folded his arms on the counter, one hand out of sight. To reach for a weapon? "Bring it here so I might see it."

Neville did not want to do anything to arouse Carter's suspicions, so he complied.

Reaching under his coat, he drew out a pair of gold and sapphire earrings. He glanced quickly at Priscilla to warn her not to show her surprise. He need not have worried. Her face displayed only her eagerness to sell the pieces and get out of the shop.

Carter picked up one earring and examined it. "This is a fine piece. Where did you get it?"

Neville leaned one elbow on the counter and scratched his side with his other hand. "D'ye truly wish to know?"

The fence drew back. Pulling out a handkerchief, he held it to his nose. "It is dangerous to try to resell items that have been stolen."

"It be dangerous to lift these items, too. My missus, she be good at it." He winked bawdily at Priscilla. "She works at the theater. Cleanin' up things, y'know. She found these in a box there." He grasped Priscilla's arm and gave her a rather rough tug forward. "Speak up, woman. Tell the man wot ye know."

She fired him a scowl that would have daunted even him if he thought it was genuine. "Let me go, ye son of a sow." Jerking her arm out of his grip, she came forward to bat her eyelashes at the fence. "Came from a fine lady who 'as no need of them."

He bent to open a drawer behind him and reached in to pull out a magnifying glass. A glitter within the drawer caught the light.

"There it be!" cried Priscilla. "There be the brooch I told ye the fine lady was wearin'."

Carter slammed the drawer closed. "You are mistaken."

"I saw it with m'own two eyes. At the theater and 'ere. In the drawer there."

"You are mistaken. Why don't you leave?"

Neville took the fence by the lapels, but did not pull Carter toward him. With his hat tipped down over his face, he doubted the fence could see his features. "Don't call m'woman a liar. She said she saw it. So she saw it."

"Same one as the lady wore," said Priscilla. "Fine brooch with blue stones in it. I wanted it, but I couldn't lift it right off 'er chest."

Still holding Carter, Neville motioned with his head for her to go around the counter. The fence warned them not to do something out of hand. Neville remained silent as he watched Priscilla open the drawer and lift out the brooch. Her fingers were trembling, and he hoped she could maintain the masquerade while holding the piece of jewelry that had been stolen from her late friend.

He was amazed at her acting ability when she tossed the brooch onto the counter next to where Carter was trying to wiggle away. There was an air of indifference in her motion as she came back around the counter.

Giving the fence a shake, he ordered, "Ye owe m'woman an apology."

"For her pawing through my drawers?"

"No, fer makin' ye see *this*." Neville shoved the man back a step and picked up the brooch. Setting it next to the earrings, he said, "See."

Carter's eyes sparkled with avarice. "Yes, I do see." He held the earring up against the brooch to compare the gold and the stones. "They do look similar."

"They should," Priscilla retorted even as her fingernails dug into Neville's arm. "Same lady wore them."

"A woman who was murdered," Neville said, dropping the street accent and pushing his hat back from his brow. He wore a terse smile.

"Hathaway!" gasped Carter. His surprise became fury. "I should have guessed you would be behind a stunt like this."

"Like what?" He scooped up the jewelry. "This is no stunt. I am trying to find where this stolen brooch had been sold. Who brought it to you?"

Carter scowled as he adjusted his coat. "Who sent you? Bow Street? I thought you had become some sort of sir."

"This is personal, Carter. The jewelry was stolen from Lady Priscilla's friend."

The fence dropped onto a stool behind the counter. Looking at Priscilla, he tried to choke out something. He could only stare. She gave him her iciest smile, resisting her urge to put him at ease. This man did not deserve the manners she used with the Polite World or her neighbors in Stonehall-on-Sea. He made a profit from the misfortunes of others.

"Speak up, Carter," Neville said. "Who brought this brooch to you after killing Lady Lummis?"

"Killed?" he whispered, his face becoming gray. "I had no idea anyone had been killed."

"Who brought it?"

As the fence began describing the man who had brought the brooch and other small pieces of jewelry to the shop, Neville felt his stomach cramp. The description of a well-spoken blond man fit Reginald

Birdwell perfectly. Beside him, Priscilla gasped.

"Do you know the man?" asked Carter.

"Mayhap." He put the jewelry under his coat. The fence did not protest. Neville did not expect him to, because Carter knew if he did, Thurmond would be sent to retrieve the brooch and put him out of business. "If he comes back again, send a message here." He set a card on the counter. "I trust you can devise some way to persuade him to linger long enough for me to arrive."

"If I try to keep him here, he will get suspicious and run."

"Use whatever methods you have short of killing the man." He rested his hands on the counter again. "Double-deal with me on this, Carter, and you will be sorry." Pushing away from the counter, he cupped Priscilla's elbow and led her out of the shop.

She said nothing, and neither did he, but he knew her thoughts were identical to his. Had Birdwell lied? Had he really killed his mistress?

Chapter Ten

St. Julian's Church near Bedford Square was a grand edifice. Corinthian columns marched in perfect precision along its front, reaching the roof far above the doorway. Over the door was a great arched window. Its stained glass depicted the tablets of the Ten Commandments in letters large enough to be read from the floor. During morning services, the colors splashed onto the walnut pews within the sanctuary. A pulpit of the same wood, simply carved, could be reached only by climbing a quartet of stairs. Above it, the sounding board hung like the hand of doom. Candles always burned on the altar and on a metal stand set to one side of the church.

But its most magnificent aspect was the pipe organ that took up most of the western wall. Its pipes slipped up through the choir loft to boom music against the ceiling. The organist played, hidden, behind a purple velvet drapery, moving from light melodies to imposing hymns that threatened to shake the church's foundations.

In a pew halfway back along the black-and-white tiled floor, Priscilla sat with Neville and her children. The service had gone long this morning, and Isaac was squirming in his seat. Leah had yawned more than once behind her gloved fingers, and Daphne seemed intent on appraising every young man attending this service. That last fact made Priscilla especially glad when the notes of the recessional exploded from the organ and those sitting in the pews began to rise.

She could not fault the children for being unsettled when she was as well. Instead of listening to the sermon, she had found her mind wandering to Harmony's murder and the fence's description, which identified Mr. Birdwell as the man who had come to the shop. Several days had passed, and nothing new had emerged from the clues. Even Neville had said nothing about the crime this morning. Was he waiting anxiously, as she was, for the killer to appear again from the shadows? Would it be the actor?

When Neville offered his arm as she stepped out into the aisle between the pews, she put her fingers on it. His smile became a frown, and she guessed he had sensed, through his dark green coat, the tremble in her fingers.

"Not here," she whispered before he could ask the question in his eyes. "And not when the children could hear."

He nodded and led her out of the church. As they spilled onto the walkway with the other worshipers, she did not slow. He said nothing as she motioned for him to walk around the line of parishioners waiting to greet the reverend.

Priscilla paused when she realized Daphne was not keeping pace with them. Looking back, she saw two men giving her daughter overly warm smiles. She tugged on Daphne's arm, and her daughter stumbled after them. Daphne's face was an enticing pink, but Priscilla did not want those two men — one a well-known rogue and the other a married man whose wife had recently given birth to his fourth son — to find anything enticing about Daphne.

The men's smiles vanished, and she discovered Neville was aiming a frown in their direction. Daphne scurried to catch up with her brother and sister. Her face remained rosy, and a smile played at the corners of her lips.

"Something is upsetting you, Pris,"

Neville said as they continued walking toward where her carriage waited.

"That is easy to guess." She glanced toward her older daughter, who was paying no attention to her siblings' prattle.

"Not just Daphne's sudden rush of admirers, for you expected that."

"Mayhap, but not at church. I thought they would show some restraint here." She tried to smile, then gave up, for her strained expression must be ghastly.

"So there must be something else disconcerting you. Could it be the banns that were read as part of this morning's service? One week of banns read, two more to go." He grinned. "You still have time to change your mind."

"Don't change your mind, Mama!" said Isaac, bouncing from one foot to the other.

"Ah, a vote in my favor." Neville lifted one finger.

"Me, too!" Leah raised her hand, waving it as if she feared she would not be seen, although there was no one else near them on the walkway. "Don't change your mind, Mama."

Priscilla laughed, grateful for Neville's jesting to keep dismal thoughts from her mind, and put her hand on Isaac's shoulder to keep him from skipping into a puddle. "I did not know that the question of whether Neville and I wed or not had become a democratic decision."

"Quite true." Neville wore a mockly stern frown as he bent toward the two children. "There appears to be only one vote that has any weight in this decision, and it is your mother's."

Leah and Isaac looked expectantly toward her. Daphne was still staring at the two men again giving her warm smiles.

Shaking her head and putting her hand on Daphne's arm to remind her daughter of her manners, Priscilla asked, "Why are you being silly? Have I given you any hint that I have changed my mind? I think you would be wiser to consider the fact that Neville may change *his* mind. I understand there is quite a bit of money wagered on whether he actually will show up at our wedding."

"How did you know about that?" he asked, obviously surprised as the children badgered him not to change his mind. Calming them with a few words and motioning for them to get into the carriage, he said, "You are an endless amazement to me, Pris. Where do you get your information?"

"All one needs to do is listen. I heard

whispers during the church service, and I believe more than a few bets were placed at the recent assembly."

"You said nothing of this."

"I saw no need." She laughed again. "And why wouldn't there be bets on our wedding? The gentlemen will wager on just about anything."

"But one should only wager when there is some question to the outcome." He drew her hand within his arm. "Those placing bets that I will not be there to speak wedding vows with you are condemned to lose."

"Mayhap I should have you place a bet for me."

"You?" He gave her a horrified glance. "A parson's widow? Gambling? I apparently have been as atrocious an influence on you as your aunt believes."

Priscilla ran her other hand along his sleeve. "No one could be as atrocious an influence on me as Aunt Cordelia believes you are."

"Where is your aunt this morning?"

"Can I dare to believe you miss her?"

He laughed. "As one would miss a burr in one's leg if it falls off. I had thought she would be here for the reading of the banns."

"I suspect she was delayed on her visit to Grosvenor Square. She planned to give her second husband's third daughter's first daughter a look-in before church this morning. Matilda recently gave birth to her fifth child, the long awaited son."

"How do you keep track of all the numbers in your aunt's family?"

She smiled. "It is not easy when Aunt Cordelia married three times, and each of her husbands had children with their first wives."

"Children she never had to raise herself."

"Aunt Cordelia always has been interested in men much older than herself." She cocked her head and paused on the walkway. "Until she met your friend Duncan last fall. She asked me if I thought you would be upset if he invited himself to stay with you for the wedding."

"McAndrews? I had no idea that she had given him much thought since she last saw him."

"Apparently she has." She stepped up into the carriage with the tiger's help. When Neville sat next to her, she included the children in her smile as she said, "It appears you may be a better matchmaker than you guessed, Neville. Who would have guessed you would have such influence on Aunt Cordelia?"

Isaac leaned forward and, putting his hand to his mouth, whispered, "Aunt Cordelia really does like you, Uncle Neville."

"Is that so?" He glanced at Priscilla who was struggling not to smile. "I suspected your aunt might have mellowed in her feelings toward me since our visit to Cornwall a few months ago."

"She has said your name a few times."

"Kindly?"

Isaac paused to consider the question, and Neville did not restrain his laughter. Ruffling the lad's hair, he sat back and stretched his arm along the back of the seat.

When his fingers brushed her shoulder, all thoughts of anything but his touch vanished from Priscilla's head. Later, she would tell him about her grim thoughts during the church service. She hoped he would keep the dreary notions out of her mind for the rest of the day.

Neville yawned as he stepped into his house on Berkeley Square. Dash it! These trips to and from Bedford Square were becoming tiresome. Propriety was an infuriating taskmaster, but he knew Priscilla would not be budged from following the strictures set by Society. Nothing must taint Daphne's first Season. If he had been thinking clearly instead of concentrating on how much he longed to hold Priscilla, he would have tried to persuade her to hold off another year on firing-off Daphne. It would not have taken much convincing, because he knew she was worried that Daphne was still too young, in spite of her burgeoning maturity, to be a part of the *ton*.

He laughed tonelessly as he handed his hat and cloak to Stoddard, his butler. The man was unlike Priscilla's majordomo. Gilbert seldom revealed any emotion. Stoddard's face beneath his graying hair displayed each one, most commonly dismay at something Neville had done or was doing.

Neville had inherited the household staff along with the town house and his title. Stoddard seemed determined to remake Neville into the form of his Hathaway ancestors, something Neville had no intention of becoming. Most of them, if he were to believe the tales, preferred drinking and gambling to anything else in life. His predecessor, Sir Mortimer

Hathaway, had been quite the opposite, never spending a farthing unless absolutely forced to. He had closeted himself in the Berkeley Square house with his art and the few friends he had. Mayhap that was why there had been no direct heir, and the title had come to the son of a disowned branch of the family.

"Good evening, sir," Stoddard said, his tone reproving.

Wondering what he had done now to distress his butler, Neville smiled. "It has been a very pleasant evening."

"Now that Lady Priscilla has returned to Town." The butler went along the hallway leading toward the back of the house and the door down into the kitchen. He paused beside the staircase, which rose as straight as a soldier's gun barrel at one side of the foyer. Behind him, a niche was edged with gilt and held a vase with fresh flowers. "You have a caller, sir."

"A caller? At this hour?" He did not bother to dress Stoddard down for failing to mention the caller until now. It would do no good, because his butler believed that Neville was the one who needed training in how a house should properly be run. Mayhap it was Thurmond, who had taken the information Neville brought about Carter and the brooch. The Bow Street Runner could have discovered something important.

"Yes, sir. He is waiting in the front parlor." His nose wrinkled. "He requested that I not send word to Lady Priscilla's house that he had arrived."

Curious at who was calling and why the caller had made the butler even more disgruntled, Neville climbed the stairs past the paintings and statues set in niches along the stairwell. He barely glanced at them as he slid his hand up the walnut banister, but reminded himself that many of the pieces the previous baronet had collected must be disposed of when Priscilla came here to live. She would not appreciate receiving guests when erotic statues and paintings were scattered everywhere.

Or would she want to come here to live? This house was grander than her Bedford Square house, but not as big. Dash it! He had to remember to discuss that matter with her.

Neville swept those thoughts from his head when he reached the top of the stairs and saw a familiar freckled face beneath black curls. A pinch of disappointment that Thurmond was not calling vanished as he smiled at his friend Duncan

216

McAndrews. Duncan was shorter than he was, but had a way of drawing everyone's attention whenever he entered a room. It might have been his good humor or the fact that he was not a stingy Scot when he sat at the card table.

His friend was, Neville noted, none the worse for almost being killed by a crossbow arrow last fall. He should not be surprised, for nothing slowed Duncan for long.

"Duncan! I had heard you were planning to take advantage of my hospitality again." He clapped his friend on the shoulder before motioning toward the book-room he preferred to the fancy parlors. One of these days, he would have to have the house redone in a manner that better suited him. He chuckled. If they decided to live here, that task would become Priscilla's.

"What is amusing?" Duncan laughed before adding in his heavy Scottish brogue, "No, there is no need to answer. I see by your moony expression that your thoughts are focused on the lovely Lady Priscilla."

"It is a bridegroom's privilege to contemplate his bride."

"Unquestionably." He frowned abruptly. "Although I had thought you might be thinking about that horrible murder at the

Prince of Wales Theater. You used to perform there, didn't you?"

Neville motioned once more toward the door. Closing it behind them, he opened it again just enough so nobody would be able to lurk nearby without a shadow crossing the open space.

Pouring himself a glass of Neville's best brandy, Duncan gulped it quickly. He refilled the glass and sat down so hard in the closest chair that the wood beneath the red upholstery groaned. "Don't chide me, Neville," he grumbled.

"Why would I do that?" he asked, puzzled.

"I don't know, but you have the expression of a man ready to scold someone."

Sitting on another chair, Neville glanced around the room. Only two walls held bookcases, and not many shelves were laden with books. The previous baronet had apparently preferred to use this room for raising a cloud, because when Neville moved in, the ceiling had been stained with smoke, and the odor of cigars remained in spite of the household's attempts in the past four years to dislodge it.

"I am sorry, Duncan." He looked at his friend who was sipping his glass of brandy. "It is frustrating to have a woman

218

murdered, and the rest of the Polite World acts as if it never happened."

"Not all of the rest of the Polite World."

"No. Priscilla is quite unsettled by this."

"The murder or the lack of talk about it?"

"Both." Setting himself on his feet, he served himself some brandy. He put the bottle on a table near their chairs. "On another topic, I understand you are here at Lady Cordelia's invitation."

"Quite a surprise it was to receive it. I had thought she had forgotten me since the debacle at Lord Stenborough's estate last Michaelmas Day."

Neville chuckled. "Lady Cordelia never forgets anything. She can recite every misdeed she believes I have committed since the day she first met me. Be wary when you call upon her, my friend."

"She is quite the interesting lady. Much like the one you are about to wed."

"Priscilla and her aunt alike? Most definitely not."

Duncan threw back his head and laughed. "They are more alike than different, Neville. Stubborn and lovely, determined and devoted to family, curious and intelligent."

"Yes," he said reluctantly, "but Priscilla

is not as unwavering in her assumptions as her aunt is."

"Mayhap."

Neville changed the subject to Duncan's journey from his estate far north in Scotland. He tried to listen to his friend, but his mind kept wandering away to Priscilla and the puzzle they had not solved.

Not yet.

Neville stared out the window of the carriage. The deep shadows of twilight were spreading across the streets and climbing up the houses on the far side of the square. With a sigh, he turned his gaze back inside the carriage.

Next to him on the comfortable seat, Priscilla was looking out the window on the other side. Her endearing profile changed with each expression, but now it was taut. She was not frowning, but deep in concentration. He did not have to ask what she was thinking. He knew.

He had gone to Bow Street this afternoon to speak with his friend Thurmond. The Bow Street Runner had had no further information about Harmony Lummis's murder to share. Neville had told Priscilla that in what he realized had been a clipped tone when he arrived to escort her to a *conversazione* at Mr. Ward's house. He had said very little since those few discouraged words.

She turned to look at him and said nothing. She just stared as she had out the window.

"Is there something amiss with me this evening?" Neville asked, glad only the two of them were in the carriage. Daphne was coming to Ward's house with her great-aunt and Duncan. As if Duncan were no older than Daphne, his friend had spent the past two hours filling Neville's head with his anticipation of the evening. "I find myself questioning your silent appraisal."

"I am sorry," she said in the warm voice that filled his dreams. "I did not realize I was staring at you."

"I don't dislike your appraisal, Pris. I am simply curious why."

"Could you not believe it is because I feel like I am going to heaven on a string? That I am so happy to be with you and happy that you love me?"

He folded her hands between his. "Sweetheart, I would be very happy to think that. However, your face is anything but happy. Have I down-pinned you with my low spirits? If so, I apologize."

"You have not upset me more than I am

already. I, too, had hoped Mr. Thurmond would have plenty to share with you."

"But he had nothing, so there is no reason to dwell on that. Let us speak of something else. There is a matter I wish to discuss with you."

"Of where we shall live once we are wed?"

He put his arm along the back of the seat and gave her shoulders a gentle squeeze. "Pris, you were chiding me not so long ago about never being able to surprise you. Now you are doing the same to me."

"Would you rather . . ." She looked up at him and pressed her hands to her cheeks. Her eyes grew wide, and her golden lashes fluttered. "A matter to discuss? Oh, my dear Neville, whatever could it be? I trust you are not displeased with something I have done or said."

He silenced her with a hearty kiss. What he had meant as a jest became far more. His arms slipped up her back as he drew her soft curves up against him. Her mouth was delicious, and he explored it with slow appreciation. When her breath, quick and eager, rushed into his mouth, he considered raising his lips only long enough to call an order to take them back to his house, where they could have the privacy to savor every inch of each other.

"That is nice," she murmured when he drew back while he still could.

"Yes."

She curved her gloved hand along his cheek. "Neville, mayhap we would be wise to speak of something other than our future together."

He groaned. "Even the most commonplace words seem to have a double meaning when I think of holding you, sweetheart. I wanted to speak of where we would live after we are wed. Do you have a preference?"

"I always have an opinion," she said with a laugh. "You know that."

"So what is your opinion, Pris?"

"My preference would be to live in Stonehall-on-Sea." She closed her eyes, and he knew she was thinking of the village and the comfortable house on the cliffs overlooking the sea. "I prefer it to London."

"Or my family's dirty acres in Cornwall?"

"Yes."

"I have given some thought to selling the estate in Cornwall."

"Isn't it entailed?"

He shook his head. "Not according to the deed I have seen, but who would buy such a dusty, fusty place at the end of the island? If it could have been foisted off on someone else, I suspect one of my ancestors would have done so long ago." He looked out as the carriage slowed to a stop in front of a brightly lit house. "We are here at Ward's. Think of what you wish to do about the two houses here in town."

"I will."

"We could always give one to Daphne when she weds."

"True." She smiled. "However, I hope that is not for a while yet."

He opened the door and stepped out. "Your hopes may be doomed if Witherspoon keeps eyeing her the way he does."

"Speak to him, Neville," she said as she placed her hand on his palm.

"About what?"

"About how young Daphne is and how swiftly she gives her heart and how swiftly she reclaims it again." She smiled. "After all, it was not so long ago that she believed herself heart-deep in love with you."

"You need not remind me of that." He walked with her to the door that was opening as they approached.

Priscilla withheld her laugh while they stepped into an entry as simple and austere as the house's exterior. The bright blue tile floor was bare, and there was only a single portrait on the wall. It depicted their host, a rotund man with white hair and bulbous cheeks.

A footman in livery of a color identical to the tile led the way up uncarpeted stairs to a large room. The furniture had been pushed against light blue walls. Servants walked quietly through the room, offering glasses filled with wine or lemonade to the two score of guests.

Neville cleared a path through the men who were so intent on their discussion of the latest bills in Parliament that they seemed barely aware of Neville and Priscilla passing. He grumbled something.

"What is it?" she asked.

"It is nothing more than the anticipation of an eternally long evening. I should have known better than to let you talk me into coming to Ward's gathering. That chicken-nabob is intolerable."

Priscilla glanced past Neville to where their host was speaking with other guests in front of a row of tall windows at the far end of the parlor. Mr. Simmons Ward, now retired from the East India Company, had too many teeth in his broad smile, but in the past she had found him a genial host. She and Lazarus had not called at this house, however. He must have purchased it while she was in mourning.

His new town house was decorated — for the most part — in the latest fashion, from the friezes lacing flowers across the ceiling to the settees covered in a rainbow of colors. Beneath her satin slippers, the cool marble floor was burnished to a shine.

"Mr. Ward is no chicken-nabob," Priscilla said. "His family has been of good standing among the *ton* for many years."

"But he augmented his inheritance with his work in India." He gestured toward the opposite side of the room. "Have you ever seen anything as gauche as that blasted elephant?"

She laughed. The stuffed creature must be life-size, and it wore some sort of fringed contraption on its back. Set in an alcove and surrounded by leafy plants, the elephant seemed to be peering out of its native jungle. She dismissed the arrangement as an aberration in the otherwise pleasant room, but clearly Neville was not so forgiving.

"Mr. Ward must have a reason for the elephant," she said. "Mayhap he wishes to recall his time in India."

"He wishes to glorify a career that was hardly glorious!"

"Neville! He is our host."

"He is a high-and-mighty block!" He offered her a conciliatory smile as he took a glass of lemonade from a passing tray and handed it to her. "You know less of him than I do, my dear. You can be assured I did not form this opinion lightly."

She took a sip of the lemonade, grateful the sour taste seemed to cut through the room's stuffy air. "Neville, if you would prefer to leave . . ."

For a moment, she thought he was going to say he would like to go. Then he shook his head. "Thank you for offering me an excuse to leave, Pris, but I prefer to stay here and enjoy your company. Duncan is sure to still be at my house, and I do not like the idea of listening to him tout again your aunt's virtues."

She put her hand over her mouth before a giggle could escape at his dour tone. She was pleased Duncan had accepted Aunt Cordelia's invitation to call. He was quite unlike her aunt's late husbands, who had been a lackluster lot. Duncan possessed a sense of humor, and he was not above being part of a prank. He was the antidote Aunt Cordelia needed for a life centered too closely on the lives of Priscilla and her children. Having her aunt distracted as the days counted down to the wedding was the best gift Duncan could have given the soon-to-be newlyweds.

When she said as much to Neville, he chuckled and hooked his arm through his. He led her to where their host was expounding on the caste system in India and his opinions on it. She was not surprised when Neville questioned Mr. Ward's assumptions.

Mr. Ward launched into reasons why Neville was mistaken, and Neville answered the examples with his own to show why he believed their host was in error. Priscilla smiled as the guests looked at each man, appalled at the heated discussion, before they drifted away to find other, more tranquil conversations. When Neville glanced at her and winked, she wondered if he had changed his opinion of Mr. Ward. Neville seldom wasted time on anyone who did not challenge him in some way, and Mr. Ward was doing that now.

"Lady Priscilla," hissed a man behind her.

She looked back and smiled at Lord Carlington, a dark-haired baron who seldom wore any expression other than one which suggested mild indigestion. He was so thin that it was doubtful he consumed much, so mayhap his countenance revealed his true feelings.

"Good evening, Lord Carlington." She offered her hand.

He bowed over it, and the trio of rings on his hand glittered in the lamplight. He did not release her fingers, astonishing her. Drawing her a few steps away from Neville and Mr. Ward, he muttered a quick apology for his untoward action. Agitation filled his deep voice as he added, "My lady, if you have any influence on Hathaway as his betrothed, you should warn him that Ward does not welcome anyone to question his experiences in the east."

"Quite to the contrary. They both seem to be greatly enjoying their conversation."

"Their voices are growing more impassioned."

"True." She plucked a glass from a servant and handed it to the baron. "Lord Carlington, this is not Parliament, where fiery discourse can create rancor. Quite to the contrary, I did not guess they would find so many different opinions in common."

Lord Carlington's bushy brows dipped toward each other. "If you are sure they are not vexing each other . . ."

"Vexing? Most likely, but they are not enraging each other."

"It does not sound that way," said Mrs. Tapper as she edged forward. Wafting her carved ivory fan in front of her full face, she winced when Mr. Ward's voice rose as he jabbed a finger in Neville's direction. "My dear Lady Priscilla, do you think you need to part them before the conversation escalates into more?"

"More?" asked Priscilla, astounded at the question. "Do you mean fisticuffs? I cannot imagine Neville giving Mr. Ward a bunch of fives simply to drive his point home."

"And Mr. Ward," interjected a ruddy-faced gentleman, "would know better than to land a facer on Hathaway. They are much better matched in a verbal debate than a physical one." He dipped his balding head toward her. "Good evening, Lady Priscilla. I am Lord Meddington. We met previously at a musicale at —"

Lord Meddington was knocked aside by a blur. As Priscilla steadied the older man before he could fall, her scold at the rude man pushing past him was silenced. The round form was easily identifiable because of the short cape the brown-haired man wore over his coat.

Mr. Wiggsley! What was the playwright doing at Mr. Ward's house? Once Mr.

Wiggsley might have been welcome among the Polite World, but his series of failed plays had exiled him from the *ton*'s company.

"Thank heavens, Sir Neville!" shouted the playwright like one of his characters bursting onto the stage. He was panting as if he had run from the theater. "Thank heavens you are still here."

"What is it?" Neville asked as Priscilla came to stand beside him.

The playwright's face was, save for his full lips, colorless. "They said you would want to know now that you are in charge of the theater."

Neville grimaced at the reminder of his obligation to the Prince of Wales Theater, but asked, "Know what? I hope you are not here because of another of Birdwell's tempers."

"No, Birdwell did not send me. He —"

"Tell Robertson I will stop by tomorrow."

Mr. Wiggsley grabbed Neville's arm and shook it wildly. The motion pushed Priscilla back a couple of steps. As she steadied herself by putting her hand on the wall, she saw a motion in the doorway. Her aunt and Duncan McAndrews were standing there, staring at the contretemps.

Priscilla wondered if matters could become more complicated.

She got her answer when Mr. Wiggsley said, "The theater manager did not send me. Mr. Thurmond sent me."

"Thurmond? From Bow Street?"

At the mention of Bow Street, Priscilla saw heads snap around throughout the room. Everyone was listening as Mr. Wiggsley choked out, "There has been another murder."

Chapter Eleven

"Cordelia, do you want to come along?" Duncan was asking as Priscilla reached the doorway.

She pushed past them without an apology because she wanted to catch up with Neville. Mr. Wiggsley was trailing her. When she heard her aunt give a faltering answer, she was relieved.

That relief vanished when she heard Duncan say, "But this is your chance to be the first to know what is sure to be *on dits* by morning."

"That is true," Aunt Cordelia replied.

"Shall we go with them?"

Priscilla groaned as she rushed down the stairs, almost running over a maid who stared as if Priscilla had sprouted a goat's horns and hooves. If she paused to remind her aunt of how horrible such a scene could be, Neville might leave without her.

"Neville," she said as she caught up with him only because the footman hesitated on opening the door, "we are going to have company."

"Company?"

She glanced up the stairs, and this time the moan escaped. Daphne was trailing Aunt Cordelia and Duncan down the stairs. How could she have forgotten her daughter was riding to the *conversazione* with her great-aunt?

Neville swore under his breath, then a bit louder before calling up the stairs, "Duncan, I thank you in advance for taking Lady Cordelia and Miss Flanders to their homes."

"By gravy," shouted back Duncan, "we are going with you to see what has happened." He flung out his arm toward the other guests gathered around the top of the stairs. "Everyone is waiting for a report on what has happened." He lowered his voice to a stygian tone. "And to whom."

"Such a sight is not appropriate for your companions." Neville stepped aside as Daphne came to throw her arms around Priscilla.

Patting her daughter on the back, Priscilla said, "Aunt Cordelia, please take Daphne back to Bedford Square."

"I will make sure she gets there safely," replied a deeper voice than her aunt's.

Lord Witherspoon stepped from the shadows as if he had been lying in wait for this very moment.

Priscilla was torn between appreciation that the marquess showed good sense and consternation at how Daphne whirled with an instantaneous smile.

"Thank you, Witherspoon," said Neville.

Priscilla hurried to add after giving Neville a frown, "I am sure Mr. McAndrews and Lady Cordelia will see my daughter arrives home without incident."

"I will insure it, my lady." Lord Witherspoon nodded toward Duncan, who was watching the exchange with a mischievous smile. "*We* will insure it."

"*I* will insure it," said Aunt Cordelia, stepping forward to put her arm around Daphne's shoulders.

Knowing her aunt would allow nothing untoward to tarnish Daphne's reputation, Priscilla took Neville's arm. They hurried out the door. Mr. Wiggsley rushed after them and climbed into the carriage with them.

The ride to the Prince of Wales Theater was not quick, but no one spoke. At least, no one spoke aloud. The playwright mumbled as he worried the third knuckle on his right hand. It was bright red by the time they reached the theater.

Neville opened the door as soon as they stopped. He motioned for Mr. Wiggsley to get out, then followed. Turning, he held out his hand to Priscilla.

As she let him hand her out, he said, "I trust you realize I was not suggesting to Witherspoon that he do anything out of hand."

"I am glad to hear that, but *you* must realize that Daphne may not be thinking as squarely," she replied.

"The reason your aunt stepped in to serve as watch-dog."

"Yes." She smiled. "But you knew that once you thanked the marquess as you did, Aunt Cordelia would jump in to protect Daphne's reputation, didn't you?"

"And Duncan would not miss a moment of your aunt's company." He gave her a smug smile. "You should be ashamed of yourself for doubting my concerns about Daphne."

She was, but she would not own that. Instead, she looked past him as she heard a shout from beneath the columns at the front of the Prince of Wales Theater.

"See here, my good man," Mr. Wiggsley was shouting, "I demand that you allow us entrance."

"Sorry, sir. I cannot let anyone enter," said a pale-haired man wearing a bright red waistcoat.

"Bow Street," Priscilla breathed, discovering that, until this very moment, she had hoped Mr. Wiggsley was mistaken.

Neville strode to where the plump playwright was standing nose to nose with the Robin Red-Breast. Elbowing aside Mr. Wiggsley, Neville stuck out his hand and spoke his name.

"I am Gatlin," said the man in the red waistcoat, shaking Neville's hand. "I am glad to see you, Hathaway. Mayhap you can persuade this man to heed the orders given to me."

"By Thurmond?" Neville asked.

"Yes."

"Is he inside?"

Gatlin shook his head, then bowed it toward Priscilla as she approached. "Good evening, my lady. Thurmond told me to tell you that he would meet you at home."

"Home?" she asked. "On Bedford Square?"

The man paused, obviously searching his mind, then said, "That is right."

"Why there?" Neville grabbed Wiggsley's cloak and jerked him back from where he was trying to slip past the Bow Street Runner.

"He did not say, but he usually arranges such meetings when he has something to say he does not want every ear in the neighborhood to hear."

Neville took a deep breath, releasing it slowly. Giving the playwright a shove toward the carriage, he motioned for Priscilla to follow. Then he turned and offered his arm.

She smiled sadly as she put her hand on it and went with him to the carriage. She was not surprised that, as he helped her in, he was calling to Stuttman to get to Bedford Square with all possible speed.

By the time Priscilla and Neville reached Bedford Square with Mr. Wiggsley, she feared the playwright would succumb to vapors in her entryway. He was taken up the stairs to the back parlor with the help of both footmen. Mrs. Moore followed close behind while she gave orders to the tweener to bring strong tea and brandy. Priscilla was thankful for the housekeeper's calm head.

"Where is Thurmond?" Neville asked Gilbert as the butler took his hat and Priscilla's evening cape.

Priscilla untied her bonnet. "First tell

me, Gilbert, if Daphne has returned."

"Yes, my lady. She was delivered here by Lady Cordelia and two gentlemen. The younger gentleman seemed very solicitous of her well-being."

"Are they here?"

"They took their leave as soon as they were assured Miss Daphne was home safely. As I said, the younger gentleman was concerned about that."

Neville waved aside the butler's comment. "Where is Thurmond?"

"Thurmond?" The butler's expression was as impassive as ever, but Priscilla thought she detected a tic by his right eye. He kept his face averted, so she could not be certain. "I am sorry, sir, but —"

"From Bow Street, man!"

She put her hand on Neville's arm, and he scowled. She did not back down before his frustration. "Neville," she said with what serenity she could delve up, "we need everyone working together tonight. Venting your aggravation will not help anything."

His fierce frown vanished. "Forgive me, Gilbert, for my sharp tone."

"No need, Sir Neville, to apologize." Gilbert did not meet their eyes as he added, "Mr. Thurmond has not yet arrived."

"Mayhap Gatlin was mistaken." Neville

struck the banister with his fist, and the whole staircase quivered. "Dash it! I should have sent him to find Thurmond."

Priscilla slipped her arm through his. "That might have created further delays, and you must own that there are many reasons why Mr. Thurmond may be delayed. Shall we go up and wait for him?"

"Dash it, Pris! Must you be so reasonable?"

"If I am not, I shall shatter into a thousand pieces."

Sadness dimmed his eyes as they went up the stairs. "I am sorry you have been dragged into the investigation of murder again."

"You have, too." She could not keep from smiling. "But the difference is that you *revel* in the pursuit of the truth."

"I don't think we are different in that, Pris." He looked past her.

Priscilla was not surprised to see her younger children peering over the railing above. Isaac and Leah came rushing down the steps, their mussed hair and nightclothes flying around them.

"What are you doing up?" she asked when the children met them at the top of the stairs. "You should be in bed."

"We heard . . ." Isaac lowered his voice.

"Someone else has had her lights put out, right?"

"Isaac, such language!"

"Neville says it all the time."

She squatted so her eyes were even with her son's. She did not have to bend as much as she had to just a few weeks ago. He was growing so fast, but he must recall that he was still a child.

"Neville is an adult," she said, "and you are not. That is why both you and your sister should be in bed. Daphne has not rushed down here with you, which shows she —"

Leah grimaced. "Since she was brought home, she has been trying to decide which gown to wear to the next party she is going to. All she babbles about is some old Lord Withered-up."

"Witherspoon," Neville said with a laugh. "And you would be wise to get his name correct in case he gives your sister a look-in."

"A look-in?" gasped Leah. "She is going to have callers now? She will be babbling on and on even more about clothes and what she has worn and what she is going to wear next. Mama, she is impossible."

"We shall speak about this more in the morning. Now it is time for you two to go

241

to bed," Priscilla said, although she was tempted to agree with her younger daughter. She thought she would get an argument from Isaac. Neither could hide their curiosity, but complied. Or they did as long as she and Neville stood in the corridor. She would not be surprised if the children crept back down the stairs as soon as she and Neville turned their backs.

Going into the front parlor, she looked at the door that opened into the back one. It was closed. She wondered if she jerked it open if one or more of her children would tumble into the room because they had an ear pressed against the door.

As if the house belonged to him, Mr. Wiggsley was stretched out on the light green settee in front of the fireplace. He had his arm over his eyes, and he groaned at the sound of their footsteps.

"Leave me be," he pleaded in a lament worthy of one of his characters emoting on the stage. "I cannot bear to speak of the unspeakable just now. There are no words, no words at all, to describe what I have seen."

"No words?" asked Neville, his exasperation returning. "You are a writer. You, more than anyone else, should be able to describe what you have witnessed."

The playwright hid his face in his hands, his whole body shuddering.

Priscilla said, "You will get nothing out of him now, Neville, and if you press him, I fear I shall have to send Mrs. Moore for the *sal volatile*."

"As you wish, Pris." His mouth tightened. "Where in perdition is Thurmond?"

He stormed toward the front windows. He ran his fingers along the writing desk set between them, but his eyes were focused on the park in the middle of the square. She wondered what he expected to see in the deepening twilight. Thurmond might be in a carriage or on foot. Either way, Neville could not hurry the Bow Street Runner's arrival by glowering at the street.

Walking around the settee, she put her hand in the center of his back and was surprised when he did not face her. She understood when she heard the anger in his voice as he snarled an oath that elicited another whimper from Mr. Wiggsley, who curled into a ball.

"Where is Thurmond?" Neville repeated with the impatience he displayed so rarely. "I thought he was supposed to be waiting here for us."

"Mayhap Mr. Gatlin was mistaken. He

did hesitate on his answer to my question. Mr. Thurmond may be at your house."

Neville picked up a bell and rang it so hard she was surprised the clapper did not burst right through its brass sides. When Gilbert answered it himself, Neville gave the butler orders to send someone to his house. "If Thurmond is there, tell him to come here immediately."

"Yes, Sir Neville." The butler bowed his head and walked out as serenely as if they had asked for nothing more unusual than a bottle of wine to drink with the end of the day.

At that thought, Priscilla wondered how much longer before the tea was brought. It was certain to be hours before any of them, with the possible exception of Mr. Wiggsley, who was snoring softly on the settee, could find sleep. The tray arrived at the very same time as she heard the door open below and a man's voice resonate up the stairwell.

"Thurmond!" Neville turned from the window and went to the doorway. He drew in a breath to shout.

"The children are in bed, Neville," Priscilla said quietly.

He gave her a swift smile after releasing the breath and waiting for Thurmond to be shown up the stairs.

The Bow Street Runner glanced at Neville, then bowed to Priscilla. "Thank you for receiving me, my lady."

"Thurmond," growled Neville, "save the nice manners for when we have a reason to use them. Tell me what happened. Wiggsley said someone else has been murdered at the theater. When we went there, we were turned away by Gatlin, who said you wanted to speak with us."

"Yes, there has been another murder. I saw the body myself." He hesitated, then said, "I thought you would want to know straightaway because it was at your theater, Hathaway."

"My . . ." Neville scowled. "Let's leave that issue for later. Tell me what you can."

"I think it would be better to show you. If you would come with me, we can discuss what has happened."

"*Now* we can go to the theater?"

Thurmond folded his hands behind his back. "I gave orders that no one was to be granted entrance because I did not want the body to be disturbed until I had a chance to speak with you."

"Why?"

"Because the victim is a member of the *ton.*"

Priscilla groped for a nearby chair, but

her fingers found Neville's hand. "Another member of the *ton?*"

"Yes."

"A man or a woman?"

"A woman." He swallowed hard, then said, "It is apparently Lady Dentford, but I was hoping you could identify her, Hathaway."

"Lady Dentford, did you say?" Neville sighed.

"Yes." Mr. Thurmond turned again to Priscilla. "If she is a bosom-bow of yours, my lady, I am sorry to have told you in this manner."

"I have never met her, although I met her husband at the first assembly Daphne attended," said Priscilla. "Do you know her, Neville?"

He nodded. "I have had the occasion to be introduced to her once or twice."

"Will you recognize her?" asked the Bow Street Runner.

"Yes." His voice grew gloomier with each answer.

Mr. Thurmond motioned toward the stairs. "Shall we go, Hathaway?"

"Do you have a carriage, Mr. Thurmond?" asked Priscilla. "You are welcome, of course, to ride with us."

His mouth gaped until he closed it so

hard she heard his teeth click. "Us? *You* are coming as well?"

Neville put his arm around her waist and smiled grimly. "Only a fool would try to halt Priscilla Flanders when she is determined to do something."

"But it is not something for a lady to see."

"I have seen such scenes before, Mr. Thurmond," she said, fighting to keep her voice even. She truly did not want to view another slain woman, but waiting here for Neville to return would be almost as ghastly. "Just a short time ago at that very theater, if you will recall."

The Bow Street Runner stared at her for a long moment, then nodded. He stepped back and motioned for her to precede them down the stairs. He started to follow, then asked, "What about Wiggsley?"

"He will not be in anyone's way if he remains in Priscilla's parlor." Neville hurried down the stairs and took the hand she held out to him. "Let's go. To quote the Bard as I seem to be doing too often of late, 'If it were done when 'tis done, then 'twere well it were done quickly.'"

Chapter Twelve

The theater seemed much bigger when it was deserted. Even the voices of the actors and those who worked behind the scenes had disappeared. Faint light came from the empty stage visible through a half-open door, but the rest of the lower level was lost in the darkness. If there were any lamps burning in the upper boxes, Priscilla could not see the light from where she stood.

Mr. Thurmond said nothing as he led them and two of his fellow Bow Street Runners up the staircase that was the twin of the one she had climbed when she had brought Daphne to watch the play. Did Mr. Thurmond have a bat's skills to maneuver without light? He seemed to find his way through the darkness without hesitation. Mayhap it was as simple as he was accustomed to lurking in shadowed places while he skulked after thieves.

"How are you doing, Pris?" asked Neville in little more than a whisper. He was walking behind her.

"I never realized how cavernous a theater would sound when no one else was around."

"It is spooky and very disconcerting, even for those of us who have spent considerable time in deserted theaters."

She did not answer as she continued to climb. Neither man had spoken of the fact that both victims had been female, but she was not surprised Mr. Thurmond and the other Runners were walking only a step in front of her and Neville close behind.

Was the murderer still within the theater? She warned herself not to assume anything, because there were many places both behind the curtain and in front of it where a killer could hide. What had Lady Dentford been doing in the theater? That was another question she hoped would be answered quickly.

At the top of the stairs where a faint glow turned the blackness to gray, Mr. Thurmond and the men he called Gill and Bintcliff waited for them. Priscilla could not fault them for hesitating to go into the dark corridor. She realized how mistaken she was when, with eyes now adjusted to the low light, she saw Mr. Thurmond reach under his coat and draw out a long item.

A pistol!

She turned to discover Neville doing the same. Not speaking the curse that would be inappropriate for a parson's widow, she asked, "Are you bereft of your senses?"

Mr. Thurmond asked from the shadows, "What do you mean, Lady Priscilla?"

"If either of you fires a pistol, how do you know you will not strike some innocent person?"

Neville's laugh was strained. "There are those who say no one in the theater's demimonde has any innocence left."

"This is no time for silliness."

"I can think of no better time than when we are surrounded by silliness, but if it makes you feel better, we shall put the guns away."

"Hathaway —" began Mr. Thurmond.

"She has a point. We have no idea who might be in the theater."

Mr. Thurmond muttered something, but a motion told her that he had heeded Neville's request.

"Take this," Neville said.

The Bow Street Runner's hand came near Priscilla's face. She sensed rather than saw it.

"What is it?" asked Mr. Thurmond.

"Your man at the door had several sticks in case someone was more persistent than we were about getting into the theater. In close quarters, they should be effective."

"As long as the murderer has Lady Priscilla's compunctions about firing off a gun in the theater."

"He will have only a single shot, so he cannot slay us all."

"If that is supposed to be comforting," Priscilla said, "you are failing."

"*You* are the one who asked we put our pistols away."

"Holding a duel in the dark is a mad idea."

When Neville's hand on the back of her waist gave her a gentle shove, she took a single step in the direction he had indicated. The floor was uneven. She did not know if only this side of the theater had boards jutting up at strange angles or if she had not noticed the bumpy surface when the lamps were lit.

Suddenly something struck Priscilla's left arm. A fierce tingle leaped from her elbow to her fingertips. An ache rose to her shoulder. She stepped back, bumping into Neville. Light blinded her, and she raised her other arm to protect her eyes. She heard Mr. Gill yell something as Neville grasped her, trying to push past her in the narrow passage.

She was hit again as she tried to shake feeling back into fingers deadened by the blow to her elbow. Hit again by a door, she realized, as a block of light emerged from the blinding brilliance. Blinking, she tried to see through it.

A woman peered out. She held a lantern. Raising it, she gasped, "Oh, my!" As she stared at the men and the sticks they held, her face was ashen.

Priscilla recognized her as the actress who had been rehearsing while Priscilla and her son watched backstage. She was incredibly beautiful, with an ethereal grace that had allowed her to appear to float across the stage.

As the woman stepped out into the corridor, Priscilla saw a motion in the room. It was a flash of red — red hair or the waistcoat of another Bow Street Runner?

"Neville, someone else is in there," she whispered.

He glanced at her, then, handing her the cudgel he held, edged toward the room while Mr. Thurmond told the woman to remain where she was. Neville looked into the room and then back at her.

"Red," she said lowly.

"Ella Ayers," the woman said in response to a question Mr. Thurmond must have asked. "I had the first female lead in Mr. Wiggsley's most recent play."

"But the play has closed," Neville said. "Why are you lurking in theater at this hour?"

"I came here to get some of my . . . things." She glanced guiltily at the large bag she was carrying. Her expression told Priscilla that the actress had helped herself to props or costumes that she could sell to give her money until she found another role.

"How long have you been here?" Mr. Thurmond asked.

Neville motioned for them to keep Miss Ayers talking. Then he slipped into the room. Priscilla wanted to watch him, but kept her gaze focused on the actress so Miss Ayers would not notice what Neville was doing.

"Long enough to know there has been another murder." She shuddered. "I did not see it, but everyone is whispering about it."

Mr. Thurmond pounced on a single word. "Everyone? How many people are here?"

"A few of the other actors were collecting their personal items when you and your fellow Robin Red-breasts appeared."

"And you decided to keep hidden?"

She raised her chin. "We actors know how others look down on us because of our profession. Men like you doubt we are telling the truth because we make lies appear so real when we are on stage."

"I will want to speak with anyone who was in the theater when the murder took place."

Neville came back out of the room and raised his hands, palms up, empty.

"If you are asking me to tell you who was here," Miss Ayers said, still paying no one but Mr. Thurmond and his comrades any mind, "you should know that I do not buy and sell my fellow thespians."

"I am not asking you to betray them. I am asking you to let me talk to them, so they can be cleared of any connection with the murder."

"They might be willing to talk to you so they are not blackballed from another theater." Her mouth straightened as she focused her gaze on Neville. "After all, nobody seems to know when our patron will be arranging for another performance at *this* theater."

"Not until," he replied, appearing unruffled by her accusing stare, "it is safe for the audience to return. Killing off an audience one by one does not lead to profit for any theater."

Before the actress could fire back more angry words, Priscilla said, "Mr. Thurmond, I think we should continue on."

"Where are you going?" asked Miss Ayers.

"If you would wait here, Miss Ayers," said Mr. Thurmond.

She gave a soft squeal when the light shone off his red waistcoat. "Do you mean *she* is still here?"

Priscilla did not bother to answer, and neither did the men as they continued along the corridor. Their shadows stretched out in front of them, because Miss Ayers followed close behind. The actress might be dismayed to see Bow Street Runners in the theater, but she clearly did not intend to miss what he was there to investigate.

"All I saw was a length of red cloth," Neville murmured as he leaned toward Priscilla.

"I saw a motion. I would take an oath that it was a person."

"There is a window in the room. A breeze could have fluttered the cloth."

"And a person could have slipped out of the window."

He regarded her with a smile. "You are becoming even more adept than I at seeing unscrupulous behavior." Turning to the Bow Street Runner, he said something too low for her to hear.

"All right," Mr. Thurmond said. "Gill, go."

The other man nodded and slipped back into the darkness beyond Miss Ayers's lantern.

When Mr. Thurmond shouldered aside a drapery, Priscilla was astonished. Another murder in a box? This made no sense. Why would someone be in one of the boxes when the theater was closed?

A nervous laugh tickled her throat. She had learned that, although in the murderer's mind the crime might make sense, she must never judge these atrocities by normal logic.

The Bow Street Runner looked at her and started to speak. Then he stepped aside so she could enter. He must have guessed that, having come this far, she would not be turned away.

Priscilla almost wished he had insisted that she remain in the corridor when she saw the corpse in the faint light edging past the drapery. Unlike Harmony Lummis, this woman was lying facedown.

Like Harmony, a knife was driven into the woman. It had pierced her heart from the back.

When Neville took the lantern from Miss Ayers and stepped past Priscilla, he hooked the lantern's handle over the lamp on the wall. Light spread across the box, glistening on the blood on the carpet. Filthy footprints obscured the rest of the carpet.

His jaw tightened, and Priscilla knew he was furious that someone else had died so horribly.

"When was Lady Dentford found?" he asked.

"Her body was discovered a few hours ago," Mr. Thurmond said, "when the manager came to the theater to make sure no one was here who should not be."

"Where is Robertson?"

"Drinking in his office," Miss Ayers replied.

"Alone?"

"With Morton when I was there several hours ago."

Mr. Thurmond turned to his companion. "Bintliff, see if they are still there or if anyone saw one of them leave."

The Runner nodded and hurried away into the darkness.

Mr. Thurmond drew the curtain closed. "You said you know the lady, Hathaway."

"Indirectly. I have met her husband several times. He is a quiet man, and I had understood that they had an excellent marriage."

Priscilla could not tear her gaze from the corpse. She went back to the drapery and pulled on one side. It snapped from its rings. Stepping forward, she began to spread it over Lady Dentford.

"Then why would she have been here?" she asked. "Is it possible that she was having an affair, too, with one of the actors?"

"Are you suggesting she has been involved with Birdwell?" asked Neville.

Miss Ayers shook her head vehemently as she pulled a handkerchief from her bodice. "That was impossible."

"Impossible? Why?"

"Mr. Birdwell . . ." She flushed and swallowed hard before going on. "He has his — um, admirers. The lady murdered the opening night of our latest play was one. The other is an actress from a theater in Drury Lane."

"Obviously he is a better man than I am," Neville replied. "I find one woman keeps me on my toes." He gave Priscilla a smile.

Drawing the drapery farther over the dead woman, Priscilla said, "Mr. Birdwell would have no reason to wish Lady Dentford dead, it appears."

"No." Miss Ayers worried the handkerchief, threatening the lace on its edges. "He has not been at the theater in several days. I doubt if he and this woman ever met. If —"

"Oh, sweet heavens!"

Neville bent toward her. "Pris, what is it?"

She pointed to Lady Dentford's left hand, which still remained uncovered. "Her third finger shows an indentation where she was wearing a ring. The ring is gone."

He motioned her aside. Priscilla rose and put her hands over her stomach as Neville knelt, lifting the dead woman's left hand to examine it. He did the same with the right.

"Find anything?" asked Thurmond.

"It appears she was wearing several rings. All of them are gone." He turned to the Bow Street Runner. "It seems you must begin your investigation of Lady Lummis's murder anew, for this is too much of a coincidence to be ignored."

"I had hoped to obtain your help,

Hathaway, in finding these murderers."

"Murderers? Do you believe there is more than one?"

"I hope so."

Priscilla glanced at Neville, then asked, "You hope so, Mr. Thurmond? Why would you wish there to be more than one murderer?"

"It would be easier to find two murderers, each with a reason to prey on a specific woman, than to have to chase down a single killer murdering rich, titled women." He glanced over his shoulder and motioned.

Mr. Gill entered the box, crowding past Miss Ayers. "No sign of anyone, Thurmond, in any of the alleys. The ground beneath the window is hard, so no footprints would have been left."

"Miss Ayers," asked Mr. Thurmond, "who was with you in the room you stepped out of?"

"I was alone," she replied, but did not meet his eyes.

Priscilla folded her hands behind her back, waiting for Mr. Thurmond to denounce the actress as a liar. Instead he asked Mr. Gill more questions about any other routes out of the theater.

Turning to Neville, Priscilla said, "If the

murderer was in the room with her —"

"She is not that skilled an actress. She would have come screaming out of the room."

"But if she did not know the person was the murderer, she would have no reason to scream."

"Wait here." Neville squeezed past where Mr. Thurmond was in intense conversation with the other Robin Red-Breast about the missing rings. Going to Miss Ayers, he spoke as quietly to her as he had to Priscilla.

The actress was defiant and started to leave. Neville caught her arm, and her shoulders sagged. She nodded, glancing at the Bow Street Runners. He patted her arm, then elbowed around Mr. Thurmond again.

"There was a man with her," Neville said. "Her lover."

Priscilla began, "If he —"

"Impossible. When the murder took place, they were — shall we say occupied?"

"But who is to say exactly when Lady Dentford was murdered? It could have been any time in the past few hours."

"Which gives the man with her a good alibi."

Her brows rose as she smiled. "Really?"

"Really." He chuckled. "He apparently is a very attentive lover." Raising his voice, he added, "Thurmond, if you want to try to find the missing jewelry, I suggest you contact a fence near the Thames. A fence by the name of Carter."

Thurmond nodded. "You spoke of him when you brought Lady Lummis's brooch to Bow Street's offices."

Bintliff appeared out of the shadows. His report was quick and concise. Morton and Robertson had been sharing a bottle in the theater manager's office. Both had fallen asleep, so neither could be completely certain the other man had been there the whole time. Just as importantly, neither had been sober enough to hear anything out of the ordinary in the almost deserted theater.

"That is no help," Neville said, frustration seeping into his voice.

"I leave you to your task, Thurmond. I assume Lord Dentford has not been notified."

"No."

"I will —"

Priscilla interrupted, "We will speak with him while you tend to what you must, Mr. Thurmond."

The Bow Street Runner drew back the

remaining piece of drapery. "Let me know if you learn anything, my lady."

"If you will share with us what you glean from those you speak with."

"My lady, you cannot expect —"

Knowing she was being rude, she halted him by saying, "I expect we all shall work together to solve the puzzle of these crimes. I know I am interested in what you learn after speaking with Carter and Mr. Birdwell."

"But Birdwell may not be involved with this lady's death. If you remember what she said . . ." Mr. Thurmond turned around, looking in every direction. "Where did Miss Ayers go?"

"She must have taken it into her mind," Neville replied, "to disappear before you asked her more questions."

"But she is not a suspect."

"In this crime."

Thurmond's mouth twisted in a wry grin. "Point well taken, Hathaway."

"And I hope you took Lady Priscilla's point as well."

Neville steered Priscilla out of the box before Thurmond could give them another argument about why he could not share any information he gathered. Neville understood why Bow Street wanted to keep its information close to its collective chest, but the fact remained that most of what it had thus far had been brought to Bow Street by Neville and Priscilla.

Mayhap the two of them *should* open an investigation agency of their own. So far, their skills had rivaled or bested Bow Street's, and they were welcome amidst the Polite World. He almost laughed as he realized he seldom had considered belonging to the *ton* a beneficial circumstance.

"What do you find amusing?" Priscilla asked as they went down the stairs.

He put his finger to her lips and motioned with his head toward where several men were arriving with a litter. He recognized at least two of them from St. Julian's Church. They must be coming to take away the lady's corpse. Nodding to them, he hurried Priscilla out into the rain and to the waiting carriage before anyone could ask them questions.

Telling the coachman to take them to Lord Dentford's house and handing Priscilla into the carriage, Neville sat. He shut the door and slapped the wall.

"Will you tell me what you find amusing now?" she asked.

He wished he could see her face in the darkness. The light from the street lamps was dimmed by the rain. "I was thinking about how we discussed establishing an agency to do publicly what we have found ourselves doing privately in the past year."

"I doubt that is legal."

"Bow Street is well within the law."

"I thought you meant this." She leaned toward him, and he found himself being thoroughly kissed.

As her lips played across his, lingering to lilt a melody he heard in her rapid breath, he swept his arms around her. The silken warmth of her gown teased him to discover the soft skin beneath it. Losing himself in her touch and touching her would be the best antidote to the horror of the murders.

Again he wondered if she knew his thoughts, because she drew back and whispered, "We must recall what we need to do."

"We *need* to do this." He kissed her deeply and smiled when her breath pulsed against him. Releasing her reluctantly, he added, "But we also need to stop this murderer." He took a deep breath and released it through his tight lips. "There seems nothing in common about these murders other than the location, Pris."

"Killing someone in a theater is a risky matter."

"Killing someone *anywhere* can be risky."

"I shall not ask you how you know that."

"That shows good sense, in this case." He leaned one elbow against the window frame and stared out at the square they were passing through. "But the theater was almost empty when Lady Dentford was slain. The question is why was she there?"

"She must have been lured there for a specific reason."

"Agreed. I suspect if we had further information, we would see something we have overlooked."

"Mayhap Lord Dentford will be able to help." Her voice quivered. "Although I hate to ask when we are bringing him the news of his wife's death. I wish we had never gone to the theater with Daphne that night."

"This is not the Season you hoped for."

"That is obvious." She sighed. "I had assumed I would spend these three weeks before our wedding trying to persuade Aunt Cordelia that I had specific ideas on how the wedding breakfast should be held."

He smiled before resting her head against his shoulder. "I am astonished that even two murders keep her from giving you her opinions."

"Duncan is distracting her."

"I should invite him more often."

"I believe I shall extend him an open invitation to Mermaid Cottage."

"He may not want to return to Stonehall-on-Sea after his previous visit there almost ended up being a fatal one."

She shook her head, then raised it. "He was eager to go to the theater tonight."

"True. Duncan is always looking for a bit of mayhem."

"No wonder you two are such good friends."

He chuckled as she placed her head on his shoulder once more. Wishing the carriage ride could continue forever was an air-dream. They could not escape the madness surrounding them.

Dentford's house was dark when the carriage halted in front of it. That puzzled Neville. Whenever Priscilla went out, a lamp shone beside the door until she came home, no matter how late the hour.

He said nothing, because he sensed Priscilla's uneasiness in how tightly she gripped his fingers as he handed her out and went with her to the door. A servant answered it quickly, further proof that Lady Dentford had intended her homecoming not to be noticed. The footman scurried away with Neville's request to speak to the viscount. He returned and asked them to follow him.

Priscilla's fingers dug more deeply into his arm as Neville climbed the stairs with her. Blast and bother! He should have taken her back to Bedford Square first. She already had endured the difficulty of telling Lummis about his wife's fate. She should not have to suffer through the conversation to come with Dentford.

"Pris," he began.

"I will be fine," she whispered. "And you may need me."

"I *do* need you." He put his other hand over hers on his arm. "But if you wish to return to the foyer, I will tell Dentford."

"Thank you, but no." Her voice was grim, and, when they reached the top of the stairs where a single lamp burned, he could see her face was bleak.

Priscilla was relieved that Neville did not press further. She wanted to be done with this errand, but she must be strong for Lord Dentford . . . and for Neville.

Another lamp was burning in a room that was too small for a parlor. Two chairs were set in the corners, and a table topped with a stack of books took up most of the center. Shadowed paintings hung along the walls.

From behind the table, Lord Dentford came to his feet. Surprise exploded across his face as he gasped, "Hathaway! What are you doing here at this hour?" He swallowed quickly, then said, "My lady."

"We are here," Neville said, "about Lady Dentford. We have just come from the Prince of Wales Theater."

"The theater?" He sat heavily on the chair. "Deuce take it! I told her she was asking for trouble if she continued going there."

Priscilla said nothing as Neville walked to stand in front of Lord Dentford. The two men were such a contrast. With much of Lord Dentford's sun scorching peeled away, his skin was a pasty white. Neville's face was bronzed. Everything about the viscount suggested a gentle upbringing, while Neville retained the coiled wariness he had needed to refine before his life was abruptly altered by his inheritance.

Lord Dentford pushed himself back to his feet. "Why are you inquiring about my wife? What has happened?"

As Neville explained with a serenity Priscilla doubted she could copy, the viscount's face grew even paler. He almost tumbled back into his chair. Priscilla put out a hand to steady the chair while

Neville rang for a servant to bring something strong and strengthening for Lord Dentford.

"And we suspect she was robbed as well," he said while he filled a glass and shoved it into the viscount's hand. "Her fingers had been stripped of her rings. If she was wearing any other jewelry, we did not see it."

"I cannot believe this," Lord Dentford moaned. He tossed back the contents of the glass and slammed it against the table.

"You mentioned trouble there, Dentford," Neville said. "Was she threatened by someone?"

The viscount shook his head and groped for the bottle. Finding it, he poured more wine into his glass.

"Then what sort of trouble?"

He downed the wine. "You know, Hathaway! It is a topic we should not broach in front of Lady Priscilla."

"I probably do know, but enlighten me."

Priscilla added, "You may speak plainly, Lord Dentford."

The viscount's fingers closed into a fist on the table. "She is fascinated with him."

"Him?"

"Your friend, Hathaway," snarled the viscount.

"Who?"

Priscilla held her breath as she waited for Lord Dentford to answer.

"That actor. Birdwell. First he fascinated her with his seductions. Now he has lured her to the theater for an assignation and murdered her." He pushed past Neville. "I am going to kill that son of a sea-cook."

She watched Neville try to keep the viscount from storming out of the house to do something stupid. Was it possible? In spite of Miss Ayers's assertions, had Mr. Birdwell been dallying with another titled woman? His description matched the man who had brought Harmony's stolen brooch to the fence. One mistress murdered was a tragedy; two were a horror she wanted to deny as impossible.

But it was possible. That she knew all too well.

Chapter Thirteen

Neville smiled during the congratulations from his friends as he emerged with Priscilla from St. Julian's Church and the second reading of the banns. It was a brittle smile, but nobody seemed to take note. Beside him, her hand stroking his sleeve, Priscilla wore an identical expression.

The message he had sent to Thurmond half a week ago had received no reply. He had been certain the Bow Street Runner would be interested in Lord Dentford's assertion that his wife was involved in an *affaire de coeur* with Reginald Birdwell. Mayhap Thurmond was busy contacting Carter to discover if anyone had tried to sell him the lady's rings. The description of them given by Lord Dentford would help Bow Street locate the missing jewelry. One ring had the family's crest engraved inside where a thief might not notice it.

He noted people talking with anxious expressions. The glances toward where he and Priscilla stood with the children announced their whispered conversations involved the topic nobody spoke of openly. Two dead women at the Prince of Wales Theater and a murderer who had not been captured.

Even the children were subdued when they returned to the carriage to go to Bedford Square. Aunt Cordelia, who had joined them for the service, agreed to stop by later, and Neville suspected she was hoping for a call from Duncan as an excuse not to have to come to the house while he was there.

He had been surprised to see her in church this morning, because he had doubted she could restrain herself when the pastor said: "I publish the Banns of Marriage between Sir Neville Hathaway of St. Julian's parish, London, and Lady Priscilla Flanders of St. Julian's parish, London. If any of you know cause, or just impediment, why these two persons should not be joined together in holy matrimony, ye are to declare it. This is the second time of asking."

He chuckled at the thought of how Aunt Cordelia's mouth had become a straight line, as if she were fighting her yearning to jump to her feet and denounce the coming marriage in front of the parishioners. Fortunately, her desire for proper decorum overruled her dislike of him.

"Aunt Cordelia will never come to call once you and Mama are married," Isaac said as he stood beside Neville while Priscilla entered the carriage with her daughters.

"That would be a great disappointment for your mother." He smiled at the lad, who never had been able to hide his feelings.

"Aunt Cordelia chides Mama all the time."

"But your mother loves her."

Isaac nodded ruefully. "That is true."

"And so do you."

"Yes." The word was reluctant. He brightened as he added, "But if Aunt Cordelia does not come to the house, I will not have to recite my lessons for her."

Neville could not argue with that. He hefted the boy up to sit with Stuttman in the box before getting into the carriage with Priscilla and the girls. Leah was sitting next to her mother. Picking the girl up, he set her close to her sister.

Leah giggled, but Daphne looked pained.

As he sat beside Priscilla, he whispered, "Is your oldest all right?"

"She is distressed."

"About Lady —"

She shook her head. "About a certain peer who caught her attention, but has not been present at any events she has attended in the past day or so."

Neville leaned back against the seat and regarded Daphne, who was staring at her folded hands. He never had seen the girl so dejected. Wanting to say something to give her comfort, he could not imagine what.

"She will be fine," Priscilla said, so softly he could barely hear her.

He wondered how she could be certain of that. His doubts remained until they reached the house on Bedford Square and were met at the door by Gilbert. The butler welcomed them before holding out a folded page to Daphne.

"This arrived for you, Miss Flanders," he said.

"For me?" gasped Daphne, her glum spirits vanishing.

"It was delivered into my hand by a footman who asked that it be given directly to you, Miss Flanders." Gilbert almost smiled. He had, like the rest of the staff, a very soft spot in his heart for the Flanders children. "I assured him it would be, and it has been."

"Thank you." She started to break the seal, then said, "Excuse me, Mama, Uncle

Neville. I think I would like to read this in private."

Daphne gave no one a chance to reply as she rushed up the stairs at a pace she had given up with her childhood. Neville wondered if her feet touched any of the risers.

"Who do you think sent it, Mama?" asked Leah.

Isaac rubbed his toe into the floor. "Probably that chap she is all moony about."

"You are growing wiser with every passing day," Neville said, ruffling the boy's hair.

He laughed along with his sister as the two youngsters climbed the stairs. Even before they had reached the top, the butler said quietly, "The note for Miss Flanders was not the only one brought to the house, Sir Neville. This was brought for you."

"Here?" He took the folded page from Gilbert. "Forgive the stupid question, Gilbert. Thank you."

The butler took Neville's hat and walked toward the back of the house.

Neville opened the page and read it.

"Is it from Thurmond?" Priscilla asked.

"No, it is from Dentford." He handed her the note.

The few words were right to the point.

Her husband had spoken with his wife's abigail and discovered Lady Dentford had left the house wearing, in addition to the rings, a pearl and ruby necklace that had been in his family for generations.

Neville glanced at Priscilla as she read the note. Her face revealed nothing, but he knew her quick mind was already sorting through the few facts they possessed.

"Should we go to Carter's shop?" she asked.

"It is a job better suited to Bow Street. I think I should alert Thurmond."

"Be careful." She curved her hand along his cheek.

"I have every reason to."

Her kiss was, he suspected, the only warmth he would have for hours to come.

"We must be certain it was not left in the box where Lady Dentford was killed." Thurmond pushed open the front door of the Prince of Wales Theater.

"Even if the necklace is there," Neville said, stepping inside the theater, "it may be proof only that the murderer missed it in his hurry to flee with her rings."

"I know, I know." Frustration tainted Thurmond's words.

That frustration deepened when a search

of the box where Lady Dentford died brought no hint of the missing necklace. When Thurmond started grumbling that the lady's maid might have been mistaken, Neville guessed his friend was assuming any clues would again lead nowhere.

Seeing a movement on the darkened stage below, Neville motioned for Thurmond to come with him. He did not have to caution the Bow Street Runner to silence when they rushed out of the box.

They edged into the stage's wing. Neville drew aside the curtain and peered out onto the stage. A pair of lanterns set on a bench in the center revealed an astonishing sight. A man was standing between the lanterns. He held a long-barreled pistol up and aimed it in the direction of the box where Lady Lummis had been found dead.

Thurmond muttered an oath and leaped onto the stage. The man holding the gun whirled with a startled cry. The Bow Street Runner froze.

Pushing back, Neville ran behind the curtain. The light seeping under it helped him avoid coils of rope and pieces of scenery. He tensed, waiting for the detonation of the pistol.

"What are you doing here?" he heard. It must be the man with the gun, because it was not Thurmond's voice.

He bent and tugged at the curtain. It was heavy, but he could raise it enough to slither beneath it. He must be careful to slip under *behind* the man with the pistol. Otherwise, he might give the man a choice of targets.

Looking around, he saw a wooden box close to the curtain. He tiptoed toward it. He got down on his stomach and pressed the bottom of his boots against the box. Lifting the curtain, he saw two pairs of feet. Thurmond's were planted solidly against the stage's floor. The other man's shifted. Was he getting ready to flee or to shoot the Bow Street Runner?

Neville had no time to determine that. Pushing his feet against the box, he propelled himself out onto stage. He jumped to his feet and wrapped his arm around the neck of the man holding the gun.

"Drop it!" he ordered. He tightened his arm, and the man gagged.

The gun clattered to the stage, hitting a small pouch. Thurmond ran to pick it up.

Neville released the man's neck. Grasping his shoulders, he spun the man to face him.

"Reeve!" He stared in disbelief at the actor's valet. "What in perdition are you doing?"

The valet struggled to answer, but coughed and coughed.

Thurmond pushed past him. "You will want to see this, Hathaway." He handed the gun to Neville.

He hefted it, surprised by its slight weight and that it was not particularly well-balanced. Checking it, he said, "This is not loaded." He shoved it into Reeve's hands.

The gun almost fell out of the valet's grip, but he managed to hold on to it. Regaining his breath, he asked in a scratchy voice, "What are *you* doing sneaking up on a man and scaring ten years off his life?"

"We saw you pointing a gun," Thurmond retorted. "What did you think we should do? Two women have been killed here in the past fortnight."

Reeve flinched, then said, "They were not shot."

"No," Neville said, "they were not. But that does not explain why you are pointing a gun at the box where one woman was slain."

"I was? I did not realize that." He swallowed roughly and put a hand to his neck, wincing. Then he pointed to a small, lace-edged garment hanging over a box farther past the one where Lady Dentford had been found. "I was aiming at that."

"What is it?" asked Thurmond. "A lady's undergarment?"

"One of Wiggsley's fancier capes."

"You were going to shoot a cape?" Thurmond sounded more and more puzzled, and Neville could not fault him. "Why?"

"I was practicing."

"For what?"

"For when I am a soldier." He held the pistol close to his chest. "I am tired of following Birdwell's silly orders to clean up messes after him."

"You would rather," Neville asked, "follow some officer's orders into a volley of gunfire?"

"At least that is heroic. This —" He gestured toward the side of the theater where the actor's dressing room was situated. "This is drudgery."

"And nothing a woman would admire? Reeve, you are being a fool to join the Army simply to obtain a woman's favors. Find another way to win her heart."

Raising his head, he glared at Neville, then at Thurmond. "If you gentlemen do not mind, I will practice handling a gun somewhere else."

Neville smiled coldly. "Take care where you aim that gun. Someone else might believe you intend to shoot something other than Wiggsley's cape."

As icily, Reeve replied, "Which was why I was practicing here where I thought nobody would see me." He bent to pick up the pouch which probably held balls for the pistol and walked toward the wings.

Thurmond wiped his hands as he looked out at the empty theater. "That was humiliating. If word of what happened here gets back to Bow Street, I will be a laughing-stock."

"Don't look at me as if I am about to run and tell them." Neville brushed dirt from his waistcoat. "Then I would have to explain how it took two of us to disarm a man with an unloaded gun."

His friend chuckled. "We make quite a pair. There does not seem to be any —"

"Reeve!" came a shout from offstage.

Neville smiled as Reginald Birdwell walked out onto the stage. The actor stopped, staring at them. His feet shifted, just as his valet's had. Was he giving thought to the idea of running, too?

Closing the distance between them, Neville said, "Hail, fellow, well met."

"What play is that from?" asked

Birdwell, his brow wrinkling.

"It is Jonathan Swift. You should read something other than plays." Putting his hand on the actor's shoulder, he steered him toward where Thurmond stood next to the bench holding the lanterns.

Birdwell halted and stared at the Bow Street Runner. "Why is *he* here?"

"We are — as you probably have heard, even though you have not been seen at the theater in the past week — investigating another woman's death."

"Another?" His face lost all color. "I had not heard that. Who was killed?"

"Lady Dentford."

He mouthed the woman's name, but no sound came out. He sat on the bench and stared out at the deserted boxes.

"Where have you been, Birdwell?" asked Thurmond.

"I have been . . ." He gulped. "I have been busy."

"With whom?" asked Neville.

Birdwell raised his chin. "It is not a gentleman's place to say. I am innocent of these crimes." He motioned toward Thurmond. "He will not believe me, but you have known me for a long time, Hathaway. Tell him that I would not have killed those women."

"Two women you knew well."

"Yes." The answer was reluctant.

"And do you own to having *affaires* with both of them?"

"Yes."

"At the same time?"

"They had no reason to complain that my attentions to them were divided."

"You are a fool, Birdwell." Neville put his foot on the bench and leaned toward the actor. "As long as I have known you, all you ever talked about was when your name was prominent on the playbill posted outside the theater. When did you find that philandering with other men's wives was more important than your career?"

Birdwell exploded up off the bench. "We are not all lucky enough to have a rich relative die and leave us plump in the pockets, Hathaway. While you went off to live a gentleman's life among the *ton,* I remained here striving in vain to make something out of another of Wiggsley's worthless productions, even after most of the audience had left to demand the return of their money."

"So you grew tired of waiting for your fortune?"

"I started to grow old." He laughed humorlessly. "I know my acting skills will never be a match for the greats like Garrick, so I have only my youthful looks to trade on. As those diminished, I had to find some way to keep from ending up starving on the street or taking bit parts that no one else wants."

"And you believed Lady Lummis and Lady Dentford would provide you with that comfortable life you aspired to?"

"They — or I should say their disinterested husbands — had more than enough blunt to give them *and* me luxury. Neither woman complained about the gifts I was happy to take from them."

"Are you so concerned about money?" asked Thurmond.

Birdwell whirled, his face pale. "No — I mean, yes — I mean I did not kill them, if that is what you are suggesting. Tell him, Hathaway! I could not have slain them."

"You could have," Neville said. "Any man or woman is capable of killing if provoked enough."

"But I did not kill them!" His voice rose to a screech. "You must believe me! I did not kill them."

"I believe you."

"You must believe me. I did not —" Birdwell's eyes widened. "You believe me?"

"Yes." Neville walked past the astonished actor to where Thurmond was listening with his arms folded over the front of his red waistcoat. "It seems obvious to me, Thurmond, that even Birdwell is smart enough to realize that murdering his patronesses would not help his financial state."

"And the robberies?" asked the Bow Street Runner.

"You know as well as I do how few shillings he would have gotten from any fence for those baubles." He looked back at the pasty-faced actor. "Those few shillings would not have kept him in the comfortable state he aspires to."

"Are you asking me to take him off my list of suspects?"

Neville laughed. "Of course not. Nobody should be removed. I simply am suggesting that he not be considered the most likely suspect in these murders. However, he might provide the key to why these two specific women were killed."

"How?"

Instead of answering his friend, Neville turned to Birdwell. "How many other women are you involved with?"

The actor flushed to the color of Thurmond's waistcoat. "No gentleman should speak of that, for the answer could tarnish a lady's honor."

"Mayhap, but a true gentleman would be more concerned with a lady's life than her honor." He smiled coolly. "Miss Ayers spoke of an actress at another theater."

"Clementine."

"Clementine Lang?" Neville frowned. "Don't I recall you having her mother as your paramour?"

"That was many years ago."

"I would hope even you were honorable enough not to bed a mother and a daughter at the same time."

"Of course," he replied, but his face grew an even brighter crimson.

"Who else?" asked Thurmond.

"Mrs. Kreller and Lady Morley and Miss Greene and . . ." He paused, his face screwed up with concentration. "I believe that is the total."

"Six women?" Thurmond's brows reached toward his nose as he frowned. "You are asking us to believe that you were keeping six women?"

Neville said before Birdwell could answer, "You forget, Thurmond. *They* were keeping him. Some men sing for their suppers. Others . . ."

The Bow Street Runner guffawed. The

laugh echoed through the theater even as he said, "Do not think of sneaking out of Town, Birdwell. We may have more questions as we try to protect your harem." He chuckled more as he walked off the stage.

Birdwell sank back to the bench. "Thank you for persuading him of my innocence. I am in your debt, Hathaway."

"Many times over, but that changes nothing. You should find a place far from this theater and go there."

"You heard Thurmond. He warned me not to leave London."

Neville's sharp laugh sounded more like a snort. "You may be able to betwattle Thurmond, but I know you well, Birdwell. There are many places you can stay in the warren around these theaters. Just keep away from any woman until this murderer is found."

"Any woman?" he choked. "Hathaway, why am I being punished when I am innocent?"

"Innocent? Hardly. An innocent man does not bed other men's wives in exchange for the gifts they give him." When the actor began to protest, Neville knew he had to find some way to reach past Birdwell's pride. "Will you start thinking with what is in your head instead of what is in your breeches?"

"I am."

"Then you know that if another of your mistresses is murdered, even *I* will find it hard to swallow your protestations of innocence."

The actor blanched again. "Hathaway, if you do not believe me, who will?"

"Mayhap you should take your cue from Hamlet and his comment about protesting."

" 'The lady doth protest too much, methinks.' " His shoulders sagged. "But Hamlet was the one guilty of murder, and I am not."

Neville put one foot on the bench. "Who is the woman for whom Reeve is determined to prove himself in battle?"

"Ella Ayers." He snorted. "She pays him no mind, even when he follows her around like a lonely pup. She has a rich lover and will not trade his wealth for Reeve."

"Do you know who her lover is?"

"No, I don't know his name. I have seen him around the theater. A tall, red-haired man with freckles all over his face. A very large nose and a pointed chin. He is not very old, but must be wealthy because he wears some heavy gold rings. I suspect she may be his first actress."

Heavy footfalls came from behind Neville. He recognized them, although he had seldom heard them on the boards of a stage because Morton preferred to remain behind the curtain. Turning, he saw the old man wore an expression as bleak as Birdwell's. Morton, looking much the worse for his time with a bottle, was holding a wooden box which he thrust into Neville's hands. It contained knives like the one that had been used on stage and the ones used to murder the two women.

"Look 'ere," the old man ordered. "There be four knives missin' from the props room."

"Are you certain?" asked Birdwell, slowly standing.

Morton gave him a withering scowl. "I know wot's in m'room. Ye should know wot's in yers." Reaching under his shirt, he pulled out another identical knife. "I found this one in yer dressing room."

"Impossible!" cried the actor. "I never handle props. I leave that to others."

Neville had to own that was true. Birdwell considered himself too grand to be bothered with such details. When he extended a hand, Morton placed the dagger on it. Neville whistled when he saw light glisten off the sharpened edge of the blade.

"It 'as been whetted," Morton said, then winced as he touched his forehead. His voice must be aching in his skull. "Could Reeve 'ave 'ad it in there for some reason?"

"Possibly. The man is obsessed with learning to use all sorts of weapons." With a tight laugh, Birdwell sneered, "He views himself as the savior for England in the battle against Napoleon, even though he has probably never shot a loaded gun. He ran like a coward when we were set upon by a thief last year."

Morton nodded. "I remember that. He took a lot of jestin' after that."

"Did Ella Ayers join in with the teasing?" Neville asked.

"I don't recall."

When Neville looked at him, Birdwell shrugged. "I did not involve myself in the pranks."

"Pranks?"

Morton sighed as he sat on the bench and gently kneaded his forehead. "The usual. People poppin' out from behind scenery to scare 'im. Anythin' to make 'im wish 'e'd stood 'is ground."

"So he looked like a coward in front of his beloved?"

"She paid 'im no mind either 'fore or after."

"Did he start talking about entering military service at around that time?" Neville asked.

Birdwell shrugged. "Mayhap. I do not honestly recall. Reeve prattles all the time about things that do not matter."

To you, Neville added silently before saying aloud, "You should ask him why he brought the knife into your dressing room." He handed the box back to Morton, who dropped the knife into it. "However, that is not what concerns me the most."

"What does?" asked Birdwell.

"That there is still one other knife missing from the box. One was in Birdwell's dressing room. One is unaccounted for. It suggests the murderer has at least one more victim in mind."

"Who?"

"A question we need an answer to before he strikes again."

Chapter Fourteen

As she sat in her front parlor and listened to the rain strike the windows, Priscilla thought that she had never seen anyone more uncomfortable in her life. Lord Witherspoon wore the expression of a man about to find himself climbing the steps to the gallows. Knowing she should put him at ease, for that was a hostess's duty, she found it difficult to concentrate on her task. She wanted to be with Neville while he went to the Prince of Wales Theater to ask more questions.

It was just as well she had not gone, because no sooner had Neville taken his leave than Daphne rushed to her with the note she had received. A note from the marquess, Priscilla quickly noted. Daphne gave it to her, explaining that it must have been misdelivered because it was really meant to be read first by Priscilla. It was a short note saying that Lord Witherspoon was planning to give her a look-in shortly.

Wondering when her daughter and Lord Witherspoon had concocted this call as an excuse to see each other, she knew it was too late to send back a reply that she would not be at home during the afternoon. They may have considered such a call an inspired idea at the time, but she suspected both had changed their minds when the conversation dragged to a halt more than once.

"Stonehall-on-Sea is very lovely," Daphne said, breaking the silence. "Have you traveled near the southern coast?"

Lord Witherspoon gave her a grateful smile. He was dressed in prime twig with a fawn-colored coat and a chocolate-colored waistcoat. A signet ring glittered as brightly as the shine on his shoes.

"I have traveled there on occasion," the marquess said, relief in his voice. "I enjoy the fresh air and the lovely vistas."

"I do believe Stonehall-on-Sea is the prettiest village between Rye and Brighton. Don't you think so, Mama?"

Hearing the pleading in her daughter's voice, Priscilla forced her thoughts back to their words. She owed Lord Witherspoon the duty of conversing with him rather than wishing she was listening to whatever sort of questioning Neville was employing at the theater.

"I agree," she said with the best smile

she could manage. "However, I must say as well that I am prejudiced on this matter."

"The green in Stonehall-on-Sea is a triangle," Daphne hurried to add, as if afraid silence would grow smothering in the parlor again.

"Very peculiar," the marquess said.

"Unique is what I prefer." Daphne held out a plate of cakes. "Do you want another, my lord?"

"No, thank you, Miss Flanders." Even though every motion was reluctant and every word suggested he wished he did not need to speak it, he came to his feet. "I have enjoyed your hospitality, Lady Priscilla, but I have finished my tea and several cakes. I do not want to overstay my welcome."

Daphne flashed her a frantic look.

Priscilla pretended not to see it as she stood and held out her hand. "It is very kind of you to call to make sure we are fine in the wake of the recent disturbing events."

He bowed over her hand. "I considered it my duty, my lady. A very pleasant duty." His neck stiffened as he seemed to be fighting to keep from looking at Daphne. "Good afternoon, my lady, Miss Flanders."

As he walked out, Daphne jumped up. A single glance from Priscilla was enough to curb her daughter's enthusiasm, which could lead her to a faux pas. Slowly Daphne walked to the door to the hallway, but went no farther. She was silent until the sound of the street door closing came up the stairs.

Daphne flounced back to the closest chair and sat on it without the grace she had exhibited during the marquess's call. A frown ruined her visage.

Putting the teacups and the plates back on the tray, Priscilla said, "You did well for Lord Witherspoon's first call on this family."

"Well?" She jumped to her feet. "It was a disaster."

"I think you are overreacting. Such calls are never easy, and you must accustom yourself to the fact that being given a look-in by someone you barely know is difficult."

"Mama, if you do not approve of him, you need only say so."

"What gave you the idea I did not approve of the marquess?" She faced her daughter, who was scowling more fiercely at her. "I have not spent enough time in Lord Witherspoon's company to form an

296

opinion one way or the other."

Daphne threw herself down upon the settee. "But, Mama, you said scarcely a score of words to him. He is going to believe you regret being at home for him."

Priscilla knelt beside her daughter. Putting her fingers over Daphne's on the arm of the chair, she said, "If you wish, I shall invite Lord Witherspoon to join us one evening for dinner. Neville speaks well of him."

"And Uncle Neville is not easy to please."

"Most especially where this family is concerned, for he wants to make sure nothing horrible happens to us."

Daphne's smile returned. "Do you think we could offer the invitation to Lord Witherspoon during a ride in Hyde Park? The marquess mentioned several times while we were dancing that he and his friends enjoy riding on sunny afternoons."

"The next nice day, we shall go to the Park. Even if we do not see Lord Witherspoon, it will be good for you to see how the *ton* spends its afternoons. If we do encounter him and he accepts my invitation, I will endeavor to apologize for my wandering thoughts during his call."

Daphne patted Priscilla's hand. "I know

you are distressed with what has happened at the Prince of Wales Theater."

"You are an insightful young woman. I will be glad when Neville returns."

"He knows the Prince of Wales Theater well."

"So does the murderer, I would venture." Daphne's voice dropped to a whisper. "*On dits* suggests it is someone who works in the theater."

"That is likely, but you must take care not always to heed what *on dits* reveals. *On dits* often proves to be less than reliable."

From the doorway, Aunt Cordelia, dressed in a lacy dark blue gown, said, "You should heed your mother on this, Daphne."

"Aunt Cordelia!" Priscilla could not hide her astonishment.

Her aunt came forward to give her a hug and kiss on the cheek. Priscilla returned both. Although Neville asked so often how Priscilla could have affection for her cantankerous aunt, there was no way to explain. Priscilla suspected it was because both she and Aunt Cordelia saw much of the same in each other and ignored the differences.

"We were unsure if you would be calling this afternoon," Priscilla continued.

"I said I was, didn't I?"

Accepting the dressing-down as her due, Priscilla gave her aunt another hug before walking with her to where Daphne was coming to her feet. Daphne greeted her aunt while Priscilla rang for a fresh pot of tea. By the time she sat facing her aunt and her daughter on the settee, Aunt Cordelia was offering Daphne commiseration.

"You should be pleased, Daphne," her aunt was saying, "that Lord Witherspoon took time to give you and your mother a call."

"Why is everyone telling me how I should feel? Why will no one listen to how I do feel?" She sighed and stirred more sugar into her tea. She put down the cup when she realized her great-aunt had not been served any yet. "Forgive me. That was my frustration speaking."

"I know." She patted Daphne's hand. "You have just embarked on your first Season. Allow events to unfold as they should."

Priscilla smiled. "The very same advice I recall you giving me, Aunt Cordelia."

"I trust Daphne will follow it more closely than you did, Priscilla, with your precipitous betrothal to a parson."

Before Priscilla could answer, Daphne cried, "Deuce take it!"

"Daphne, you need to watch your language," Priscilla said quietly.

"I have heard Aunt Cordelia utter far worse."

Priscilla waited for her aunt's explosion, but Aunt Cordelia said in a surprisingly even tone, "But I am not a young miss in need of Society's approval. Dear child, it distresses me to see you in a flutter."

"Then stop deriding my mother. Aunt Cordelia, you have married three times. Certainly you know as well as anyone that the heart listens to no sense other than its own." Flinging out her hand toward her mother, Daphne continued, "Mama and Papa were the happiest married couple I have ever seen. Yes, they had their differences, because neither of them ever held back their strong opinions. But they loved each other, and they would not have been happy without each other." Tears filled her eyes. "You know that is true, Aunt Cordelia. Even if you doubted it before — and I have no idea how you could — you must have seen it after Papa died. Mama was strong for us, but when she thought we were not aware, she gave in to her grief at the idea of a life without Papa."

Priscilla took her daughter's hand. "I thought I was keeping my sorrow from you. I did not want you to have a heavier burden."

"What did Papa say so often? A burden shared is a burden halved?"

"That is true."

Daphne looked back at her great-aunt, who was regarding her with both amazement and vexation. "Aunt Cordelia, I love you, and Mama loves you. I know you love us, but sometimes how you speak and act makes me question that. Mama was happy for you when you last married. I remember that. Why can't you be happy for her that she found love with Papa and now with Uncle Neville?"

In lieu of an answer and admission that Daphne was correct, Aunt Cordelia changed the subject to the arrangements for seating in the pews during the upcoming wedding.

Daphne squeezed her mother's hand before taking the fresh teapot from a maid. The squeeze told Priscilla that Daphne was over her rare passion and all was forgiven. It was the comfort she needed amidst the chaos caused by a killer who had left too few clues in his wake.

"Oh, Priscilla," her aunt moaned, breaking the spell spun by Daphne's solace, "I had so hoped you would come to your senses before the plans got to this point. You have let *that man* beguile you."

"That is true." She smiled. "However, there is talk that *you* are the one who has most recently been tripped the double by romance, Aunt Cordelia."

"Me?"

"You and Duncan have been much in each other's company since his arrival in Town."

"I never imagined one of *his* friends would be so charming and genteel."

"*His* name is Neville, Aunt Cordelia. I had thought you agreed to address him by it."

"I have, but I prefer not to drop names into conversation over and over."

Daphne began to giggle, for Aunt Cordelia liked to mention often the names of her well-placed friends in the Polite World. Daphne doused the sound with a quick sip of tea. Even so, her great-aunt gave her a glower cold enough to freeze a pond.

"Would you like a frosted cake?" Priscilla asked as she held out the plate to her aunt as a peace offering.

"What I would like is for you to close this house and take the children and return posthaste to Stonehall-on-Sea."

She tried to swallow her vexation at the resumption of a brangle they had had too often. "Aunt Cordelia, I have told you more than once that I intend to marry Neville at St. Julian's Church."

"You could marry him at St. Elizabeth's in Stonehall-on-Sea. The banns have been read there as well."

"You want me to marry Neville in Stonehall-on-Sea? Why?" She frowned as she set her cup back on the tray. "If you think I should leave Town because I am ashamed of my betrothed, then you are wrong."

"No, *you* are wrong." Holding up her hand to halt Priscilla's reply, Aunt Cordelia said, "This has nothing to do with Neville. It has to do with keeping you safe."

"Me?"

"Two women have been murdered."

"Aunt Cordelia, why do you think that *I* would be a target for this murderer?"

"Both the women were married to wealthy men and had a title. Your father did not leave you destitute, and you have a title."

"I could say the same of you."

Her aunt shuddered, and Priscilla regretted her words. Upsetting Aunt Cordelia further had not been her intention. Before she could apologize, her aunt said, "That is true, and I will be glad to return with you to Mermaid Cottage. This time of year is lovely by the sea."

"We have had this argument many times in the past, Aunt Cordelia, and every time you become perturbed when I say I will not leave when Neville insists on remaining here. I will not leave him in danger."

"I understand your concern on his behalf, even though I believe it to be misplaced. *He* has shown over and over that he has learned how to protect himself from his onetime cronies."

"What he has learned will safeguard us as well." She forced a smile. "I appreciate your kindness in worrying about us, Aunt Cordelia."

"But you will not change your mind?"

"No."

"Even though you may be a target for this bedlamite?"

"I do not believe the murderer is mad. His targets have been quite carefully chosen."

Her aunt folded her arms in front of her, and Priscilla knew she had pushed Aunt Cordelia too far. Whenever her aunt took that pose, it warned that she would not listen any longer, for her mind was completely and irrevocably made up.

"One fact you ladies may not have," Neville said as he entered the room, swinging off his rain-splattered cloak, "is that both slain women were having affairs with Reginald Birdwell." Dropping his cloak on another chair, he lifted Priscilla's hand and kissed it. "I trust you are not also, sweetheart."

"On that you can rest very assured," she replied, holding back the questions she wanted to ask him. As she smiled up into his dark eyes, she heard her aunt's grumble at his suggestion Priscilla would be interested in the actor.

"I am happy to hear that, Pris." He bowed his head toward her aunt. "How pleasant of you to call this afternoon, Aunt Cordelia."

"You need not sound as if you are already the master of this house." Aunt Cordelia set herself on her feet, scowling at how he had addressed her.

Priscilla looked hastily at the teapot. She did not want to see her aunt regarding her with disapproval or to behold the amusement in Neville's eyes at her aunt's irritation.

"Mr. McAndrews is calling later this

afternoon," her aunt continued, "so I must ask you to excuse me. It is clear that anything I say will be disregarded."

Rising, Priscilla took her aunt's hands. "You know that is not true. I listen to everything you say to me."

"Then choose to do exactly the opposite."

"I am sorry if it appears that way to you. I truly thought you would understand why I cannot leave London now." She hesitated, then knew she must say the words clamoring against her lips. "After all, when last you saw Duncan McAndrews, you were determined to see him healthy before you returned home. You did not leave him. Would you ask me to be less loyal with Neville?"

Aunt Cordelia said nothing, but paused to stroke Priscilla's hair before she left.

"Uncle Neville, you need to keep a closer eye on Mama," Daphne said with a grin.

"To protect her from that virago?"

"Neville!" chided Priscilla.

Daphne chuckled. "No, she can handle Aunt Cordelia, but she did have a very handsome gentleman giving her a look-in this afternoon."

"Is that so?" He turned to Priscilla and grinned.

"That does not look like a jealous face," Priscilla said.

"Why should it be when your caller is more interested in another lovely lady in this house than in you? Or so I would guess from what Gilbert happened to mention when he opened the door for me." He looked back at Daphne. "I hear your name has been on Witherspoon's lips quite often of late. He fancies himself quite your protector after making certain you were returned home safely from Ward's *conversazione*."

When her daughter's color rose, staining her cheeks pink with pleasure, Priscilla said, "Daphne, see that these dishes are returned to the kitchen. Neville, if you will come with me."

"Anywhere . . ." he drawled, but his easy grin faded as soon as she closed the door on her book-room at the rear of the house. He leaned back against her desk that was set near the overflowing bookcases. "Thank you for understanding I wanted to speak with you alone."

"What did you discover at the theater?"

She listened as he told of speaking with both Reeve and Mr. Birdwell. When he listed the many women the actor had seduced, she shook her head in amazement.

307

"But no further clues to the murderer?" she asked.

"Save for the missing knife — which, quite honestly, could be missing for any of a score of reasons — there was nothing I noticed."

"You do not believe the knife just happens to have been lost, do you?"

"No. Morton is too compulsive to let a knife vanish without his taking notice of its disappearance. The box being upset and the knives scattered might have been the killer's attempt to allay suspicion in our minds."

"Not in *yours*. I think you were born conjecturing others have ulterior motives."

"Much like you, Pris, as I have learned through recent events." He pushed away from the desk and put his hands on her shoulders. "Pris, Thurmond would like you to come to Bow Street."

"Me? Why?"

"He wants you to explain to his superiors what you know about Harmony Lummis. Lord Lummis refuses to come back to Town while in mourning."

She sighed. "A reasonable response when he lost his wife in such tragic circumstances."

"He lost her long before she was killed."

Priscilla had no answer to that, so she remained silent as she sent for her cape and a straw bonnet that would not be ruined by the rain. She told Gilbert only that she was uncertain when she would return and to have Mrs. Moore serve the children's supper on time. If he was curious where she and Neville were bound when the rain was swirled about by the wind, she saw no sign of it.

Neville hurried to his carriage and handed her in. Priscilla brushed rain from her cloak as he jumped in beside her, closing the door. The carriage lurched into motion.

The interior was brightened by intermittent flashes of light from the street lamps. Not all had been lit at this early hour, but some had in order to guide drivers through the storm.

When Neville's arm curved around her shoulders, she smiled up at him. "Does Thurmond really need help with his superiors?"

"Yes."

"But he could have come to the house."

"Your house is busy. Your aunt and your children seem to want your attention far too often for a man who needs some of your time just for himself." He feigned a frown. "And now you have that young pup calling, too."

She searched his face, seeing the grim determination in his eyes. "What took place at the theater that has unsettled you?"

"Couldn't you believe *you* are what unsettles me?"

"When I do, you wear a very different expression." She ran her fingertip along his lowered brow. "Now you look like a man who has lost his way in a wood with a highwayman close by."

"The murderer has to be connected with the theater. He knows his way about it too facilely to be an outsider. As well, anyone not belonging to the theater would gain everyone's interest. If you recall, when we went to see Morton, every eye was focused on us."

"On you. They were hoping you would announce the theater was reopening."

He nodded. "True, but, under customary circumstances, they would have waited to hear from Robertson. The theater manager brings such tidings."

"Where has Robertson been during this?"

"In his office." A suggestion of a smile tipped his lips. "When he is not drinking to escape the horror, he is preparing all the books for when I assume ownership of the theater, or so I have been told. I have not checked, because I want to avoid having him thrust those books at me and insist I take on the duties of the owner."

"That leaves Birdwell, Reeve, Miss Ayers —"

"And the rest of the employees at the theater. We need to speak with someone who can help us gain some insight on this."

"Who? Mr. Thurmond's superior?"

"Not likely, from what Thurmond says. He is hoping not to be pulled off the investigation again and given other work to do."

"Then who should we seek out to help us see what we obviously cannot see?"

"That is the crux of the matter, isn't it, Pris?"

"Then what can we do?"

"Pris, you always ask the most enticing questions." He framed her face in his hands and tilted her mouth beneath his. The remembered fascination of his lips faded before the thrill coursing through her as he gently — thoroughly — kissed her. As his hands slipped down her back to draw her to him, her fingers curved along his nape to comb through the coarse silk of his hair.

The furtive touch sparked alive embers deep within her. She clung to him, every brush of his body urging her closer. Her hands stroked him in rhythm with the leap of the fires blazing within her. Finding his ear so close to her lips, she laved it with the tip of her tongue. When she felt his breath catch against her, she smiled. The pulse of his breath, rapid and warm, matched the tempo of her heartbeat.

When he recaptured her lips, he eagerly wooed them to soften beneath his gentle assault. His tongue delved within her mouth, stroking hers. Overmastered by the longing consuming her, she pressed to him. A gasp of unrestrainable delight burst from her when his mouth seared that flame along her neck.

Drawing his mouth to hers, for she ached for his lips on hers, she heard his muted chuckle. She opened her dazed eyes to see his smile.

Before she could speak, he whispered, "You are dazzling in my arms."

"Don't speak," she answered as quietly. Each word fought its way through her breathlessness. Teasing the dark hair along his forehead, she whispered, "Actually, you talk too much, Neville Hathaway."

"When I am teasing you?"

She shook her head as her fingertip traced the uncompromising lines of his face. "All the time!"

"Then I shall say nothing more."

"Good."

"You shall miss my teasing."

"I doubt that."

"I —"

She pressed her mouth to his. In the moment before her eyes closed, a spark of longing in his eyes urged her to melt against him. One thing he had *not* said. Each time he went to the theater, seeking answers, he might be taunting the murderer, risking his own life if the investigation closed in too tightly and the killer struck out with that missing knife in an effort to escape detection. As he held her and kissed her with such passion, she did not want to imagine ever again losing a man she loved.

Chapter Fifteen

Priscilla had no interest in a ride in Hyde Park, even though the day was sunny and warm. Greeting acquaintances and listening to gossip and speculation had no appeal for her. However, she had promised Daphne they would visit the Park on the first pleasant day, and she did not want to break that promise.

She hoped Thurmond's superiors were as unwilling to turn their backs on a pledge they had made. The interview with them had been brief, and they had seemed disinterested in the few facts she had to share. Even Neville's reassurance that she should not judge by the Runners' outward reaction failed to ease her disquiet.

When she stepped out of the house, two horses waited next to Neville's phaeton. One was a tall bay, and the other a gray horse with a black mane. Neville held the reins of both. He was dressed in jaunty riding clothes, his dark coat over his buck-skin breeches looking dull next to his hair, which glistened blue-black in the sunlight. He held his tall, black hat under one arm.

Priscilla lifted the long hem of her green wool riding habit as she walked toward him. The length, which would be perfect when she was riding, made walking difficult.

"Horses *and* a phaeton?" she asked.

He brushed her cheek with a kiss that was appropriate for standing in the open square. "I thought they would allow us the excuse to give Daphne and her admirer a chance for some conversation that would be overheard only by a footman." He gestured toward the phaeton. "Stuttman has driven the phaeton for me before."

"That is a good idea."

"Especially because it will allow us some time for private conversation, too." He took her hand and bent over it. Tipping her hand palm up, he pressed his lips to it. The heat from his mouth surged through her thin leather gloves.

"You are aiming to ruin my reputation," she whispered.

"Then I shall have to do the honorable thing and marry you, Pris." A slow smile spread from his lips to his eyes to light them with the expression that seemed to soften her bones into a sweet, perfumed pool.

Daphne rushed up to them, twirling about so Neville could admire her ivory gown with the matching parasol. She twittered like a songbird, rejoicing in the return of the sun after several rainy days. Giggling over some jest Neville must have made, Daphne let him hand her into the phaeton.

Priscilla watched as her daughter kissed Neville on the cheek. Two years ago when Lazarus died, she could not have guessed either she or her children would be so happy again. Neville had brought joy back into their lives. Since then, it had been threatened time and again by their disbelief that friendship could evolve into love. Finally owning the truth to themselves and each other when they could no longer deny it, they reveled in what they had found.

Juster stepped forward. "May I help you, my lady?"

Startled out of her contemplation, Priscilla nodded. "Thank you, Juster." She let the footman assist her into the saddle on the gray horse.

"Too slow, I see," Neville said, coming back to stand beside the horse.

"My lord?" asked the footman, puzzled.

"Not you." He clapped Juster on the shoulder. "I speak rather of my being too slow helping Miss Flanders so that I did not return in time to throw Lady Priscilla into the saddle."

"I am —"

Neville laughed. "Do not apologize, Juster. I suspect I shall have a time or two to help Lady Priscilla before she is too old to ride." He swung up onto the bay. "What do you say, Priscilla?"

"I say you should recall that you are older than I."

"Ouch!" He put his hand over his chest. "That one pierced me right to where I am young at heart."

Priscilla rolled her eyes before guiding her horse to match the pace of the carriage slowly driving toward Tottenham Court Road. By the time she reached the corner of the square, Neville had caught up with them.

As they rode toward Oxford Street and Hyde Park, she forced her dreary spirits aside. It was a lovely day, and she wanted to enjoy the chance to be out of the house and away from the wedding arrangements, which had taken on a frantic pace now that the final reading of the banns and the ceremony were only days away.

The busy streets gave way to the serenity of the Park. The open expanse leading down to the Serpentine was filled with people enjoying the day. A few had placed blankets on the grass and were enjoying an alfresco meal, but most were wandering about and talking with friends.

Priscilla made an effort to keep a smile on her face as she greeted people she knew. More than once, she considered asking Neville to slow the pace, but refrained. Her low mood seemed to wash up over her again and again like the tiny waves slapping the shores of the Serpentine when a boat was pushed out onto the water.

When the carriage abruptly turned to the left and the trees along Park Lane, she heard Neville laugh.

"What is funny?" she asked, urging her horse to keep up with the phaeton.

"Your daughter needs to learn to hide her thoughts." He pointed ahead of them to where a man was standing in the shade beside his horse. "Otherwise, she is going to ride Witherspoon down."

The man stepped out into the sunshine, and Priscilla saw Neville was correct. The marquess was dressed, as always, in prime twig, with his navy blue coat open to reveal his waistcoat and with black breeches tucked into well-polished boots. Beneath a tall hat, his face was brighter than the reflection of the sun off his gold buttons as he watched the carriage approach.

"I would suggest the same lessons for Witherspoon," Neville said dryly. "I think Daphne's calf-love is reciprocated."

"Don't let her hear you describe it that way," she murmured as they drew even with where the carriage had stopped and Lord Witherspoon had come to stand on the side where Daphne sat.

"Good afternoon, Witherspoon," Neville called.

The young marquess tore his gaze from Daphne. "Good afternoon, Hathaway." He tipped his hat toward Priscilla. "And to you, my lady. I am pleased you decided to ride today. Ah, Sitwell."

Priscilla smiled as another horse stopped on the far side of the carriage not far from the marquess. The red-haired man, swinging down off his mount, was introduced to her as Lord Sitwell, the younger son of a duke. He had many freckles scattered across his long nose, which seemed to be trying to reach his chin.

When Neville drew in a sharp breath, she turned to him and asked, "What is it?"

"Sitwell," he murmured. "He matches the description Birdwell gave me of Ella Ayers's lover."

"His red hair could have been what caught my eye."

He nodded. "That is not a subject we can discuss now."

She looked at her daughter. Neville was right, for she could not speak of Lord Sitwell's paramour in her daughter's hearing. "I trust you will call on him later."

"Most definitely."

"You are a dashed fool," Lord Witherspoon said when Priscilla turned her attention back to the conversation by the carriage.

"Me?" asked the redhead.

"Look at you. All that glitter is dangerous now."

Lord Sitwell held up his hand where two rings, one topped with a red stone, shone. "I will not be frightened by some coward into putting aside my finery. I have been wearing these rings since I left school, and I do not intend to hide them away in some musty box."

"Then you are a fool." The marquess looked back at Daphne. "I am pleased to see you are much wiser, Miss Flanders. Anyone wearing jewelry now marks themselves as a possible victim for that murdering thief."

Neville leaned forward. "Isn't that a bit of an overreaction?"

"Ride around the Park," Lord Witherspoon said, "and you will see I am not the only one who shares that concern. Even the matrons who usually bedeck themselves in their family's heirloom jewelry are as plain as monks. Nobody wishes to be a target."

"The two women were killed at the theater, not on an outing."

"No one wishes to take chances, save for Sitwell."

Priscilla listened as the two young men argued, then moved her horse a few steps away. She could chaperon her daughter from this distance, although she suspected Neville's orders to his footman about acting as a watch-dog had been very precise.

As soon as Neville moved his horse closer, she said, "A quick ride about the Park should tell us if Lord Witherspoon is correct or panicking."

"He does not have a reputation for panic, Pris." His face was shuttered again, and she knew he was trying to make these comments fit in with what else they knew about the murders.

"Will you ride about and confirm his opinion?"

He nodded. "I shall be back quickly. Stay close to the carriage."

"You sound as if you expect the murderer to jump out from behind a tree and stab me."

"I will not make any assumptions at this point, Pris."

Priscilla turned her horse toward the carriage and was glad to discover Lord Witherspoon and his friend had changed the subject. They both were focused on Daphne, which her daughter was clearly relishing. Her smile seemed almost as broad as the Serpentine. Even when Priscilla was welcomed into the conversation, Daphne continued to glow with excitement. Neither man acted as if they had noticed Neville's departure. Even if they had, such comings and goings were commonplace in the Park, where conversations shifted as people met up with other friends.

Again, as when she had been hosting Lord Witherspoon in her front parlor, Priscilla's attention drifted. She could not keep from wondering what Neville might discover and was eager for him to return and share that information with her. Mayhap the very clue they needed was here in the Park.

★ ★ ★

"Ride a bit longer with me, Pris," Neville said when they paused in front of her house on Bedford Square.

"Aunt Cordelia expects me to call on her to go over a few final details for the wedding breakfast." She smiled as her daughter waved before going into the house.

"I would rather speak of what I have seen without other ears overhearing."

"All right." She set her horse to a walk to match his horse's pace. "Is Lord Witherspoon right? Are people eschewing their jewelry because they are afraid they will be the next victim?"

Neville nodded, even as he scanned the closest houses. He lowered his voice. "Pris, people are terrified. They had persuaded themselves that Harmony Lummis's death was the result of a lover's quarrel or a jealous husband. That theory was credible when Lummis left town and did not return."

"He went to bury his wife."

"I know that, and so do you." He sighed. "So does the *ton*, but they overlooked the facts in exchange for resuming their festivities. That fiddling while Rome burned came to an abrupt end with Lady

Dentford's murder. Now they are scared."

"Panicked?"

"Close." He raised his voice slightly as two carriages came into the square from opposite directions. "If the murderer is not halted and hanged soon, I suspect some of the *ton* will make good their threats to leave London now. Once a few leave, the migration back to daisyville will become a race to escape the killer. Some have already given him mythical abilities to sneak in and out of the theater unseen. I need to speak with Sitwell and find out if he saw anything at the theater during his trysts with Ella Ayers."

"Do you think he will own to anything?"

"Most men are not reluctant to share information about time spent with their convenients."

She did not have a chance to reply. An explosion resonated through the square. Something whizzed past her ear like a swarm of maddened bees. Stone flew as the house in front of her was struck.

Neville jumped from his horse and grabbed her by the waist. They tumbled to the walkway. He pulled her into the garden in the center of the square and behind a bush. He pressed her to the ground as another ball was fired at them. She heard someone shriek. Was it her? And the rattle of a carriage being driven away at a high speed. Another scream. Savage curses.

The last came from just above her. She tried to get up, then winced as her elbow ached. Tears sprang into her eyes as she whispered, "Neville, let me up."

He mumbled something, then moved so she could sit. She heard someone calling for the watch. Doors slammed all around the square. When he tipped her face toward him, she wondered if her face was as colorless as his.

He ran his hands along her as he asked, "Are you all right, Pris?"

"For someone who has just been shot at, yes." She looked in the direction the carriage had vanished. "Did you see who shot at us?"

"A blond man."

"Birdwell?" she choked.

"He is not the only light-haired man in London. Did *you* see anything to identify him further?"

Even if she had noticed anything about the carriage and the man driving it, Priscilla had no chance to tell Neville anything. They were smothered by a frightened crowd pressing closer to discover if they were still alive. All the people were discussing the shooting, although she wondered, hearing their comments, if any of them had seen the same thing.

Daphne rushed up to them with Gilbert and Mrs. Moore on her heels. "Mama!" she cried. "Mama! Uncle Neville! Are you hurt?"

Neville came to his feet and held out his hand to Priscilla. She reached for it, then saw her right glove was torn and her palm scraped. She took his hand with her left and came slowly to her feet.

Blood was running down his face. She pulled out a handkerchief and gave it to him. Nodding his thanks, he pressed the linen to his raw cheek. He must have scraped it on the walkway. It could have been much worse. When he put his arm around her shoulders, she rested her head on him, glad for his strength.

"We are fine," Neville assured Daphne and everyone else. "Has someone sent for the authorities?"

A dozen answers came back.

Neville said beneath the cacophony, "Gilbert, if someone has not alerted Bow Street, send word to Thurmond right away."

"Yes, sir." The butler remained as calm as always, although the tic by his right eye was twitching faster than she had ever seen.

Mrs. Moore cleared a path through the crowd. She sent some boys to bring the horses to the stables in the mews behind the house. Leading Priscilla, Neville, and Daphne into the house, she offered to bring something strong upstairs to the back parlor.

"Just tea for me," Priscilla murmured.

"Just tea," Neville seconded before adding, "and brandy."

The housekeeper smiled, then hurried toward the stairs to the kitchen.

"Mama, if you want to leave London, I will understand. You do not need to stay in Town because of me." Daphne blinked back tears. "As much as I have waited for the opportunity to be part of the Polite World, I would trade every minute of it to make sure you are safe."

"Lord Witherspoon wants you to leave London, doesn't he?" Priscilla asked with a smile.

"Yes, but, Mama, it is more than that. I could not bear to think I put you in danger because I wished to spend time with Burke."

Priscilla arched an eyebrow at her daughter's easy use of the marquess's name. Either Daphne did not notice, or she was so immersed in despondency that she could not muster a reaction.

"I am in no more danger than anyone else in the *ton*," she said.

"But the murderer clearly knows you and Uncle Neville are asking questions."

"Yes." She reached for the banister, wishing her head did not ache so much.

"Do you need help getting upstairs, Mama?" Daphne asked, flitting about nervously.

"I should be fine —" She yelped as Neville put his arm under her knees and lifted her up against his chest. "Neville, don't be silly. You are bumped up as much as I am."

"Pris, for once do not argue when I am doing something for your own good."

"For once." She leaned her head against his shoulder and closed her eyes while he carried her up the stairs.

The all-too-brief respite came to a halt when they reached the top. Leah and Isaac were waiting. They began asking questions, each louder than the previous one.

"Daphne, explain to your brother and sister," Neville said.

"But I don't know what happened," she replied, her eyes wide.

"Neither do we." He carried Priscilla into the back parlor and closed the door.

As he placed her on the settee, she said, "Neville, the children are frightened on our behalf. You cannot close them out."

"You need to rest."

"I shall not be allowed to rest while they talk right outside the door."

Neville did not want to agree, but he knew Priscilla was right. Going to the door, he opened it and went out. He closed it behind him as he gave each child an intense look. Both Isaac and Leah grew silent while Daphne sighed with relief.

"Your mother is fine, save for a few bruises and scratches," he said. "Those, I regret to say, were most likely caused by my haste to get her to safety. What she needs now is quiet. However, she wants to see you and soothe your fears herself. If you promise to be quiet and gentle, you may go in."

"I will be quiet!" shouted Isaac, waving his hand. He deflated when Neville gave him another stern glance. In a whisper, he repeated, "I will be quiet."

"I will, too." Leah grasped Neville's hand.

He winced and realized he must have scraped it, too, but he did not release her fingers. Opening the door, he ushered the children in. Isaac and Leah ran to their mother.

Daphne looked at him. "Uncle Neville, how are you?"

"Playing your mother's knight in shining armor can be hazardous at times." He patted her cheek. "Go to your mother. She wants to see you, too."

Neville watched as Priscilla allayed her children's qualms about her safety. She spoke quietly, and after several minutes had passed, their voices grew calm. When Leah placed her head on her mother's lap, he recalled how cozy a perch that had been for his own. He would have liked to usurp Leah's place, but that would have to wait.

Slipping out of the room, he closed the door quietly behind him. He smiled at one of the maids who was coming up the stairs with a tea tray. He took the bottle of brandy and motioned for her to go into the back parlor.

He did not follow. Before he faced Priscilla again, he had to get his emotions under control. She was far more serene — or *appeared* more serene — than he. Now that she had calmed the children, he could not allow his fury at whoever fired the gun to upset them again.

Opening the bottle of brandy, he tipped it back. The maid coming out of the back parlor stared at him in astonishment, but rushed away when he scowled at her.

He walked to the front of the house where he could see the garden in the square's heart. His phaeton remained in front of the house, but someone had taken the horses away from the crowd that was only now dispersing.

So many people. Yet, not a one seemed sure of what he or she had seen and heard.

He swore under his breath, then a bit louder. Priscilla could have been killed because he had let his pride blind him. He had been so assured that he could keep her and her family safe from this murderer.

He had been wrong.

The shooting must serve as an admonition to him. He needed to find this killer soon, and, until that killer was found, he could not relent in guarding Priscilla and the children. The murderer may have been trying to frighten them, rather than kill them. If so, the ploy had succeeded. If the murderer had hoped to curtail their investigation, he had failed utterly. The killer had made the chase personal now, and Neville intended to make him rue hurting Priscilla.

Turning on his heel, he strode toward the back parlor. He took another drink from the bottle as he reached to open the door.

The door opened below, and he heard Thurmond's voice. Leaning over the railing, he waved to the Bow Street Runner to come up the stairs. He started for the front parlor, then turned to go into Priscilla's book-room. It was far more private. He hoped Thurmond would have some insight into this incident. If the Runner did not, they were still at the mercy of a madman who had decided it was their time to die.

Chapter Sixteen

"But you are not seating the guests in proper precedence." Aunt Cordelia tossed aside the list Priscilla had made up with Mrs. Moore's help. "You cannot expect a countess to sit with a baron's wife."

"If you will recall, Aunt Cordelia, the countess and the baroness are sisters." Playing with the pearl necklace she wore to complement her ivory morning dress, Priscilla tried to ignore her aching head. She had not thought the attack yesterday would leave her with a head that still throbbed. Or mayhap it was no more than she was growing exasperated with her aunt. "They specifically asked if they might sit together. As the breakfast will be informal, we are not conforming to every canon of propriety. I would rather the guests have a pleasant time."

"But propriety —"

"I will leave propriety to you, Aunt Cordelia, if you and Duncan set a date for your own wedding."

Her aunt flushed, but her voice remained firm as she set herself on her feet. "Priscilla, I shall never understand you. Your older daughter is the talk of the *ton* with the attentions a marquess has been showing her, and your son creates curiosity wherever he goes because there is much interest in how much influence your fiancé will have on him. As for Leah . . ." She shook her head.

"I have chided Leah for sneaking out into the square in hopes of finding the balls shot at us. She will not be so unthinking again."

"She should not have been so unthinking to begin with." Aunt Cordelia sighed. "I cannot expect anything else when you have allowed *him* to run tame through your house."

"Are you speaking of Lord Witherspoon?"

"No, of your fiancé. You must have known that."

Priscilla had known that, and she regretted baiting her aunt. Coming to her feet, she said, "I am sorry, Aunt Cordelia. I am sorry, as well, that the arrangements for the wedding are not what you expected. As we will be celebrating a second marriage for me, I thought it would be better to have the wedding breakfast less formal than it will be when the girls marry."

"Marry? The girls?" Aunt Cordelia's eyes began to glitter. "Are you saying that Lord Witherspoon has offered for Daphne already? It would be a prime match. The Witherspoons' title is as ancient and revered as our family's. He would not care if Daphne's dowry is small —"

"Daphne's dowry shall be taken care of."

"You have only the little left to you by my brother and the pittance you inherited from your late husband. Isaac cannot give her any money because his inheritance is in trust for him until he reaches his majority." She tapped her chin. "I may be able to help you arrange for some funds to be transferred, and, of course, I intend to contribute to each girl's dowry."

Priscilla hugged her aunt. "Thank you, but that is not necessary."

"Nonsense! You may have this lovely home and the cottage in Stonehall-on-Sea, but you have little more money than a poor church mouse."

"Neville will see to the matter of Daphne's dowry."

"What?" Aunt Cordelia bristled like a frightened hedgehog. "Priscilla, how can you allow *him* to do such a thing?"

Sitting again, Priscilla clasped her hands

in her lap. She had anticipated a storm of protests from her aunt on this matter, but even Aunt Cordelia must be sensible.

"Aunt Cordelia," she said as evenly as she could manage, "Neville will be their stepfather. It would be expected he would provide for this family."

"But with the money from *his* family. You know where it came from." She lowered her voice, even though every servant in the house knew how Neville's ancestors had made a fortune by bamboozling excise men through the centuries. "Smuggling money, Priscilla. Do you want your daughter to go into marriage with such unclean money?"

"You are getting yourself all distressed for no reason. Lord Witherspoon has made no offer for Daphne."

"Oh." Her aunt's shoulders sagged as if she once again were taking on the weight of the whole world.

"They have known each other such a short time. Daphne has seen firsthand how foolish it is to fall in love without considering the consequences."

"She has been offered for before?"

Priscilla smiled. "No, it was another case of calf-love, which she is well over now." She would not speak of how Daphne had believed herself, in spite of his efforts to dissuade her, in love with Neville not many months ago. Aunt Cordelia would see that only as another sign of the appalling influence he had over the family.

"I am glad to hear that. She does not need her mind befuddled during her first Season. She —" Aunt Cordelia frowned. "Good *morning*. Do you often call at such an unreasonable hour?"

Priscilla was not surprised to see Neville in the doorway. His face was drawn, as it had been since they were shot at, and she realized he was wearing the clothes he had yesterday.

He ignored her aunt as he came to where Priscilla was standing and drew her to her feet and into his arms. She put her arms around him, not caring that her aunt would be scandalized by such a public display between a couple not yet married. When she felt him tremble, she drew back and looked up at his scratched face. He was not fearful. He was furious.

"Tell me," she said.

"There is little to tell. Thurmond came to my house a short time ago. He is waiting downstairs and wants me to go with him to the Prince of Wales Theater. I insisted on coming here first to tell you there has been another murder. This time, it is a man."

She heard her aunt gasp and sit heavily on a chair that creaked in protest.

"Who?" Priscilla asked.

"Lord Sitwell."

"Oh, no!" She grasped the front of Neville's coat, not trusting her abruptly weak knees. "The man we met at the Park yesterday?"

"One and the same."

"Daphne told me that he and Lord Witherspoon belong to the same club. They are not close friends, and they often disagree as they did yesterday." Her eyes widened. "They argued about wearing jewelry. Lord Sitwell said there was no danger. Now he is —"

He put his finger to her lips. "Sweetheart, take a deep breath."

She tried, but sobs rattled in her chest. "Was he robbed, too?"

"Yes."

Aunt Cordelia gasped, "This is madness. No one is safe from this killer."

"Your household is safe, Pris," he whispered against her hair. "I promise you they will stay safe."

"How? I cannot cocoon them in wool and believe they will be protected."

Leading her to the settee, he sat with

her. His arm around her shoulders was the only invitation she needed to lean her head against him. She did not care if Aunt Cordelia was watching.

"Do not let any of them go out alone," Neville said quietly. "All the people who have been killed apparently have been alone when the murderer attacked them."

"We were not alone yesterday. We were with each other."

He nodded. "I thought of that, but that assault does not match the pattern of the others."

"But he has killed a man now. That does not match the pattern of the other murderers."

"In some ways, it still does. The murder was at the theater, and the victim was a member of the Polite World. Also, he was robbed of those rings, which were family heirlooms."

"Was Lord Sitwell involved with Birdwell in some way?"

"Birdwell has shown his definite taste for women, and there is no possible way they could have been in business together. I suspect Sitwell may have done just as Witherspoon feared. He taunted the murderer into killing him for the gold he wore."

"This murderer must be stopped!" announced Aunt Cordelia in a tone that suggested nobody else had given credence to such a course of action before.

"I agree." Neville came to his feet. "Thurmond is waiting, so I cannot linger any longer. He has kept his men and anyone else in the theater from tramping through the scene of the murder, so we may be able to find some clues that were lost with the previous murders."

"An excellent idea." Priscilla stood. "Aunt Cordelia, if you will excuse us . . ."

"Pris, you should stay here," he said.

"Why? Because of the danger?" She put her hands on her waist. "You did not flinch from asking me to go with you through the bowels of London."

"You went where?" asked Aunt Cordelia.

Neville ignored the older woman, who scowled and strode out of the room, calling for her carriage to be brought.

"This has nothing to do with danger, Pris. Thurmond wants to interrogate everyone who was in the theater when the murder took place. Those working at the theater may be willing to speak to me, but they will not be so forthcoming with an outsider."

"But you are an outsider now."

"Most of them still accept me as one of them, for they believe once one is a part of the theater, one always will be. Others, like Birdwell, see me as a traitor who turned my back on them once I was given my title."

"Don't they know about your patronage of the theaters where you worked?"

"I never mentioned anything about that to you."

She curved her hand along his cheek. "There was no need to. I know you, Neville Hathaway, and I know you would never turn your back on anyone in need."

"I would not go that far."

"All right. You would never turn your back on a friend who needed something."

He held her chin between his forefinger and thumb. "And you look as if you need a kiss right now."

"A kiss could hurt you. That cheek looks painful."

"Pris, you will note that a scratched cheek does not impair me when you need a kiss."

"You are trying to change the subject and persuade me not to go to the theater with you. I will not let you go alone."

"Are you going to nag me like this when we are married?" He grinned as he put his arm around her waist. "Should I expect a curtain-lecture every night?"

She laughed. "You have made it clear that marriage will not change you, Neville. I do not intend for it to change me, either."

"Is that what you think?" He slipped his fingers through her hair as he tilted her mouth under his. "Are you telling me you will continue to need this? That you will continue to need me?"

He gave her no chance to answer as he claimed her mouth. She tasted his anxiety for her and his frustration at not being able to stop the murderer. Then, as the kiss deepened, only his longing for her remained on his lips. It was everything she wanted.

Thurmond shot furious glares at Neville as they entered the Prince of Wales Theater. Neville paid them no mind. Even though he wished Priscilla had stayed at Bedford Square, he hoped she would have some insight into the murder that the others missed. She often did.

Unlike the last time they had come here to see a corpse, the front of the theater between the staircases was full. All the people waiting for word that the theater would be reopened had been gathered by Thurmond's men with the help of the local watch.

Neville saw rage as well as fear on their faces. Morton sat on the lowest riser of the right-hand staircase and glowered. No doubt he was anxious that someone might go into his props room and disturb it again.

"This is all of them," a scraggly man said, scratching his nose. "We pulled a few of them out of a tavern where they'd 'oped to 'ide." The Charley's grin revealed most of his teeth were gone, and he leaned on a long staff. "Lucky fer us, some of the others were willin' to tell us where t'look."

"Good work," Thurmond said. "Just keep them here."

"Wotever ye say." He turned to look at the people gathered in the entry and rested his arms on the staff again.

"This way." Thurmond opened a door and motioned for them to enter.

Neville said nothing as he led Priscilla through the doorway and out onto the ground floor of the theater. It was lit with lamps from the stage. Looking up at the boxes hanging overhead like raptors waiting to swoop down on unsuspecting prey, he remained silent.

Thurmond walked to the right, where the shadows from the boxes concealed the bare floor. He paused by Lord Sitwell's body. It was lying facedown next to the bench that ran along the full length of the wall. As with the other victims, a knife was driven into him.

"This accounts for the missing knife," Neville mused. "I trust you have men watching the props room to make sure nobody runs off with another."

Walking back to the door they had entered, Thurmond shouted for one of his men to guard the props room. He came back. "A good suggestion, Hathaway. You know this theater far better than I do. What else do you suggest?"

"Nothing at the moment. Sitwell was stabbed, and the rings he wore are gone. It looks like the other murders."

"Not quite," Priscilla said, pointing to the floor. "Look at those marks."

Neville knelt and examined the black marks that stretched more deeply into the shadows. Ignoring his stomach that threatened to explode, he picked up one of Sitwell's feet. The toe of his boot was rubbed dull, although the rest shone with obvious attention.

"He was dragged here," he said. "Mayhap in hopes that the shadows would conceal him long enough for the killer to elude us again." He peeled Priscilla's fingers, which were digging into him, away from his shoulder as he stood. "Three members of the *ton* murdered and stripped of their heirloom jewelry."

"And other robberies before the murders began," she added. "Being robbed is the one thing all the crimes around this theater have had in common. Could it be the robberies that connect the murders, as well as Mr. Birdwell?"

He smiled at her. "By Jove, Pris, why didn't we think of that earlier?"

"We had no reason to think of it earlier. We considered the victims themselves because they *did* have Mr. Birdwell in common. Considering the victims is a logical way to look at the crimes."

"But we should have looked beyond the obvious," Thurmond said, amazed.

"Do you mean that *you* should have?" Neville asked.

His friend's lips twitched with a smile. "I have to own that I know better than to consider only the most obvious aspects of a crime."

"As we all should," Priscilla said.

"Yes, Pris, you are becoming all too familiar with murders."

She took his hand and squeezed it. "I do

believe you remarked once that we would never again be invited anywhere if the stigma of murder continues to stalk us."

"Then we shall have to remain at home."

A screech drowned out anything else he might have said. When a woman rushed toward them, Neville caught her to keep her from tripping over Sitwell's body.

"My beloved, my beloved," she moaned, and he knew he held Ella Ayers.

"Let me," Priscilla said.

With a grateful look, Neville nodded. He stepped back, but kept himself between the actress and Lord Sitwell.

Priscilla put her hands on either side of the woman's face. "Miss Ayers, listen to me."

"My beloved, my beloved!"

"Listen to me."

Her stern voice must have reached the frantic woman, because Miss Ayers looked at her. "Lady Priscilla! You must help me."

"I will be glad to do all I can, but you must be calm and heed what we tell you."

"Is he — ?"

"Yes, he has been killed."

Another scream threatened to burst Neville's ears. When Priscilla shook the actress gently, Miss Ayers pressed her face against Priscilla's shoulder and wept.

"It is my fault," the actress choked out.

"Why?"

"I wanted him to give me some token to show he truly loved me."

"A piece of jewelry?" asked Neville.

"Yes, but I asked for that *before* these killings began. I told him not to come back here. He was stubborn. He sent a note this morning saying he would be stopping by with a gift for me."

Neville stepped closer. "Could anyone else have seen the note?"

"Everyone could have. It was not sealed."

"Who brought it to you?"

"It was slipped beneath my door."

Neville swore vividly, and Thurmond muttered something. Every clue led nowhere.

Taking Miss Ayers to sit on the bench closer to the stage, Priscilla went back to the body. She knelt and tried to see something that would reveal the truth.

"What is this?" she asked aloud, pointing to his right hand.

Neville looked over her shoulder. A furry clump as wide as her thumb and as long as her longest finger lay on the floor between the dead man's fingers. "Hair. Blond hair. I would guess our murderer is missing what Sitwell pulled out of his head while trying to save his life."

"That is a lot of hair. If he had a full handful, he —"

"Let me through!" came a shout from the door. "By all that's blue, I say you shall let me through."

Neville was amazed to see Witherspoon come toward them with two men hanging on him, trying to stop him. He pushed forward like a bull intent on breaking through a fence. When Thurmond shouted for his men to release the marquess, he walked toward them without a backward glance.

"Lady Priscilla! Hathaway!" Witherspoon smiled. "I am very glad to see you here." He looked past them to where his friend was lying dead. "I did not want to believe the tidings when they were brought to my door."

"How did you hear?" asked Thurmond.

"Daphne," Priscilla answered before the marquess could. "She sent you word, didn't she, after getting the information from one of my staff."

He nodded. "You are very astute, my lady." Turning to the men, he said, "Tell me what you know."

Neville began to outline the few facts they had. When he saw Priscilla go to where Miss Ayers was hunched on the bench, sobbing, he sighed. Three dead people, too many people grieving, and still no answers.

"That is not much information," Witherspoon said after Neville finished.

"We have very little."

Thurmond said, "We may have more when we question the others in the theater." He glanced at the body, then walked toward the door. He reached it just as Priscilla did while escorting Miss Ayers out.

When Neville started to follow, Witherspoon grabbed his sleeve. The marquess motioned with his head toward the stage. Puzzled, Neville went with him.

"What is on your mind, Witherspoon?" he asked when they emerged from the shadows.

"This is not the proper time to bring up this subject, but I must."

"I know Sitwell was a friend and —"

"I do not wish to speak to you about Sitwell." Witherspoon sighed and shook his head. "Don't think me heartless, Hathaway. I have known Sitwell for more than a year, but he did not heed common sense."

"Say what you want to say." He did not want to remain here. Priscilla probably had

349

no need of his help with Miss Ayers, but she should not be given the responsibility of seeing to the actress's welfare by herself.

"You are going to be Miss Flanders's stepfather before the week is out. I wanted to get your permission to call on her."

Neville was startled into silence, a rare occurrence. He was about to lambaste Witherspoon for speaking of such mundane matters when a man was lying dead not far away. Then he paused. How many times had *he* pushed aside Society's rules, especially where Priscilla was concerned? Weren't his thoughts now of Priscilla?

He smiled at the marquess. "It is something I must discuss with Miss Flanders's mother. After all, I am not yet a part of the family."

"Will you discuss it?"

"I shall." Putting his hand on the marquess's shoulder, he said, "Now let us see what Thurmond may have learned from any witnesses."

Witherspoon gave him a relieved and grateful smile as they went out into the theater's entry. Chaos had erupted. Everyone seemed to be shouting at once, and several people were being held back from the door to the street.

Neville pushed his way toward the front

of the crowd. Raising his voice, he called, "If any of you want to work in this theater again, you will be quiet and cooperate with the authorities. Now!" He repeated himself twice before the frantic people began to calm.

"Thank you again," Thurmond said as he watched his men begin to question the potential witnesses once more.

"What set them off?"

"Who knows? Some rumor, no doubt."

Neville chuckled. "In that way, the Polite World and the demimonde are very much alike." He scanned the entry. "Where is Lady Priscilla?"

"She was with Miss Ayers last I saw her."

He saw the actress being comforted by two seamstresses and Morton. He did not see Priscilla. Hurrying to them, he tried to ignore the tightening in his gut.

"I have not seen her for several minutes," Miss Ayers said in answer to his question.

"Did she tell you where she was going?" The ache in his middle was becoming a cramp.

"She said she wanted to check something."

"Where?"

"With the body." Tears fell from the actress's eyes. "My beloved, my beloved."

Neville thanked her, but he doubted Miss Ayers heard him. Pushing through the crowd once more, he rushed into the theater. He called Priscilla's name, his voice resounding through the empty theater. He ran to the corpse.

His foot struck something, and it bounced off Sitwell's boot. Bending, he picked it up. The cramp deepened until it crunched his bones as he stared at the pearl.

Just like the ones in the necklace Priscilla had been wearing.

"Pris!" he shouted. "Pris, where are you?"

All he heard was his desperate voice echoing a taunt back to him.

Chapter Seventeen

Darkness surrounded Priscilla when she forced her eyes open. What had happened? She remembered going back to Lord Sitwell's corpse to examine the blond hair by his hand. Something about it had bothered her. She had been bending over the man's hand when she saw a shadow move.

Before she could react, a hand clamped over her mouth as an arm around her waist hugged her so tightly to a hard body that she could not catch her breath. She had struggled, but could not escape. The arm pressed into her abdomen, and everything had disappeared into ebony.

Now it was dark, too. How much time had passed between then and now? She had no idea. Her head throbbed, and thinking was difficult.

She tried to move, then realized her arms were bound. She inched her fingers outward. Slowly she realized that she was lying on a soft carpet. It whispered beneath her questing fingers. At least she was not lying in a coffin.

She saw a hint of light coming from her right. Silencing the groan that rang through her skull like a sword on a shield, she turned her head to discover it was a sliver of light slipping beneath a door.

She was alive, but what should she do now? Trussed up like a Christmas goose, she could not move much other than her fingers and her head. She considered screaming, but guessed whoever had brought her here would have made certain it was a place where her screams would reach no other ears.

Trying to shift as her arms ached more, she banged her head against something wooden. "Deuce take it!" she moaned.

"Are you awake, Lady Priscilla?" came a voice out of the darkness.

"Mr. Birdwell!" she gasped. Had their suspicions been right all along? Was the actor deeply involved in these murders? "Where are you?"

"Here." He put his hand on her arm. When she tried to flinch away, he said, "Do not worry. I will not hurt you."

"You already have."

She heard a metallic sound, and a small circle of light illuminated the floor. The actor must have a dark lantern.

When he leaned toward her, she saw his face was lined with fear. "I did not mean to, but you struggled. I was afraid you would scream, and I did not want to alert *him*. I bound you to make it easier to carry you here." He began to untie her hands. "I did not want to do anything to let *him* guess what I was doing."

"Neville?"

"No, the murderer."

Her eyes widened as she shook her hands to get feeling back into them. "Who was wearing one of your wigs! That is why Lord Sitwell was able to pull out a tuft of hair. It was from a blond wig. I was checking that when you sneaked up behind me. But why do you have a blond wig? You have blond hair."

He thought for a moment, then said, "It must be the one I used during a farce that Wiggsley wrote back when he was capable of great things." He touched the middle of his upper arm. "It is of this length, because I was playing a man pretending to be a woman."

"But why a wig?"

"To shift suspicion onto you and away from him. If it was cut shorter, the wig could make the killer look from a distance like you."

"Very good, my lady," said a voice from behind her.

In disbelief, she looked over her shoulder to see Reeve standing in the doorway. He held a gun in one hand and a bottle of wine in the other. On two of his fingers were the gold rings stolen from Lord Sitwell. He kicked the door closed behind him.

Mr. Birdwell squealed like a frightened child and jumped to his feet. "Reeve!"

"Open the lantern wider," Reeve said. "I do not want to trip over Lady Priscilla and cause this gun to fire prematurely."

The actor hastened to obey, and Priscilla realized they must be in Mr. Birdwell's hallowed dressing room. A fine carpet was spread across the floor. Costumes hung on pegs nailed to the walls. On either side of a large mirror set over a table topped with goblets and several dusty bottles of un-opened wine, shelves held cosmetics and wig boxes. One was open and empty.

"Reeve —"

"Shut up, Birdwell. This conversation is between Lady Priscilla and me."

Priscilla stood. "I would prefer to speak without a gun pointed at me. The last time you aimed at me, you fired."

"That incident in Bedford Square?" He

laughed. "That was to persuade Hathaway to stop trying to uncover the truth." He shoved the bottle into Mr. Birdwell's hand. "Open it."

"Now see here," the actor said, "I do not take orders from my own valet."

"No?" He pressed the gun against Priscilla's side. "How many more deaths do you want on your hands?"

"My hands?" choked Mr. Birdwell as he struggled to open the bottle.

Priscilla saw the door open a crack, but quickly shifted her gaze back to Reeve. The door might be swinging ajar on its own, or there might be someone on the far side ready to come to their rescue. Either way, she could not alert the madman.

"I asked you for the loan of money for my military career," snarled Reeve.

"I told you I did not have the money you wanted."

The bottle spewed liquid all over the actor and across Priscilla's skirt.

Motioning for the actor to pour some of the contents into goblets on his dressing table, Reeve said, "No? You recall quite well? The last time I asked was after Wiggsley's last successful play. The one where you played the army officer who saved his beloved from the pirates. The one where you wore the wide gold ring Lady Lummis gave you."

"You asked me to lend you money to buy a lieutenancy. I did not think you were serious."

"I was!"

"So you decided to get the money for a commission another way," Priscilla said carefully. "First you started stealing from Mr. Birdwell at the house which Lady Lummis provided for him."

"Yes." Reeve glowered at Mr. Birdwell before he spat, "But you were like a miser counting his coins, always taking inventory of the gifts your adoring ladies bestowed upon you."

"So you started robbing people around the theater?" From the corner of her eye, she saw the door push open wider. She did not dare to look at the mirror to see if the motion was reflected there.

"A glass of champagne, Lady Priscilla?" asked Reeve, taking one from Mr. Birdwell.

She kept an emotionless mask on her face. "To celebrate the purchase of your commission with dirty money?"

"Why not? Soon I shall be the hero I have aspired to be. A real hero, not like this foolish fop who pretends to be one on the stage." With a flourish, he handed her the bubbling liquid. He held out his goblet in a salute. "To you, Lady Priscilla, and to me."

She held her glass to her lips and pretended to drink. Mayhap if he drank, he would become so foxed she would be able to slip away.

Mr. Birdwell choked, "But you killed people! You did not just rob them."

"The first lady's death was a mistake. I did not mean to kill her, just to take the jewels I knew I could sell." His mouth worked before he spat, "But she fought me! She impaled herself on the knife. I took the jewels and slipped away."

"Wearing Mr. Birdwell's shortened wig," Priscilla said. "And your work smock covered up any blood that might have splashed on you. Quite clever of you, Reeve."

"I thought so."

The door opened wide enough so she could see a hand pushing it aside. Someone was out there! She wanted to shout for help. She wanted to call out to whoever was on the other side of the door to take care so Reeve did not fire the gun still against her side.

Reeve chuckled. "I could have been a great actor, too. You never saw that,

Birdwell. I tried to convince Ella that I would be a great success, but she cared only for that whimpering young lord of hers." His lips curled in satisfaction. "Killing him was very pleasing, as it will be killing you, Birdwell." He pulled another pistol from under his coat and aimed it at the actor's feet.

"Go, and I will not say anything to anyone," pleaded Mr. Birdwell. "Don't kill me!"

"How gallant!" he sneered. "Begging for your life, not for Lady Priscilla's."

Quietly, Priscilla said, "Reeve, the theater is filled with the watch and men from Bow Street. You cannot escape now. Firing that gun will bring them running to stop you."

He jabbed the gun into her ribs and smiled when she moaned. "You will provide my way out of here, my lady, after you give me that ring on your left hand."

She clamped her left hand closed. "No."

"No?" He scowled.

"Give him the ring, my lady," urged Mr. Birdwell.

"No," she repeated. "Neville gave it to me as a betrothal gift, and I will not give it to you."

"Hathaway will get you another. Give it to me, and we will leave. Don't worry, my lady. We will leave the theater without further trouble. Hathaway will never allow anything to happen to you."

"You are right about that, Reeve!" Neville shoved the door open, knocking Reeve forward.

Priscilla tried to leap aside, but became caught up in the costumes hanging on the wall. They fell atop her when she tumbled to the floor. Pushing them off her head, she saw Reeve on his knees. He was raising his gun and pointing it toward the door. With all the strength she had left, she kicked his elbow. The gun fired, the ball hitting the ceiling. Wood and plaster cascaded down on her.

Then the room was filled beyond capacity with men, all shouting. She scrambled back under the remaining costumes on her hands and knees, so she was not trampled. She recoiled, horrified, when another gun fired. She closed her eyes, afraid of what she would see when something thudded on the floor.

Something . . . or someone?

A hand cupped her chin. She opened her eyes to see adored ones looking at her with concern.

"Neville!"

"Reeve is dead," Neville whispered. "He

proved he was a coward to the end, shooting himself when he saw he would be captured. I am sorry we were so slow getting here, Pris."

"Thank you for coming when you did," she whispered as she threw her arms around his shoulders. Her arms ached from being bound, but she did not think of that.

"I hope this is the last time you have to tell me thank you for saving your life," he said. "Or I have to say that to you."

"Somehow, I doubt you will get what you wish for."

"But I already have. *You* are my greatest wish come true, Pris." He pulled her into his arms, and she forgot about everything else in the room.

In Priscilla's estimation, the kiss that sealed the vows she had spoken with Neville was too hurried. It was a pleasant kiss. All his kisses were, but it had lasted no more than a pair of heartbeats.

Cheers rose as Reverend Dr. Horwood of St. Julian's Church closed his book and announced, "Congratulations and blessings on your union."

She took her bouquet from Daphne, who stood beside her. In the front pew, Leah and Isaac were clapping wildly. Aunt Cordelia sat beside them, dabbing a handkerchief to her eyes. The tears might be of joy or despair, and Priscilla knew better than to ask.

Looking up at Neville, who stood beside her, she smiled and whispered, "How much did you win in the wager that you *would* marry me?"

"You have been my wife only a few seconds, and already you are asking me about my gambling." Laughing, he drew her hand within his arm and led her back up the aisle. "I should have known you would be a bothersome wife, Pris."

"Yes, you should have known."

He paused as they reached the church door. Behind them, her children halted, startled. The other guests exchanged looks, clearly wondering why they had stopped.

He took the flowers from her and handed them back to Daphne, who began to smile broadly.

Framing Priscilla's face with his broad, gentle hands, he tilted her face toward him. Too low even for the children to hear, he whispered, "I feared I had lost you in the theater, Pris. Reeve's murderous capers nearly stole you from me. I promise you that all our capers from this point on will be of the sweetest sort."

"A promise I am sure will be broken quickly."

"Why do you say that?"

"You were talking about joining forces to open an investigative agency and —"

He laughed again, a low, husky laugh that erupted through her with sweet fire. "The only way I want to join forces with you now is . . ." He captured her lips, and this time their kiss lasted many heartbeats, each one more joyous than the one before.

Author's Note

Some ill winds *do* blow good.

Bianca Dunsworthy does not expect an earl, suffering from a gunshot wound, to arrive at the house she shares with her sister and aunt. As she nurses Lucian Wandersee back to health, she realizes he is the answer to two problems. Napoleon, whom she blames for her brother's death, is aboard a ship in Plymouth, and that is where Lucian is bound. *And* the earl would make a splendid match for her shy younger sister.

Lucian has no interest in a bride or escorting three women to Plymouth, but he owes Bianca a debt for saving his life. He would rather that she allow him to repay her with a few kisses. But why is she so fascinated with Napoleon? Lucian needs an answer before he can show Bianca that no bride is perfect . . . without love. Look for *The Perfect Bride* in October 2004.

Readers can contact me at:
PO Box 575
Rehoboth, MA 02769

Or visit my website at:
www.joannferguson.com

or by email at
jo@joannferguson.com

We hope you have enjoyed this Large Print book. Other Thorndike, Wheeler or Chivers Press Large Print books are available at your library or directly from the publishers.

For more information about current and upcoming titles, please call or write, without obligation, to:

Publisher
Thorndike Press
295 Kennedy Memorial Drive
Waterville, ME   04901
Tel. (800) 223-1244

Or visit our Web site at:
www.gale.com/thorndike
www.gale.com/wheeler

OR

Chivers Large Print
published by BBC Audiobooks Ltd
St James House, The Square
Lower Bristol Road
Bath BA2 3SB
England
Tel. +44(0) 800 136919
email: bbcaudiobooks@bbc.co.uk
www.bbcaudiobooks.co.uk

All our Large Print titles are designed for easy reading, and all our books are made to last.

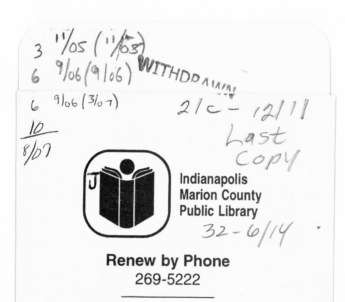